CANDLELIGHT REGENCY SPECIAL

CANDLELIGHT REGENCIES

THE BEST LAID SCHEMES

Joyce Lee

A CANDLELIGHT REGENCY SPECIAL

Published by
Dell Publishing Co., Inc.
1 Dag Hammarskjold Plaza
New York, New York 10017

Dell ® TM 681510, Dell Publishing Co., Inc.

ISBN: 0-440-11011-4

Printed in the United States of America
First printing—April 1980

The best laid schemes o' mice an' men
Gang aft a-gley.

To a Mouse
ROBERT BURNS

THE
BEST
LAID
SCHEMES

CHAPTER 1

Berkeley Square in 1817 was the showplace of the British Empire. Noted for the beauty and opulence of its houses and the lighthearted gaiety of its noble inhabitants, it was a shimmering backdrop for bals and routs and musicales, where the costliest jewels, the most lavish fashions, and the sleekest horseflesh were paraded daily, dignity and condescension were the prescribed mode of conduct, and eccentric behavior was rarely exposed to view.

Therefore, when on a bright day in April a dynamic brunette lady with smoldering eyes stood in front of the Earl of Deverill's house, jabbing her umbrella at it in a threatening way and mumbling, "Marlum quidquill nuxum pallor, warts and aches and abject squalor . . ." a small group of interested passersby gathered to watch her.

"Fleas and ticks and cooties rampant," the lady continued, turning herself twice to the right. She was in the middle of a great sweeping motion with her left hand when she stopped suddenly and, with an air of remorse, clapped a hand to one cheek.

"Zounds!" she muttered. "What am I doing to my poor Kate?"

Immediately she began turning to her left, dipping and bogging and mumbling, "tnapmar seitooc dna skcit dna sealf . . ."

11

She had just completed a series of gestures with her right hand and had paused for breath, when an upstairs window of his lordship's house opened and the Countess herself put out her head. She was dressed in daffodil yellow, a conceit she often affected on bright spring days, and her hair was arranged in its customary pile of massed yellow curls which gave the impression of a full-blown head of cauliflower.

Her ladyship, who had looked down in time to observe the last few undulations of the figure below her, peered at her apprehensively for a moment. Then she called in a slightly quavering voice, "Sophia . . . my love?"

Sophia's jaw tightened. "Yes . . . my dear?"

"If you could contrive to send Katie to us before Friday . . . Not if it is too much trouble, of course . . . but we are all so eager to know her . . . Serena especially . . . And I have planned a small rout party . . . I must be certain she is properly gowned before I present her to the ton." She fluttered her hands.

The brunette lady's eyebrows drew together in an ominous scowl. "Kate will arrive on Thursday," she said.

"Excellent, excellent," her ladyship said. But as she drew her head back inside the house and watched her cousin Sophia flounce across the square and out of sight, she exhaled unevenly, a pall of misgiving settling over her.

There had been a time, when they were girls together, that her ladyship (then the Honorable Frances Wadsworth, known to her intimates as Fanny Dear) and Sophia (then the Honorable Sophia Thorpe, known to her intimates as Yes Sophia) had been wonderfully close. Often, unfortunately, Sophia's strength of character—the unalterability of her opinions and her lack of patience with anyone who was the least bit timid or agreeable—had caused strains on their relationship. But Fanny's sunny disposition and eagerness to remain fond of her cousin had usually put any alienation to rights—until a bright spring day in 1797 when Sophia had carried her obstinacy so far that she had frightened Fanny into a breach of intimacy which lasted for twenty years.

The two girls had been walking through an open

12

meadow together, Fanny holding her skirt delicately high to prevent wetting the hem, Sophia striding through the damp grass unaware of the dew and stains and bits of leaf and stem she was depositing on her new sprigged muslin gown.

Suddenly Sophia had exclaimed in ringing tones, "I'm hungry! So hungry I could eat an entire bullock raw!"

Fanny shuddered, grateful that no one else had overheard. At that moment they reached the edge of a small orchard and Sophia stopped under a peach tree that was heavy with half-green fruit.

"If only it were ripe," she said.

Fanny was looking up into the branches. High above her, hanging alone and lovingly framed by a halo of curling green leaves, was one ripe peach. It was a large peach, soft and golden, slightly blushed with pink on one side and so obviously rich with juice that Fanny felt her mouth filling with water.

Sophia walked over to her cousin's side and looked up. "Umm," she said. "Delicious!" And she raised a lean brown finger, pointed at the peach, and muttered, "Mijum, mijum, mijum . . ." Then cupping both hands under it, she shut her eyes and mumbled steadily, forming her words into a rhythmic, insistent chant. Fanny watched her, eyes round and mouth sliding indelicately ajar.

For a moment the peach hung motionless, looking for all the world like any other normal ripe fruit on a normal healthy fruit tree. But after a few seconds of being assaulted by Sophia's incantations, it began to tremble. It shivered, twitched, gave a monumental jerk, then suddenly dropped from its branch into Sophia's waiting hands.

"There," she said, turning to Fanny and holding the peach out to her. "It's yours, Little Mouse. I'll get another for myself."

But Fanny, whose teeth had begun to chatter, backed away from her and, blubbering incoherently, fled across the meadow, stumbling through the sticky grass until she reached the manor house where her mother was visiting Sophia's mother.

13

"Peagoose!" Sophia shouted after her.

From that moment on, Fanny was afraid to be alone with her cousin. That evening, during supper, Sophia sat across the table from her, scowling, occasionally putting a finger to her eye and leering in a threatening way. Finally, before Fanny's horrified eyes, she pointed a commanding finger at one of the spoons alongside her plate and whispered throatily to herself; to Fanny's dismay the spoon rolled over on its edge and curled itself into a circle.

That night Fanny was visited by terrible nightmares in which Sophia performed a series of atrocities. With a flick of her finger, she transformed Fanny into an apple, then a mouse, and finally into a fountain; and although Fanny wept and shrieked and wrung her icy stone hands, pleading for release from her gushing prison, no one could hear her voice above the plash of her waters. She woke up sobbing, her face so wetted by her tears that she wondered if it were possible that she had really been turned into a fountain during the night and had only just come back to being herself.

After that, she had clung to her mother, refusing to be separated from her for so much as a second, until the woman, in exasperation, had taken her home.

During the years that followed, while Fanny avoided all contact with her cousin, she had put the incident out of her mind, deciding that she had behaved foolishly and had been deceived by her imagination, as her mother insisted that she had. And after twenty years of exercising strong family loyalty, common sense, and her innate conviction that good always triumphs and everything turns out for the best, she had come to doubt the reality of those long ago events—almost.

But as she stood in her private sitting room, a grown woman, Countess of Deverill, mother of two grown sons and a marriageable daughter, she felt a shiver of misgiving and wondered if she had not, perhaps, been hasty in inviting Sophia's daughter, Kate, to spend the Season with her in London, as companion to her own charming Serena.

14

After all, she had never seen the girl and knew nothing about her.

Fanny, as usual, had acted on the spur of the moment when she made up her mind to bring Kate into her household. But she had been desperate. Much to her disappointment, Serena had already been on the marriage market for two Seasons with no encouraging results. Fanny had long ago accepted the fact that her daughter, though sweet and accomplished and rich, was not the world's most vibrant beauty; but when, the week before, the girl had come home early from a rout party at the Countess of Buffton's, tears in her eyes, to announce that she had been introduced to the Duke of Nellingham three times during the evening and he had said, "Charmed," each time, not remembering that he had met her a few minutes before, Fanny made up her mind that something had to be done. And it occurred to her that if she could find someone even paler and more diffident to use as a background for Serena, her own daughter might be brought to the fore. Before she considered the wisdom of such a move, she remembered the words of another cousin, the Marchioness of Gyle. "Such a poor, silent, colorless little thing," she had said after meeting Kate. "Not a bit like Sophia." And without giving herself time to think out all the pros and cons or consider possible pitfalls, and convinced that any daughter of Sophia's must undoubtedly be a quiet, suppressed sort of girl, Fanny sent off a letter to her cousin. But she had no sooner mended her relationship with Sophia and invited her daughter to town, than she began to experience grave misgivings.

Kate arrived late Thursday night, swept into Berkeley Square on a high wind filled with driving rain. Fanny had despaired of her and retired for the night; but unable to sleep, she had leaped out of bed and rushed to the streaming windows each time she heard the rumble of carriage wheels on the cobbles below. The third time she was rewarded by the sight of a battered old traveling coach drawing up to her front door. Jerking on a negligee, she rushed

15

to the landing in time to watch Judson, her butler, herd Timothy, the second footman, into the vestibule. Timothy was carrying a bundle in his arms—a voluminous fur carriage robe with a tiny white face peering out of its folds.

"Katie, my love!" Fanny called down to the face. "Thank heaven, you have arrived at last!"

But to her alarm, as the footman set the girl on her feet at the foot of the stairs, she appeared to swoon, quickly putting out a hand to grasp the banister and steady herself.

"Oh, dearest!" Fanny exclaimed. "Are you ill? Please, Timothy, bring her up to the silver room."

The footman nodded, and lifting the girl again in his arms, bore her lightly up to the landing. As he passed her ladyship, Fanny caught sight of two extremely bright black eyes looking out at her.

By the time Fanny had bustled along the hall in Timothy's wake and reached the silver room, the footman had again set Kate on her feet and was on his knees on the hearth, lighting the fire.

"You'll be warm in a moment, my dearest," Fanny told her. "Are you ill?"

Kate shook her head and the robe fell away from her, releasing a mass of tangled black curls which tumbled out onto her shoulders in glorious profusion.

"It's only that I am tired," Kate said softly. "The trip was very long."

Fanny slid an arm around her. "Poor child, you should be tucked into a warm bed and soothed with healing draughts. Then tomorrow, when you wake up, everything will be like heaven. Your cousin Serena is planning every sort of delight for you. 'It will be like having a sister,' she said. Next week we shall hold the most charming little rout party to introduce you to the ton. I shall buy you the prettiest dress you have ever seen. And Brill shall arrange your hair à la Grecque. And there will be music and dancing and laughter and handsome young men and lobster patties and ices and all sorts of delightful things. Will that not be wonderful?"

Kate nodded, but to Lady Fanny's dismay there was a large tear in each eye.

"Oh, my dearest!" she protested. "You must not be unhappy!"

At that moment a door opened and a capable-looking young woman dressed all in brown hurried in, buttoning her sleeves and smoothing her hair with a hand. "Begging your pardon, ma'am," she murmured.

"Ah," Lady Fanny said with satisfaction, "here is Sara Brill, your abigail." She turned to the maid. "Brill, please make this child comfortable and happy immediately." She patted Kate's arm. "Brill will know exactly what to do for you. Sleep well, my love." And she hurried out of the room, her thoughts in a hopeless tangle.

As she scuttled down the hall to her own bedroom, she scolded herself for having acted so impulsively—for inviting the girl without taking time to investigate her appearance and her character more thoroughly. Why her cousin, the Marchioness, had labeled her *colorless,* she could not imagine. With her black hair and dark eyes, she was anything but that. And there was something so wistful and appealing about those eyes when they were full of tears— Fanny feared that they would melt the hearts of all the eligible young men in London—at least, all the ones she had singled out to marry her own daughter.

Even worse than the fact that the girl was pretty, however, was the fact that she appeared to be unhappy; and unhappiness was something Lady Fanny could not endure. Discomfort of any kind was her sworn foe, and she kept it ruthlessly at bay with determination, a modicum of intelligent effort, and the expenditure of large sums of money.

She crawled into her bed and pulled the comforters up under her chin, trying to restore some order to her anguished brain. If Kate did not appear to be more cheerful in the morning, she decided—and if a new dress or pretty string of pearls did not set her to rights—Fanny would seek advice from some of her intimates—from her cousin, the Marchioness, for example, who had a much wider knowledge of the world than Fanny. At least, each time a friend

17

or child of a friend came to grief, the Marchioness always said, "Just as I expected," which indicated knowledge of a sort. She would be able to contrive a solution to the problem, certainly.

Fanny sighed. Life was so full of problems. One was constantly obliged to make decisions—which dress to wear to the Countess of Buffton's, or what color satin to make up into a new gown to wear with the Deverill emeralds. Or even worse, what refreshments to serve at one's parties—they never seemed to be quite right.

She snuggled deeper into her bed. Warmth was gradually seeping through her limbs, soothing and melting them; peace was easing its way gently into her soul. And it occurred to her that if she could not make Kate happy, instead of plotting and suffering, she could simply send her home to her mother.

She smiled to herself and settled deeper into her bed. Life was really uncomplicated and wonderful, if one burrowed deeply into it. There was no need to cudgel one's brains and cause one's complexion to come out in blotches. One could lie back in comfort and allow the tides of goodness and mercy to wash over one. And all would come right in the end.

With that reassuring thought driving all else from her mind, Lady Fanny closed her eyes and sank into deep, blissful sleep, unaware that her niece, wracked by misery, was crying herself to sleep down the hall.

CHAPTER 2

Kate's invitation to visit her aunt in London had come at the worst possible time; she had, that very morning, suffered a crushing disappointment in love and was in the throes of despair.

It was not the first disappointment in love she had suffered—in fact, it was the seventh of 1817 (with the year barely begun), and she had suffered twenty-six the year before and fourteen the year before that. But this disappointment had been the worst, since she had thought that, perhaps, she really cared for the young man, and because he had about him the air of a loyal person who would not be lured away by the superficial charms of a certain type of young lady.

She had known John Wiggins all her life. His father owned a large house nearby on the high road beyond Throcklestoke village. During their mutual childhood she had not found him to be the least bit attractive, always considering him a stolid child who was not quick-witted and was prone to chubbiness and double chins.

Then one day, during a holiday from Cambridge University, he had come riding past on a new hunter, taking him over a few walls to see how he performed, and he had jumped right over the top of Kate, who had been under a creek bank, collecting watercress. He had ridden back immediately to be certain she was not injured, and it had been love at first sight—John, in the meantime, had lost his extra chins and the roll around his middle, and had acquired a fashionable tailor who knew how to fit his riding togs. He had exclaimed, in the most charming, sophisticated way, "Good God! Is it Kate Ashworth? What a beauty you've grown to be!" Kate had promptly given him her heart. They had then spent the entire morning together, John dragging his bored hunter around behind him while the horse jerked its head about in an effort to find delicious green shoots to munch and his master was impressing the young lady with his vast knowledge of the world.

Then John Wiggins saw Kate's sister, Lorna, and Kate's happiness came to an end. John promptly fell in love with Lorna. It was nothing new: everyone fell in love with Lorna. She had been variously described as Helen of Troy, Venus, and an assortment of goddesses whose names Kate could not remember. The term *beautiful* was inadequate to describe her; she was dazzling—so breathtaking that everyone who came near her fell under her spell.

Nor was there anything anyone could say to comfort Kate, who was merely beautiful, intelligent, and charming. When her father pointed out to her that Lorna's allure would fade—that in twenty or thirty years she would no longer be sought after—Kate pointed out in turn that she, too, would be withered and unlovely by that time.

He had then tried to cheer her by reminding her that she was the clever one, and that brains lasted longer than beauty. "You can always find something to interest you in a book," he said. "It is easy to draw your thoughts away from these disappointments."

But it was not easy—it was impossible. She was hard at work trying to convince herself that she did not care if John Wiggins preferred Lorna, when Lady Fanny's invitation was presented to her.

"This is the perfect diversion for you, my dear," her mother told her, removing her bonnet and placing it in its box. "You shall go to London and see a bit of the world."

Kate had been ready to protest—to decline the invitation

on the grounds that it would be unnerving to visit relatives she did not even know, and such a sojourn might result in quarrels or boredom, or even great personal danger—when Lorna rushed over to her mother, clasped both hands, and exclaimed, "Oh, let me go, Mama! I am the beauty, not Kate. I am the one who would use the holiday to best advantage. I am the one who can capture the heart of every man in London. I shall dance, I shall laugh, I shall smile at them all and put their heads in a whirl. And I shall find a rich, handsome important duke to marry. Let me be the one to go."

"No," Sophia said firmly. "Fanny has asked for Katie, and she is the one who shall go."

"But she does not want to go," Lorna announced. "I can tell by her face. Do you, Katie? You want me to go in your place, do you not?"

Kate looked at her sister pensively—the glistening golden curls, the alabaster skin, the adorable dimples—and a slow smile curled the corners of her mouth. "No," she said, "I shall go myself."

Lorna tried—at first sweetly—to dissuade her. Later, when coaxing, cajolery, and mild threats had all failed, she lost her temper and shouted many unkind things at her sister.

"I shall make my way to London," she promised, " . . . sooner than you think. And when I do, I shall take the shine out of your adventure, mark my words!"

But despite the fact that she raged at her for two days— arguing, weeping, stamping her feet—Kate packed her clothes into an enormous trunk, allowed herself to be tucked into Squire Wiggins's dilapidated old traveling carriage, and started on her way to town.

By the time she arrived, however, she was regretting her decision. It was spring in the country, with budding trees and burgeoning fields of wild flowers; the city was cold and stony and forbidding. During the journey, the driving rain chilled her to the bone. The badly sprung old coach bounced and jostled and tossed her back and forth against the hardened squabs until she ached in every joint. She de-

21

cided that her Aunt Fanny was probably a cross, vindictive old woman who would make her visit miserable, and her cousin Serena was undoubtedly as selfish and mercenary and hatefully beautiful as her odious sister Lorna.

When Brill finally tucked her into a soft warm bed, she fell into troubled sleep, yearning to be home again with her mother, where the clean fragrance of a dew-washed countryside could bathe her face. Instead, she awoke in a stuffy urban room, the air around her motionless and oppressive. There were no singing birds. There were no pungent odors of a wild countryside—only the smell of stale wax and carpeting and the heavy mustiness of dried flower petals.

Cautiously Kate raised her head. The world tilted crazily. Then she discovered that her nose was swollen shut, her eyes felt gummy, and her mouth might as well have been full of cotton wool. Unhappily she crawled out from under the covers and put a foot on the floor, then stumbled to the window which overlooked the square.

The sun was not up, but Kate could see that it was preparing to rise beyond a gnarled tangle of bare branches which had been so ruthlessly pruned that they looked like a cluster of broken fingers atop an emaciated arm.

She sighed heavily and stared at the horizon. "Ah," she said to herself, "I see part of my problem. I have slept with my head to the west. No wonder I feel all at sixes and sevens."

She leaned heavily on the bell pull. Three minutes later there were scampering sounds outside her door and Brill burst in, buttoning her cuffs and smoothing her hair with a hand, as she had done the night before.

"I'm sorry, miss," she said. "Were you unable to sleep?"

"Sleep?" Kate asked in surprise. "At this hour? It is almost sunrise."

Brill paled momentarily, but quickly recovered her composure. "What dress will you be wishing to wear this morning, miss?"

"Oh," Kate said in a disinterested voice, waving a hand, "the blue muslin, I suppose. But before I think of dressing, I must have my bed moved. Will you please call in that enormous footman who brought me upstairs last night? I want him to put the bed over there."

"But, miss," Brill protested, ". . . begging your pardon, but surely you're not thinking of moving his lordship's furniture."

"I must," Kate explained. "I slept last night with my head to the west—I was literally dragged backward through space by my hair for seven hours or more. And today I feel stuffed and muggy. It'll take all morning to get my magnetic fields properly aligned again." And she pressed a hand unhappily against a throbbing temple.

The abigail bobbed her head. "As you wish, miss. But if we're to move the furniture, we must secure her ladyship's permission."

"Very well," Kate said. "I'll go get her permission immediately."

"But, miss! Her ladyship never opens her eyes before eleven o'clock."

"That's all right," Kate said, and strode out into the hall. Brill scampered after her.

"Wait . . ." she began. Then she stopped, realizing that Kate did not know the location of her ladyship's room; and Brill was determined not to enlighten her. With a complacent smile on her face, she padded along behind the girl.

To Brill's dismay, Kate walked unerringly to the door of her aunt's bedroom and opened it. Lady Deverill was buried under mounds of sky-blue down comforters, a single fringe of ruffled nightcap showing.

"Aunt Fanny," Kate began in a voice which had been strengthened by a night's sleep, "I should very much like your permission to move my bed, if you please."

"What?" came a garbled sound from under the covers. "What time is it?"

"It is five twenty-seven," Kate told her, reading the face of a small gilt clock which stood on a mantelpiece across the room.

"Five? At night?" her ladyship cried, trying to fight her way out from under the bedclothes. "Have I been turned into a peach tree?"

23

"No, no," Kate assured her. "Please don't be alarmed. It is five twenty-seven in the morning, and I only wish permission to move my bed from one side of the room to the other."

"Oh," Fanny groaned. "Anything, my love. Only leave me until the day is properly begun."

"Thank you," Kate said in a soothing voice. "Sleep peacefully, dear aunt." And she motioned Brill to follow her back to her room. A few minutes later she was giving directions to Timothy who, with no inconsiderable effort and much grunting and heavy breathing, moved the head of her bed from the west wall to the north.

Serena had slept poorly, overcome by impatience to meet her cousin. Like her mother, she had rushed to the window each time she heard carriage wheels on the cobblestones, but eventually she had fallen asleep and had only half roused when she heard activity in the house. When she awoke the next morning, she was not sure whether Kate had arrived or not.

Her sleep was disturbed for the first time a little after five thirty when she heard scraping sounds and a heavy thump in the silver room. Opening her eyes, she looked around her own chamber, and was on the point of leaping out of bed when she read the face of a nearby clock and, noting that it was barely daylight, decided that she had been mistaken. Kate, if she had arrived, would surely be asleep, Serena told herself.

But then she heard more scraping and another thump. And after that she had lain quietly for a time, deciding to get out of bed, then deciding to go back to sleep. Then, deciding to rise, she heard a scraping screeching, which made her think of a window being forced up in an unused frame.

Finally she decided to investigate the strange noises—she would go back to sleep if Kate had not arrived. Bundling herself into a dressing gown, her hair covered by a pudding-bag nightcap, she tiptoed out into the hall and gingerly pushed the door to the silver room open a slender crack.

For a moment she could see no one inside. To her surprise the bed had moved from one side of the room to the other, but there was no sign of an occupant. The bedclothes, however, had been thrown back and there was an indentation on the pillow. Hopefully Serena put her head in farther and looked around.

Still there was no sign of Kate or an abigail, or any other form of life. Then she looked beyond the room and saw something which, for an instant, caused the entire world to tilt out of perspective. A window overlooking the square was wide open and a dark-haired girl in a blue dress was outside it, caught in the limbs of a tree.

Serena let out a shriek and rushed across the room. The girl—who wore a singularly calm expression for one who was in such dire peril—was perched on a large bare limb with both arms outstretched, clutching a branch in each hand.

"Oh!" Serena cried. "Oh, my dear! My darling girl! Don't move! I'll get Judson! I'll get Timothy! I'll get someone! Please don't move, my dearest! Hold tightly! Help is on its way!" And she turned to rush back toward the hallway.

"Wait!" Kate called to her from the tree. And before Serena's horrified eyes, her cousin stood up on the broad limb where she had been sitting, let go of the branches, and with a light spring, leaped over onto the windowsill and stepped down onto the floor inside. Serena, convinced that she was falling, let out an agonized scream and sank onto the floor in a pile of ruffled dimity.

"Here, here, now," Kate soothed her. "Please don't be upset." Raising her gently to her feet, she led her to a chair where she settled her comfortably and gently applied a soft linen handkerchief to her cousin's streaming eyes.

"Oh!" Serena wept helplessly. "Oh, my dearest! Don't ever . . . You mustn't . . . How could you risk your life so?"

"I was not risking my life," Kate explained. "I'm in and out of trees all the time at home. There was no danger.

25

And I had a much more comfortable view of the square from out there."

"You must promise me . . ." Serena continued, bursting into fresh tears.

"Please, Serena," Kate chided gently, concerned that her cousin would make herself ill. "It is Serena, is it not?"

"Yes. And you must promise me that you will never take such a chance with your life again, my dearest Katie. If you had any idea of the way I've longed for your arrival—how I've dreamed of the way everything will change with you here—you'd never run the risk of ending it with an accident that would send you back to your mother."

Kate felt a rush of affection as she looked at her cousin. With her Little Miss Muffet hat askew and her reddened eyes the only spots of color on her otherwise monochromatic face, she presented a remarkably pathetic picture. Kate patted her hand.

"There, there, now," she soothed her. "Everything is going to turn out for the best."

Serena pulled a handkerchief out of a pocket and dabbed impatiently at her nose, stirring it to an even redder hue.

Kate looked at her curiously. "But why should you want things to change? Is not your life—and this house—the epitome of everything that young ladies are supposed to desire?"

Serena waved a hand impatiently. "That's what my mother keeps telling me. But what does she know? She was a girl so long ago."

Kate nodded. "That is true."

"Anyway," Serena went on, "it was different with her. She was a beauty. She fell in love with my father and married him, just like that." She snapped her fingers. "I, on the other hand, have no admirers. I have been put up for bids, as it were—like a piece of flawed china or a cloisonné vase."

"No," Kate protested.

"Yes. I am put on display and someone says, 'Earl's daughter for sale—only viscounts, earls, marquises, and dukes need apply.' And nobody wants me because I have no face."

"That's absurd," Kate chided. "You have a face."

"But no eyebrows or eyelashes," Serena pointed out. "You see? They have no color, and I look as though they don't exist. My hair, too." She peered owlishly into Kate's face and raised her cap on one side to reveal a tangled mass of limp pinkish-yellow curls.

"Well . . ." Kate said, examining the pale strands which appeared to melt into her cousin's slightly sallow complexion.

It was true—Serena gave the appearance of having no eyebrows, eyelashes, or hair. All blended into each other. Even her eyes were so light as to be almost colorless—like clear glass.

"Never mind," Kate said. "That is easily remedied."

"Oh, if only it could be!" Serena cried, clasping her hands together. "If someone could give me a real face—even if it is not a beautiful one—I am sure I can find a wonderful rich handsome peer who will marry me. You've no idea how much I have suffered, Katie. Only last week I overheard my second brother, Sonny, talking to Lord Sumpton, who is the most odious man alive and certainly not handsome in any way. But when my brother said, 'You should get to know my sister, Egmont; she's a delightful gel,' Sumpton said, 'Sorry, old man—no offense and all that—but I'm not about to attach myself to someone who looks like a leek.' And then he laughed rudely."

"Outrageous!" Kate exclaimed, snorting with indignation. "How could anyone be so horrid! And so unjust! You and I shall snub this disgusting man on every possible occasion. In the meantime, I shall cast a spell which will transform you into the most captivating blonde beauty in London."

Serena's pallid brows knitted together. "Spell?" she said, her voice trembling slightly. "You're not a witch, Katie?"

"I'm not," Kate admitted. "But I would like to be, and I am trying very hard."

"You mustn't," Serena whispered, putting a restraining hand on hers. "It is very wicked."

Kate tossed her head. "It is not at all wicked. You've been listening to people who have no powers, and they always suffer the most excruciating pangs of envy."

"Well . . ." Serena began.

"Just think how delightful it would be to be able to coax everyone into liking you, simply by casting a spell. You could pick the young men you like and cause them to return your affection."

"Well," Serena began again, "but what would I be obliged to give in return?"

"Not a thing," Kate assured her. "It's an old wives' tale that one must give something to the devil in exchange for the good things. What I'm discussing with you is not devil worship but clean, happy spells to enhance the charms we already have."

"Oh," Serena said, brightening.

"Just think how pleasant it would be if one were forever happy and charming and pretty and generous . . ."

"Yes, yes," Serena agreed. "Let's do it. I'm most anxious to marry and live happily ever after. What is the first step I must take?"

Kate put the tips of her fingers to her temples and thought deeply. "Let me see. . . . We must brew ourselves a nice little potion—a sort of tea. And we need comfrey and mint and camomile . . . some anise . . . I've brought all the other ingredients in one of my bandboxes."

Serena waited a moment for her to continue. When she did not do so, she asked, "Is that all that's required?"

"Of course I must say a few words—a short incantation."

Serena stood up and capered happily around the room. "I shall start making plans for my wedding." She giggled. "My cousin, Tiffany, will be so snappish, for I shall select a very important man as my bridegroom, and he shall be an even bigger catch than her own Lord Diremore, whom she is to marry in May."

As Kate watched her cousin caper happily about the

room, she felt a surge of satisfaction. How good it felt to be a benefactor! Perhaps, she thought, this was the answer to all her problems—she would devote her life to helping others, and forget that her odious sister existed; she would guide the bitter and the lovelorn. For a moment she envisioned herself in flowing white robes, standing on a raised place, holding out her hands to the multitudes as she smiled at them beatifically.

Yes, she thought, that was what she would do. She would give up all interest in personal gain or happiness, and devote herself to a life of service; and she would begin with Serena.

"Who is it you wish to marry, my dear?" she asked her.

"I don't know," her cousin said, frowning thoughtfully. "There are several young noblemen who might prove suitable."

Kate threw up her hands. "Several! No, no, no! You must *never*—even for an instant—consider marriage unless you are overwhelmingly, profoundly, hopelessly in love! If you had any idea of the pain which always results from a loveless union . . ."

"Yes, yes," Serena said quickly, alarmed by the warmth of her cousin's reaction. "I know. Actually I am in love—although I have not admitted anyone into my confidence."

"Ah," Kate said. "Who is the fortunate young man?"

Allowing her mind to run quickly over the current crop of beaux who were frequenting the marriage market, Serena picked one at random. "Well," she said, with an air of conspiracy, "it is Drew Wale, the Duke of Asgar. He is the most courteous, handsome young man—a friend of my brother Willie, and one of the richest . . ."

Her voice trailed off into silence as she looked at her cousin's face. Kate was scowling darkly. "You must forget him, Serena," she said. "I could never be a party to a match between that loathsome family and any young woman of whom I am fond. The Duke is a monster, I am convinced—humorless, of low intelligence—and I am willing to wager that he suffers from an exaggerated opinion of his own importance, as do all the Dukes of Asgar."

29

"You know him?" Serena asked in surprise.

"I have never met him," Kate admitted. "But all of the family are the same."

"Oh, you're wrong, love," Serena assured her. "Drew is not a bit like your description. Although he has the dignity which befits a duke, he is quiet and self-effacing."

Kate snorted. "If he has a modest opinion of himself, it's an exaggeration of his worth, I assure you!"

"But I love him!" Serena exclaimed, tears beginning to swell into her eyes as she suddenly realized how much she cared for the gentle young Duke. "Everyone in my family is exceedingly fond of him, and I love him! I cannot live without him!"

"My poor dear," Kate said, nesting her arms comfortingly around Serena's shoulders. "If you truly love him, you shall have him. But it will cause me great pain to visit you in the ducal palace, after your marriage."

"You are so good to me," Serena sniffled, twining her arms around Kate's waist. At that moment, while the girls effected their heart-warming tableau, Lady Fanny opened the door and bustled in.

"Oh, my dears!" she exclaimed in delight. "How splendid to see you getting on so well! Charming, charming!"

Kate, flustered, would have moved away, but Serena clung to her, murmuring, "Oh, yes, Mama, we're such good friends! It's as though dear Katie and I have known each other all our lives."

"Just as it should be with cousins," Lady Fanny assured her.

Serena disentangled herself from Kate's arms and went over to twine herself about her mother's neck. "And, Mama," she added, "now it can be told. I have chosen the man I am going to marry—Katie is going to help me."

"Excellent, excellent!" Fanny said. "Who is he?"

"It's someone we all know and love," Serena told her. "Willie's dear friend, Drew Wale."

"What!" Fanny shrieked. "The Duke of Asgar! Never!"

"But, Mama," Serena protested, "you are fond of him yourself. You've said so many times."

Fanny nodded. "Of course I am! He's a dear boy. But I won't have you marry him. Remember the prophecy."

"What prophecy?" Serena demanded. "I've never heard of such a thing."

"Of course you have," Fanny insisted. "Everyone has heard of it. Not that I believe in such things—silly superstition—but one should not take chances. Where there is smoke there is fire, you know."

Serena began to sniffle. Quickly Kate took her hand and patted it reassuringly. She turned to the countess. "I have not heard the prophecy, Aunt Fanny. What is it?"

"Very simply, my dear," Fanny told her, and she wagged her head solemnly at her niece, "that one day a Duke of Asgar will go mad and fly off to live with the birds."

CHAPTER 3

"Fiddle!" Serena snapped. "Drew is quite the most level-headed person I know—to the point of being a thorough bore at times." She glanced quickly at her mother and Kate. "Not that I ever find him so, of course."

Kate was running her free hand along the edge of her dressing table, frowning thoughtfully to herself. "I am not entirely comfortable with this match, myself, Aunt," she began.

"Oh!" Serena exclaimed in exasperation. "How can you criticize him? He is precisely what everyone wishes for—the perfect complaisant husband. He is kind, excessively rich, of a pleasant appearance, and a rank which cannot be scorned. In fact, my cousin, Tiffany, cast out every kind of lure for almost two months, and only accepted that odious Lord Diremore when she had given up all hope that Drew would ever come up to scratch." She smiled. "Think how envious she will be when I announce my marriage to him." She giggled.

Lady Fanny, whose frown had melted during Serena's speech, began to smile. "And her mother, my dear cousin Maria, will be livid. Good! Let us arrange it. How shall we begin?"

To Kate's surprise, her aunt and her cousin both turned to her and waited expectantly.

"Well," she began, folding her hands in contemplation. "We must first contrive to put you into his company."

"That should not present a problem," Serena told her. "He visits here every day. Comes to see my brother, Willie. They are bosom friends—had 'digs' together at Oxford."

Kate shook her head. "That will not do. We must put you into a romantic situation together—preferably an adventure charged with emotion. If he could rescue you from a dreadful accident—a team of runaway horses, perhaps . . ." She noted that Serena's face had turned pale. "Or, perhaps, if he could foil a kidnapping . . ."

Her cousin opened her mouth, made a faint rattling sound, cleared her throat, then managed to say, though in failing accents, "That would be most difficult to contrive . . . and terrifying!"

"Yes," Kate agreed. "It would be too dangerous. We must not place you in unnecessary peril. We shall be compelled to resort to dancing parties, and tête-à-têtes during which you can say charming things and blush prettily at his witticisms."

Serena shook her head. "Drew never invents witticisms."

"Then you must invent some yourself and laugh prettily at your own humor. Somehow you must contrive to sparkle in his presence."

"I know what we shall do," Lady Fanny announced, seating herself at Serena's desk and drawing out a sheet of paper and a pen. "We shall invite Drew to our rout party next week, and you shall sparkle at him there, my love." She entered the Duke's name at the top of the page. "And I shall add your cousin Tiffany, because she always says, 'Serena, how pretty you look,' and draws attention to the fact."

"But you know she only says it to mock me, Mama," Serena pointed out, "as it is never true."

"It shall be true this time," Kate assured her.

"And we shall invite Tiffany's fiancé, Lord Diremore, of course," Lady Fanny went on. "I have already received an acceptance from Clarissa Undersette." She turned to smile at Kate. "Clarissa is Serena's very dearest friend—from the cradle." She turned back to her paper. "For Clarissa we shall invite the Duke of Nellingham. I have heard that he is in town and is making an effort to give up his wayward life. He is looking for a young pretty wife with 30,000 pounds in order to mend his fortune and settle down to produce an heir. Perhaps poor Clarissa would not be averse to such a match. She has been on the marriage market for two years without an acceptable offer and, after all, dear Nellingham is of the first rank, and is closely allied to the throne, even though he is impoverished and no longer in the first blush of youth."

"First blush of youth!" Serena exclaimed. She made a derisive face. "Indeed, Mama, has your eyesight failed you completely? Old Nellingham is ancient! Positively decrepit! He is nothing but a mass of wrinkles and folds and hanging flesh. And he is the most profligate, debauched, antiquated, decayed . . ."

"Enough!" her ladyship protested. "He is the same age as your father."

"Oh," Serena said meekly. "I should never have guessed it." She turned to her cousin. "Wait until you see him, Katie—a complete ruin. He has lived the most dissolute life! Looking for a *young* pretty wife, indeed! With 30,000 pounds!" She sniffed indignantly. "I would run away from home and become a swineherd before I would ever submit to such a marriage."

Lady Fanny laughed. "Swineherd, indeed! Serena! You must say something like that to dear Drew the next time you are with him. He will consider you a wit of the first rank." She chirped happily to herself for several seconds, then rose, carrying the guest list in her hand, and moved toward the door. "I shall take this to my room and muse for a time. You must take Katie downstairs and eat a nourishing breakfast, my love. Then we shall go to Madame Antoine's and purchase a few pretty things for our party." She glanced at her list. "Let me see: if we have dear Drew and Clarissa and Nellingham and Tiffany and Diremore . . . and I shall invite Sonny and Letitia to present a picture of connubial bliss . . ." She wandered out of the room.

After the two girls had nourished themselves with rolls and tea, Serena took her cousin into the garden to collect herbs for their potion. The terrace outside the morning room led to a beautiful balustrade which had three shallow steps leading down to a grassy place. Shrubs and flowers were blooming in breathtaking profusion. While Serena went in search of a small kettle, Kate made her way around the beds, collecting leaves and twigs. Then she arranged a little pile of dry debris in a secluded corner behind some thick foliage and attacked it with her tinder box. By the time Serena returned, Kate had produced a tiny flame which was sending up wisps of gray smoke. She drew a vial of clear liquid from a pocket and poured its contents into the kettle, then set it over the flame. Finally, producing a tiny packet of dried herbs from another pocket, she crumbled them into the liquid, added several pieces of fresh leaf and root, moved her hands back and forth over the brew several times, closed her eyes, and began to mumble to herself.

"Drees hobbis . . . drees hobbis," she murmured.

Suddenly the kettle made a whirring sound and the liquid boiled out at the top. Kate quickly lifted it to one side, setting it on a flat stone. She blew out the flame. "Now," she informed her cousin, "when it cools, we are ready to begin."

Twenty minutes later, in Kate's room, they poured the decoction into a delicate china cup. Kate seated Serena in a chair facing a mirror and began to weave her magic. Whispering all the while, she painted her cousin's eyebrows and eyelashes with the potion. Then she dampened a handkerchief with the liquid and smoothed it over her hair. "There," she said. "In no time you shall be a raving beauty."

"How soon?" Serena asked.

Kate shrugged. "It's a slow-acting spell. Sometimes it takes longer, sometimes not so long, but I expect to see results in an hour or two."

Serena jumped up, squealing with delight. She clasped her hands and did a little jig around the room. "Oh, I can't believe it! By the time we go to Madame Antoine's I shall be able to enchant everyone we see! I shall bow to my friends . . . thus." She demonstrated, smiling archly at her cousin. "And they shall say, 'Good God, Willie! I had no idea Serena had grown to be such a pretty girl!' Words to that effect."

In a state of happiness bordering on delirium, she danced down the hall and into her room to prepare herself for the excursion. Every few seconds she rushed to the mirror to see if there had been any change, and while her abigail was arranging her hair, she wriggled and bobbed so incessantly that the maid finally put up her hands in consternation.

"Miss Serena," she protested, "you must try to sit still. You keep pulling your curls loose the moment I have them in place."

Even after she had put on her pelisse and taken up her reticule, she came back to the mirror for one last peek. "Are they changing?" she asked herself.

"Are what changing, ma'am?"

"Never mind," she giggled, wagging a finger. "You shall know soon enough."

She met Kate in the hallway outside their rooms. "How do I look, love?" she asked her. "Are they darkening yet?"

Kate examined her face carefully. "Mmm, perhaps there are signs."

Serena wriggled with delight. "Come along quickly. I must look in the vestibule mirror." And she drew Kate down the steps beside her, skipping and bouncing so erratically that Kate was afraid they would both miss their footing and plunge headlong to the bottom.

They had barely reached the marble entryway, and Serena was dragging her cousin toward the heavy gilt mirror which hung between two doric columns, when the door to the library opened and the Earl strode out. He was a tall, muscular man with a remarkably youthful face, his hair brushed into the most elaborate of casual styles, and his clothes the first order of perfection.

"So!" he exclaimed in ringing tones. "This is my niece,

37

Kathryn Ashworth. Pretty little puss. Don't look a bit like your father." And he roared appreciatively at his own joke. Then he leaned over Serena and pinched her cheek affectionately. "You're looking especially fine today, my child. Are you in love?" He drowned out any answer she might have given, with another explosion of laughter.

"I am!" Serena cried, rushing toward the mirror.

At that moment Lady Fanny swept down the stairs, in a walking dress of seafoam green. Her husband eyed her appreciatively. "Ah," he mused, "I am the luckiest fellow in London." He turned to his niece. "Your aunt is a treasure indeed, Kathryn! Would you believe she is still as beautiful as the day I met her?"

Fanny giggled prettily and waved a hand in denial.

"She is very beautiful, sir," Kate agreed.

"Nonsense," her ladyship chided. "But you shall see how our girls can shine, at our rout party next week. And now we are on our way to Madame Antoine's to buy them some finery."

"Indeed, indeed!" Deverill exclaimed. "You must buy the prettiest things she has and send the bill to me. Select anything, Fan—spare no expense—as long as it costs no more than a shilling." He tipped back his head and roared again.

While her ladyship gave him a withering look, he ushered them out the front door, still laughing at his own humor. He caught Serena's arm and pulled her away from the mirror.

"You can admire yourself when you finish your shopping, puss," he told her. "I don't want my horses standing in this wind." And he handed them into their carriage and bowed them on their way.

The rain of the night before had washed the city clean. A stiff wind was blowing in from the North Sea, and as the carriage clattered over the cobbles, Kate peered curiously at the houses which lined the sides of the square. Alongside Deverill House stood an unusually beautiful building of silvery stone, its windows framed by graceful arches.

"Is this not the most beautiful street you have ever seen,

Katle?" her cousin asked her. "Do you have such houses in the country, where you live?"

"No," Kate admitted. "It is quite a sight to see so many together. Who lives in this one we are passing?"

"Oh," Serena said with a disinterested toss of her head, "that is where Young Lester lives."

"He must be very rich to have such a beautiful house," Kate observed.

"Yes," Serena said, "but he is not even a peer." And she dismissed him with a wave of her hand.

Beyond Young Lester's house they passed another pile which was even larger. "My goodness!" Kate exclaimed. "To whom does this palace belong?"

Serena beamed. "That is Drew's London house. Is it not beautiful?"

Kate, who found it lacking in beauty but excelling in size, nodded politely. "It is certainly one of the most impressive I have ever seen."

All the way to Regent Street and down its long avenue of shops, Serena continued her prattle. "Is this not the most beautiful avenue . . . the most charming building . . . the most daring phaeton . . . the most beautiful park?" Kate nodded and exclaimed in appropriate tones.

They had no sooner disembarked in front of Madame Antoine's and made their way into the establishment than they encountered Cousin Tiffany and her mama. The young lady was dressed in an elaborately frogged royal-blue pelisse and dashing bonnet, and she looked so much like Lorna—though not nearly so ravishing—that Kate disliked her on sight. Tiffany had brittle blue eyes which ran quickly over Kate in an appraising way while her mouth held itself in a tight little smile. She sat watching her cousins with narrowed eyes as Lady Fanny selected three pieces of silk for new party gowns, a piece of cherry merino for Kate, and a sky-blue merino for Serena to be made up into new walking dresses.

"It will cost more than a shilling," her ladyship laughed, "but I shall send the bill to Dev, all the same."

They had completed their purchases and were making

their way toward the door when the Marchioness of Gyle burst in, a magnificent figure in purple and puce, her elaborate superstructure of chestnut hair supporting a cartwheel hat with no less than seven ostrich plumes on it.

"Well, well!" she trumpeted. "Here you are! I saw your carriage outside. So you have brought little Kathryn to town, have you, Frances? Let me look at her." Grasping Kate roughly by the elbow, she turned her to the left then to the right while she scrutinized her intently through a quizzing glass.

"You have made a mistake," she announced at last. "She is not such a drab little thing as I thought. It is only in contrast to the exquisite sister and the vivacious mother that she looks like a mouse."

"Oh, Gussie!" Fanny protested. "Of course she is not drab! She's a dear sweet girl and we love her very much."

The Marchioness made a rude noise. "We shall see! Ha, ha, ha! We shall see!" And with a perfunctory nod to Serena and Kate, she swept regally out of the shop.

"Oh, dear," Lady Fanny murmured, "Augusta is such a . . ." She fluttered her hands. "So many problems . . ."

The moment they reached Deverill House, Serena dashed into the vestibule and confronted her image in the gilt-framed mirror. She frowned. "Do you see any change, Katie?"

Kate shook her head. "It is impossible to see anything here, this mirror is so dark."

Serena rushed up the stairs to her own well-lighted bedroom. There Kate found her in front of her dressing table, pulling off her bonnet. Two large tears were welling up in her eyes.

"Oh . . ." her voice quavered. "I look just the same! I am not a beauty yet, and I never shall be. The spell did not work." Her chin began to tremble.

"Please don't cry," Kate urged, putting an arm around her shoulder. "It will make you look all swollen and red. I told you these spells require time. I used a very gentle incantation to make this transformation."

"But why not use a strong one which will take effect immediately?" Serena coaxed. "After being ugly and humiliated for so many years, I should love to burst into full bloom all at once."

"Because," Kate explained, "if one is not extremely proficient, the strong spells are difficult to control. Think how distressing it would be if something should go wrong and you were to find yourself suddenly cursed with enormous bushy black eyebrows, or something of the sort."

Serena was silent for a moment. "Well," she admitted, "that would be dreadful indeed."

"Then you must be patient. But you must remain confident that these spells will work, given time. Certainly by the night of our rout party, you'll be glowing and beautiful."

"Very well," Serena said with a sigh. "I shall have to resign myself to another week of suffering." She walked over to her bed and flopped disconsolately down on it.

"I shall give you a treatment before you go to sleep," Kate told her. "They often work more effectively on subjects who are completely relaxed and receptive."

She hurried to her room, threw off her bonnet, and divested herself of her pelisse. Then, as she went over to her dressing table and put out her hand to pick up the potion they had brewed that morning, she hesitated. For a moment she stood thinking.

"I shall do it," she said, and turning away from the potion she had already used on Serena, she stepped to the clothes press, dug deep into its recesses, and from a back corner where she had secreted it under a pair of boots, drew out a tiny black vial. It contained a dye which her mother had concocted for her several months before and which, when applied frequently, caused brows, lashes, or any type of hair to darken slowly. Kate applied it frequently to her own eyebrows to keep them dark for, although she had black hair and black lashes, her brows had a tendency to be rather light—which gave her a perpetually blank expression if not kept under control.

She stood for a moment, holding the vial in her hand. "I should not use this," she thought. "I should rely on the spells and potions; but if I am never able to make them work . . ." She sighed. "Poor Serena." Without further hesitation, she stuffed the vial into her pocket and hurried back to her cousin.

"I have another potion," she told her. ". . . One which was brewed at home; and the ingredients may be stronger. They were all collected from the wilds—from mossy banks and dark forest recesses, and that sort of place—and they were gathered at precisely the proper time—during the dark of the moon."

Serena lay back against her pillows, watching her cousin without enthusiasm. Carefully Kate extracted a bit of liquid on a tiny brush and stroked it on, whispering, "Drees hobbis . . . drees hobbis . . ."

When she had finished, she stood back to observe her handiwork. The result, alas, was not what she had hoped for. The dye, which had been mixed for a brunette, imparted an orange, slightly metallic hue to Serena's blonde hairs. While Kate was frowning, trying to decide what she could do to modify the garish effect, Serena's eyes flew open and she started to her feet.

"Wait!" Kate protested, catching her arm. But Serena rushed to the mirror, dragging her along with her. She gasped.

"Katie!" she cried, clasping her hand. "It is working! Look at me! I have eyebrows! Oh, happiest of all days! Did you ever see such a beautiful sight in your life?"

CHAPTER 4

Drew Wale knew why he had been invited to the Countess of Deverill's rout party: she had singled him out to pair with Serena. And while he had been fond of the girl when she was a child, he was damned if he was going to be leg-shackled to her for life.

There had been a time—when she was still in the school-room and he and Willie were down at Oxford together—that Serena had been one of his pets. She had been a rather pathetic, but engaging child, with a flat little face that looked like the underside of a copper basin; and she had formed an attachment to him the first time he visited Willie's family for the holidays. After that, each time he set foot in the house, she had hurled herself into his arms, twined her own arms around his neck, and shouted ecstatic greetings into his ear.

After he had gone down from Oxford, his duties had kept him at home and he had seen her only once. By that time, she had aged enough to consider herself too old to hang around his neck, but she had greeted him with a smile, slid an arm around his waist, and leaned her head affectionately on his shoulder. All in all, he had enjoyed a warm and comfortable regard for little Serena.

That was why, several years later, when his mother finally convinced him that it was his duty to give up the

43

comfortable life he was leading, find a suitable wife, and produce an heir, he had immediately thought of his friend's little sister. By doing some simple arithmetic, he calculated that Serena was now eighteen or nineteen years old. And they had enjoyed such complete rapport in the past that Wale hoped he might be able to make a quick trip to town, approach the girl and her father in a straightforward manner, and save himself the discomfort of going through an entire Season of parties and bals, and such nonsense.

With this reasonable plan in mind, he made his way to the city, took up temporary abode in a hotel, attired himself properly for a formal call, and hurried to Deverill House to complete his business as quickly as possible. There he had received a rude shock. Serena had changed. Her looks had not improved—though that would not have deterred him—but her behavior had undergone a startling transformation during the intervening years.

Instead of rushing into the room and throwing her arms around him, she came sidling in through a garden door, crouching behind a fan, giggling and blushing and simpering. Each time he tried to talk to her, she minced and snickered and beat the air with her fan, while she fluttered her eyebrows in the most disconcerting manner. And during the entire interview she had said not even one sensible thing to him.

But to Wale's further dismay, Lady Fanny, who had treated him in the kindest and most level-headed way during his Oxford days, appeared to be alarmed when she found him talking to her daughter; and when the Earl came into the room and made several bewildering remarks about birds, accompanied by winks and booming laughter, the young duke fled as fast as courtesy allowed.

He would probably have lost all contact with the family at that point, if he had not encountered Old Willie on the front steps. There the two friends greeted each other with roars of delight, pounded each other's shoulders, and went off together to set Wale's affairs in order.

But it was a grim set of tasks which confronted the Duke. Forced to spend the Season in town searching for a suitable girl, he was obliged to open Asgar House—which turned out to be an even colder, bleaker pile than he remembered—and set up residence there. Old Willie dragged him to Weston's where he was supplied with an assortment of painfully uncomfortable clothes, then to a carriagemaker's where he was browbeaten into buying a new sporting curricle which was "all the crack." After that, Wale had begun presenting himself at bals and parties and gatherings where he immediately became the prime target for the ambitious mamas of the ton, unmarried dukes being always in short supply.

He had submitted himself to all manner of indignities, skipping inanely across ballroom floors in mating rituals known as minuets, quadrilles, and country dances; he had spent evening after evening listening to Italian tenors whining at the tops of their lungs; he had promenaded at the Pantheon and sat through four operas in coats and neck cloths that were so tight he could not turn his head. He had examined the ranks of available females, hoping to hurry his business and spare himself as much suffering as possible. But he discovered, to his dismay, that not only did all the young hopefuls behave in the same unsettling way Serena did, but they all looked so much alike in their dress and hair styles, copied exactly one from the other, that he could barely tell them apart and spent most of his time trying not to address Miss White as Miss Black, or Miss Brown as Miss Green. This caused him no small amount of consternation, as he prided himself on his well-ordered mind.

It was a stultifying experience for Wale, who customarily enjoyed a feeling of good, solid worth. From his earliest childhood he had been imbued with a sense of his duty to king, country, and all his dependents; and as the owner of five major estates and several minor ones, he was daily reminded of the dignity of his position and the influence his actions exerted on the lives of his people. To be stranded in London, hopping about from one foot to the other while there were important things to be done at home, was an ordeal which he found difficult to endure.

And there was another factor which contributed to his nagging unrest: he was a scientist, and the springtime—which was the season when London Society indulged in its most frenzied whirl of activities—was the most productive period for research, collecting specimens, and delving into the mysteries of the universe. It was the time to be bending over one's frog eggs, recording the temperature of their medium each time a pollywog broke out of its sac; it was a time to lie in a bog and count the number of toad croaks emitted per minute by those rotund denizens of that fecund domain; it was a time to crawl through ferns and over rotting timbers on the forest floor, observing the movements of tree frogs and insects, and occasionally, if one were especially fortunate, a newt.

Most Noble Andrew Gilbert Adolphus Wale, Duke of Asgar, Marquis of Brumley, Earl of Marr, Baron Wale of Glenalven, Baron Wale of Havernly had, in addition to his other dignities, the reputation for being the world's foremost authority on amphibians. His life's work had been decided for him at the conclusion of his seventh birthday party, while he was still Marquis of Brumley. After receiving a perfect miniature phaeton with an exquisite pair of ponies, the income henceforward from all the estates of Glenalven, and his grandfather's eleven-karat emerald ring, he had also received from Good Old Jock, the seventh undergardener's boy, the largest, most magnificent toad he had ever had the privilege of examining.

" 'Tis the one from that monstrous ta'pole I 'ad in me dinner mug, Your Lor'ship," Jock explained as he pulled it gingerly out of a canvas pouch, "an' I'd like ye to 'ave it."

And Jock had laid it tenderly on young Wale's eager, outstretched hands. As he stood looking down at it, his heart thumping in his throat and the great, glistening eyes peering back at him steadily, the entire purpose and direction of his life had suddenly jelled. He had rushed into the house, leaping up the stairs to his room, and set the toad on his bed, arranging the folds of the hundred-year-old lace coverlet to make the toad more comfortable. He had gently opened its mouth and peeped inside, noting the way the tongue was fastened to make it possible for the beast to catch insects some distance away. He had drawn out its legs and measured them, thrilled by the difference in length between the front and the rear. And after several hours of examining and measuring and sketching, he had gone out with Old Jock and collected several other specimens—all sadly inferior to the original—to examine and measure and catalog. From such an auspicious beginning it had been an easy step to frogs and newts.

Over the years, his collection of data had become unparalleled, but the necessity to go to London during the 1817 mating season had rudely interrupted a series of tests he was doing on incubation time for various kinds of eggs. And as the Season wore on, and Wale was no closer to finding a proper bride than he had been on the day of his arrival, he grew more and more restless, until he decided to throw over his search and return to Asgar while there was still time to observe a few transformations.

He had set Thursday as the date for his departure, and ordered his staff to commence packing for the journey home; but on Wednesday he encountered difficulties. When Old Willie joined him for breakfast, he was so obviously blue devilled that Wale set about trying to cheer him.

"It's this dashed party at home tomorrow night," Willie repined. "You're coming, of course. Promised. But it's going to be a rum go. All the marriageable gels will be there—that sort of thing—and Sonny with Letitia to present a picture of connubial bliss. Wish Mama would give up on Serena and let Elfan marry her. He's an earl, after all—don't think she'll do much better than that."

Wale frowned and shook his head. "Wouldn't do, Willie. Elfan's a gazetted fortune hunter. On the edge of dun territory. Has to marry an heiress before the summer or go under completely."

Old Willie shrugged. "What's the harm in letting him have her? He'd be grateful—wouldn't poison her tea. And he wouldn't be hanging about her neck like a lover—would keep himself busy and not clutter up her life. Seems like a perfect arrangement—but no one has asked my opinion."

Wale smiled at his friend. Good Old Willie had always been the best kind of chum anyone could have—standing by when he was needed, and in their Oxford days, full of ideas for good solid pranks that broke the monotony without lowering one's self-esteem. But as for having any understanding of human nature, Old Willie was blissfully unaware of everyone's needs but his own. Even so, Wale was fond of him—and he could never bring himself to abandon anyone who needed him.

Therefore, he postponed his departure for another day, and on the night of Lady Fanny's rout party, reluctantly allowed his valet to dress and polish him and send him off, probably for the last time in his life that he would ever submit himself to such indignities.

At Deverill House, the night before the rout party, Kate prepared a special potion. She had brewed it for herself several times in the past when she was trying to compete with her sister and retain the affections of certain young men. It had never been successful; but she thought that, perhaps, this time she could bring all the ingredients together and make it work for Serena to give her that little extra measure of allure which she needed so much.

As the two girls readied themselves for the entertainment, they were in a state of high glee. They donned new silk gowns, had their hair arranged à la Grecque, and painted their brows and lashes with the dye which Kate's mother had prepared for her. Then Kate dug out the special potion she had prepared, and started down the hall with it, toward her cousin's room. But halfway there, she paused, thought deeply for a moment, then turned around and made her way quickly downstairs to the library, where she added a dollop of her uncle's best brandy—just in case.

"You must drink this," she told Serena, after she had hurried back upstairs to her room. "It is a special potion which will make you irresistible to all men."

Serena raised it quickly to her lips and drank. Before she had drained it completely, however, she hesitated, then lowered it and held it out to Kate. "Please," she urged, "take a little yourself. You do not need it as much as I do; but I should like to be sure you will enjoy the evening, too."

Kate smiled at her. Since her cousin had drunk most of it, she accepted the glass, raised it to her lips, and drained off the remainder.

Serena giggled. "Now we shall be the most adorable and desirable girls in all England."

Kate nodded and they moved sedately to their places beside Lady Fanny in the entryhall. Within a very few minutes, they both began to feel giggly. The most delightful and humorous notions kept popping into Kate's head, which she felt impelled to share with her cousin, and while her ladyship scowled and chided and shushed them, it was not long before the two girls were barely able to suppress outbursts of riotous mirth.

"I'll know your Duke the moment I see him," Kate giggled.

"No, you shan't," Serena tittered. "You are looking for someone with a face like a pickle."

They were immediately obliged to cover their mouths and indulge in a fit of stifled hysterics before they could continue. Finally Serena squeaked, "He is not like that at all. He is the most charming, the handsomest, the most intelligent . . ."

"Please," Kate begged, "spare me your besotted opinion. There is only one way to resolve our difference—I shall guess which one he is. In fact, I shall guess who each one of our guests is."

Subsequently she judged her cattle as they arrived, bestowing on Serena, amid giggles and gurgles, her pithy summaries of their attributes and vagaries.

The first person to arrive was the Duke of Nellingham, and when she saw his wrinkles and multiple eye pouches, Kate was able to whisper, "This ruin must be his Grace of Nellingham." Serena was obliged to concur.

But then Kate's position became less secure as an extremely handsome young gentleman arrived. He was

49

sporting glossy black locks which were brushed into the fashionable "windswept," and a neck cloth of such elegance and dash that Kate was tempted for an instant to identify him as the odious young Duke. But as she was preparing to pronounce the words, Judson opened the front door again and Tiffany appeared with her mama. She threw out both hands to the gentleman and exclaimed in ardent tones, "Diremore, my love!"

The gentleman quickly turned and bestowed a lingering kiss on Tiffany's upturned fingers. She smiled at the ladies over the top of his head. "How pretty you look, Serena," she called.

Diremore looked back at Serena and surveyed her in some surprise. "You do, indeed," he agreed. "You look dashed pretty this evening!"

Serena dimpled and giggled and held out her hand to be kissed.

Kate had no sooner been presented to Diremore, who with Tiffany and Aunt Maria were quickly led away by Aunt Fanny, than two young gentlemen arrived simultaneously. Both were tall and blond and well-made; both wore cream breeches smoothed tightly over neatly turned thighs; both wore immaculate, intricately folded neck cloths and dark coats which fit so perfectly that they appeared to have been pasted onto their torsos.

And their burnished locks, also arranged in the "windswept," were identically brushed and perfectly molded . . . But, no—one had a clump of disarrayed strands over the right ear where he had impatiently run his fingers through it. And the same young gentleman's neck cloth was not quite right around the throat where he had inserted a finger and jerked at the fabric to release the pressure and allow himself to breathe.

Kate smiled confidently. "The perfect one on the right is his Grace of Asgar," she whispered to Serena. "I admit I didn't expect him to be so comely, but there is no mistaking the perfection of his appearance and the general air of self-appreciation."

50

Serena giggled. "Wrong, wrong, wrong! That's Carlton Elfan, Lord Clangarry."

Kate would have protested, but Elfan was already upon them, bowing over their hands. He was looking eagerly at Serena—undoubtedly captivated by her bubbling charm, Kate thought. He bowed briefly over Kate's hand, barely seeing her, and turned quickly back to her cousin.

Kate watched Wale curiously. He was moving toward them slowly, gazing off toward a side room in a preoccupied way. She wondered how she could have made such a mistake in identifying him—it was so obvious to her now that he was the Duke, walking forward with his brows slightly tightened and his thoughts a hundred miles away, as though he was bored by the necessity of mingling with such lowly mortals as mere earls and viscounts.

He reached them and paused, now staring at the floor, as he mused over some weighty problem. Then, still without looking at them, he bowed over Serena's hand and murmured, "Reena . . ." He pressed her fingers to his lips.

"And this is my cousin, Kathryn Ashworth," Serena announced in a voice which rang with pride and affection.

The Duke raised his eyes. For a moment he stared at Kate in surprise. "Good God!" he exclaimed. "Grandmother!"

At that moment Lady Fanny descended on them. "Ah, here you are, Drew, my love. You're to take Serena into supper." Crooking his arm for him, she placed Serena's hand on it and pushed them rather roughly toward the dining room. Wale looked back over his shoulder at Kate. He opened his mouth, but Lady Fanny forestalled any desire he might have had to speak by wagging a finger in his face.

"You can indulge in your pretty little chitchat when you are seated, my dear," she told him. And, placing Kate's hand on Elfan's arm, she herded them all into the dining room.

Kate felt that the evening was off to a bad start. Her partner, Elfan, kept staring longingly at Serena, while Serena's partner kept trying to catch Kate's eye. During the

51

meal she found Wale's attention turning constantly in her direction, and it was soon obvious that he was attempting to communicate something to her but, as they were across the table from each other, he was unable to do so.

In the meantime, Diremore, who was on the other side of Serena, perhaps in an attempt to compensate for Wale's neglect of his partner, began laughing and talking softly with her. Watching them, Tiffany began to pout. For a few minutes she sat picking at her food and, with one finger, twisting a curl at the side of her neck. Finally she scowled defiantly at her fiancé, turned her attention to her other side and began to flirt archly with Old Willie.

During this performance Kate had ample time to observe Wale. She was surprised by what she saw. He was a rather good-looking young man—not an Adonis, but with an open countenance, even features, and dark gray eyes ringed with thick black lashes which she especially liked. He had, above all things, a look of glowing health, and the easy manner she had grown to expect of persons who were in positions of authority. Despite her determination to dislike him, she found herself approving of the warmth and defer-ence he displayed toward Lady Fanny, who obviously re-turned his affection.

As soon as the meal had been completed, the company withdrew to a large sitting room which had been prepared for dancing. Wale, with Serena on his arm, joined Kate and Elfan in front of a refreshment table which had been laid out alongside a window that opened into the garden. Elfan quickly contrived to engage Serena's attention and draw her away from them. Wale picked up two glasses, taking champagne himself and presenting ratafia to Kate with a flourish.

"Miss Ashworth," he began in a pleasant, husky voice, "I hope you will accept my apology for addressing you in such a manner, but—this will surprise you, I am sure—you bear the most striking resemblance to a portrait of my grandmother, Kathryn Havernly-Brumford, the seventh duchess, which was painted when she was a pretty young girl your age. The painting now hangs over the fireplace in the main hall at Asgar." And confident that he had set everything to rights, he took a long refreshing draught of wine.

Kate gave him a gracious smile. "It does not surprise me in the least that I look like your grandmother," she told him, "as she is my grandmother, too. My father is Harley Ashworth, our mutual grandmother's illegitimate son by Gawain Ashworth, Monseigneur of Krenull Isle."

She had expected him to respond with a fair degree of interest to her revelation, but to her consternation, he clapped a hand over his mouth and departed abruptly through the open window. A moment later she could hear him outside in the garden, coughing his mouthful of champagne into a flowerbed. Before he returned, Lady Fanny bustled up to her with Elfan on her arm, and putting their hands together, steered them out onto the floor to start the dancing.

"Now where is Drew, the naughty boy?" she muttered. "He is to partner Serena for this set." She scowled down the room to a spot where her daughter was chatting animatedly with Tiffany and Lord Diremore.

Kate barely had time to set down her wine glass before she found herself steered into line by the most inattentive partner she had ever been obliged to endure. She had been skipping back and forth for several minutes, watching Elfan's every move to keep from colliding with him on each of his returns, when Serena danced past with Lord Diremore. She was wagging her golden eyebrows at him, her cheeks brightly pink from the potion, and a blissful smile on her face.

"Dashed roué!" Elfan muttered to himself. ". . . Pay his devilish compliments to his own fiancée!"

When the music came to an end and the couples began to drift toward the sides of the room, Elfan bowed low to Kate, thanked her for the honor she had bestowed upon him, and deserted her. Fortunately, at that moment, Wale walked back into the room, patting his mouth with a handkerchief, which he proceeded to stuff into a coat pocket, instantly ruining the perfect symmetry of his appearance. He came quickly over to Kate.

"Miss Ashworth," he addressed her in a low voice, "it is apparent that you know more of my grandmother's history than I do." He ran a hand thoughtfully over his chin. "I often heard her say, 'I miss my Harley,' but I thought it was a place rather than a person." He frowned. "What I do not understand is why it was necessary for her to miss him. Had there been an estrangement?"

"There had been an estrangement between your father and mine," she explained. "Your father ordered mine out of the house and forbade him ever to show his face there again or to live on Asgar soil."

Wale was frowning. "That was extremely harsh. What could they have quarreled about which was so serious as to result in a permanent breach?"

Kate lowered her eyes. "They quarreled about my mother," she said softly. "My father married her against your father's wishes."

At that moment Lady Fanny swept up to them, her brows knitted and a decidedly annoyed expression on her face.

"Katie, my love," she said crossly, "where is Serena? Did she not promise this country dance to dear Drew?"

Across the room, behind her ladyship's back, Serena was deep in an animated conversation with Lord Diremore, smiling prettily and leaning her head close to his. While Kate watched them, Serena linked her arm through her partner's, and they strolled out through an open window into the garden.

"Ah," Kate said, "I see her. I shall remind her of her commitment."

As she moved away, Wale made an effort to follow her, but Lady Fanny put out a restraining hand. "Dear boy," she said, "I wish to speak to you . . ."

Kate made her way hurriedly across the room and stepped out onto the terrace. To her surprise, Serena and Diremore were nowhere in sight. To her additional surprise, Wale came out through the windows almost immediately and strode over to her side.

"How strange," she said to him. "I saw my cousin come this way." She started to walk briskly across the terrace.

"Miss Ashworth," Wale began, striding along beside her. Suddenly Kate gasped and stopped in her tracks, barring his way with a peremptory hand.

"Don't move!" she cried. Dropping down in a billow of silk, she gently picked something off the ground from in front of his right toe.

"You almost stepped on a frog," she scolded, rising again beside him and sheltering the creature in her two cupped hands.

"A frog!" he exclaimed. "What kind is it?"

"I'm not sure," she said, opening her hands a tiny crack to peer in at it. "It's not like any we have at home. The markings are different."

"Please," he said, "let me see it." And he put out his hand.

"Oh, I could never allow you to hold it," she said. "Frogs are very delicate animals. Most men are too rough—they injure them."

"Not I!" he assured her. "I have never injured an amphibian in my life, and I have examined thousands. In fact, I'm something of an authority."

"Are you really?" she said, looking up at him curiously. "I would never have thought it. I should have expected you to be concerned about . . ." She stopped suddenly, her face flushing a bright pink. "Well, let us say I expected you to be quite different from what you are."

Wale chuckled. "Did you really? What did you expect?"

"Please . . ." she said, moving toward the parapet. "It is much too beautiful a night to talk of such things." And she gently carried the frog to the wall, holding her hands together in front of her. Wale's brows knitted.

"Let's stand here so he won't hurt himself if he leaps out of my hands," she said.

She laid the back of her left hand on the cold stone balustrade and slowly raised the other to reveal a small, bright-eyed croaker who looked up at them resentfully, poising itself for a moment as it gathered its strength to leap.

From somewhere beyond and below them, in the shelter of flowering bushes, there were little rustling sounds of which Kate and Wade, fascinated by their frog, were unaware. "Oh!" someone squeaked. "You naughty boy!"

There was a murmur, a throaty chuckle, and a deep voice rumbled happily, "Delicious ear . . . delicious throat . . . delicious beautiful nymph."

"You're right," Wale said, peering at the frog. "I've never seen one exactly like it before. I shall name it after you, Miss Ashworth. Dash it, I wish we had more light here. We must preserve this specimen until we are able to examine it properly—put it in a box."

But before he could cover it with his hand—before Kate could close her hands around it again—the frog gave a mighty leap and flew off the balustrade through the flowering bushes beyond it. There was an ear-shattering cry.

"Oh, horrid! It's cold!" a voice shrieked. "What is it? . . . A frog!" There were more screams.

Kate put a hand on the balustrade and, with a quick shove, vaulted over it, descending through the leafy branches and landing on a grassy patch beyond. She found herself standing beside Lord Diremore, who was reaching out spasmodically with his hands while Serena danced up and down in front of him, squealing and slapping at the back of her neck with her fan.

"Oh, Katie!" she shrieked. "I'm going to be sick! It's raining frogs, and one of the horrid things landed on my skin! I can't bear it!"

"There, there," Kate soothed her. "It's going to be all right."

But Serena could not stop jumping and wriggling, even after Kate put a restraining arm firmly around her waist. Wale, who had come around the corner of the balustrade and walked sedately down the steps, stood watching them quietly. Diremore had withdrawn and was leaning against the stone wall.

56

"Please, sir," Kate urged the Duke, "if you would take Lord Diremore back into the house, I'll be able to soothe my cousin."

Both Wale and Diremore hesitated for a moment. Then they bowed stiffly to each other and walked together up the steps and through the open windows.

"Now stop, you peagoose," Kate scolded. "You must stop this instant or your Duke will think you've taken leave of your senses."

"I don't care what he thinks," Serena snapped, breaking away from Kate and hopping in a circle. "I'm all sticky and crawly and I can't stand still. That dreadful wet creature actually landed on my bare skin! I'm going to contract a horrid disease."

"Not from that harmless little frog," Kate chided. "And if it makes you feel itchy to think about it, then put it out of your mind. Don't forget that this party was planned for the express purpose of fixing the Duke's attention—and I know for a fact that he considers frogs . . ."

"Oh, fiddle!" Serena cut her off. "I don't care a whit for what that silly Drew thinks. My heart is . . ." She put a hand expressively to her slightly rumpled bosom.

"Is what?" Kate asked, a flicker of foreboding nibbling at her own heart.

"Broken!" Serena moaned and took a long shivering breath. "My life is ruined!"

There was a clatter of feet on the terrace as Lady Fanny scurried down the steps. "Ah, there you are!" she exclaimed. "This will never do. Everyone is ready to start a country dance. You're to devote your attention to Drew from this moment on, Serena. No more self-indulgence or shyness. Come along, Katie. I have paired you with Sonny for this set."

Fanny caught her daughter's arm and hustled her back into the house while Kate followed meekly at her heels.

"But Mama," Serena protested.

"Tell me later, dear," Fanny said. "You're looking so exceptionally well this evening that I don't want you to waste a moment of it. I'm only sorry I didn't invite more eligible young peers—there's always a chance that Drew won't come up to scratch. But we can coax Willie to drop a few hints which might do some good."

As Fanny led Serena back to the resigned young Duke and firmly placed her daughter's hand on his arm then nudged them out onto the floor, Sonny held his hand out to Kate. She took it, giving him a preoccupied smile. To her surprise, as they stepped into their places and waited for the first few bars of music to lead them into the set, she saw Wale look wistfully over at her, and she felt a sudden rush of embarrassment, hoping that her aunt was not watching.

"So," Sonny said, as they linked hands and scampered down the line together, "you and Mama have decided to make a match between Serena and our friend Wale."

"Nothing is settled yet," Kate informed him.

"Nothing, indeed," Sonny agreed with a smile. "In fact, from the stormy expressions on certain faces, I'd say you've already made a muddle of things."

CHAPTER 5

As the last guests stepped out through the front door and it closed heavily behind them, Lady Fanny emitted a groan of happy misery, hobbled into the blue withdrawing room, and with a heavy sigh, sank onto a sofa, kicking her shoes off her swollen feet.

"What a dreadful evening," she moaned. "I am utterly exhausted!" She turned toward the girls. "It was a total success, would you not say so, my loves?"

"Indeed, Aunt," Kate agreed. "I overheard Lady Undersette tell Cousin Tiffany's mama that it was the most delightful party she has attended yet this Season."

"Ah," Lady Fanny sighed, her face alight. "Then it was worth all the suffering." She smiled at her daughter, who was standing behind the sofa staring glumly into space. "Serena, my angel, is everything going well between you and dear Drew? I observed how charmingly he bent his head close to yours when he brought you a glass of ratafia at the end of the country dance. Has he made any declarations as yet?"

Serena's chin began to tremble. "Drew Wale can take himself off to the moon, for all I care! My life is ruined and I have no further desire to live!" And she threw herself onto a sofa, buried her face against her arm, and began to sob bitterly.

59

With an exclamation, Lady Fanny leaped up and rushed to her side. "My darling!" she cried. "What on earth can be wrong? Has he offended you in some way?"

"Of course not!" Serena snapped. "Drew has nothing to do with it. Can you not get that silly Duke out of your head? I have fallen in love with the only man I will ever be able to care for and . . ." She pressed a hand to her mouth. ". . . He is engaged to marry another woman!"

Lady Fanny let out a squeak. "You cannot mean that you have fallen in love with that odious Lord Diremore?"

"Odious! Mama! He is the kindest, the gentlest, the most loving . . ."

"Serena!" Lady Fanny shrieked. "He is Tiffany's fiancé! Do you not remember how envious we were going to make her feel when she heard of your engagement to dear Drew—and her pompous, self-satisfied mother, too—after all her snubs and mockery? Have you forgotten our delightful plan, my love?"

Serena rose to her feet, shaking with indignation. "Indeed, how can you concern yourself with such a trivial emotion as envy, when we are speaking of true and undying love! You will never understand!" And she rushed out of the room.

"Wait!" Lady Fanny cried, starting after her. But she had not taken more than three steps before she stopped and turned back to Kate. "You must go to her, my dearest. She will listen to you. Somehow we must coax her out of this dreadful aberration."

"By morning she may have thought better of it," Kate suggested.

Her ladyship sank back onto a sofa. "Perhaps. But if she has not?"

"Then we must help the Duke to win her heart again. We must contrive some situation which will show him to better advantage. Though, why Serena cannot see that Wale is infinitely more charming and handsome than Diremore, I am sure I cannot imagine."

"True," Lady Fanny agreed. "What sort of situation shall we contrive?"

Kate frowned. "Well . . ." she said slowly, "nothing comes to mind at the moment, but I shall think of something."

Fanny's troubled look returned. "We must do so, my love! And they must be clever situations which will capture Serena's heart and secure it forever."

There were heavy footfalls in the hallway and Deverill strode into the room, his face grim. "What's this, what's this?" he demanded. "I met Serena on the stairs and she informed me that she is in love with that rascal, Diremore! I do not know what mischief you are contemplating, Fanny, but rest assured, I shall not stand by and allow a scandal to involve this family!"

Her ladyship squeaked and wrung her hands. "No, no, my love!"

"Please, sir," Kate explained, "we are also shocked by this development, and we are planning certain schemes which will end the attachment immediately."

"Good!" he growled. "I shall not be subjected to the humiliation of having my daughter make a cake of herself over someone else's fiancé!"

Kate did not waken the next morning until after ten o'clock. With a decidedly murky head, she dragged herself out of bed, marched to the window, and for several seconds stood breathing rhythmically while she concentrated on re-aligning her forces. The air was not salubrious, she noted, being full of smoke from thousands of kitchens and the dust from endless lines of horses and carts which were bearing goods and produce into the city. She had been huffing and puffing and concentrating for several minutes, to no avail, and was on the point of collapsing back into bed for another hour's sleep, when the door opened and her abigail bustled in with a tray of tea and buttered eggs.

"The Countess is rising early herself this morning, miss," Brill informed her, "to greet callers who'll be coming to pay their respects after last night's party. Her ladyship suggests that you wear your light green muslin, which is so especially becoming to you."

Thirty minutes later, feeling remarkably refreshed, Kate found herself downstairs in the blue withdrawing room greeting Lady Undersette and Clarissa, and before she could draw Clarissa aside to enlist her aid in weaning Serena's interest from Diremore, Lord Elfan and the Duke of Asgar were ushered in. Smiling, Wale came across the room to her immediately. He bowed over her hand.

"Excellent party last night," he told her. "First one I've enjoyed since I came to town."

Before Kate could reply, Elfan joined them and bowed with elaborate ceremony. "So radiant this morning, Miss Ashworth." But he was looking over her shoulder, peering eagerly around the room. Suddenly his face lighted up. "Ah!" he exclaimed, and left her.

"What's the matter with Serena?" Wale asked, also looking over the top of Kate's head.

She turned to observe her cousin, who had slipped into the room and was making her way to a far window, her face heavy with gloom. Serena paused to bow briefly to her guests, then leaned against the jamb and stared unhappily out into the sun-strewn garden. Kate hurried to her side.

"Please, dearest," she whispered, "come speak to your guests. Pretend to be more cheerful."

Serena stared at her sullenly, her eyes brimming with tears.

"Good gracious!" Clarissa exclaimed in surprise from across the room, "How beautiful your eyes are this morning, Serena! You grow prettier every time I see you."

Kate gave her a nod of approval.

"Indeed," Elfan agreed, moving toward them, " . . . beautiful . . . exquisite eyes . . . most delightful . . . charming . . ."

While he rambled on and Serena stood grimly accepting his homage, her face bleak with suffering, Wale contrived to draw Kate aside. "Miss Ashworth," he said, "I should like to make a tour of Lady Deverill's garden to find the frog we were examining last night, and any other specimens which I do not have in my collection. Would you care to accompany me, or should I approach Old Willie and enlist his aid?"

Kate was watching Serena unhappily. Despite the flow of compliments which Elfan was pouring over her, she was still a picture of woe.

"I think," she said softly, "as soon as the others have departed, you and Serena and I might make a tour of the garden. She will not wish to help us collect frogs, but the fresh air will be beneficial."

Wale nodded. "Poor girl. She looks moped to death."

While Serena continued to stand by the window staring out gloomily, Lady Undersette and Clarissa chatted with Lady Fanny, and at the end of twenty minutes called cheery farewells to her and went on their way. Elfan, realizing that his gallantry was falling on deaf ears, reluctantly withdrew, also. Kate then explained to her aunt that Wale wanted to tour the garden in search of specimens, and with many arch smiles and nods, Lady Fanny bundled her glum daughter into a warm pelisse and bonnet, and sent her out into the yard on his Grace's arm.

They were no sooner out of Lady Fanny's sight and earshot than Serena drew away from Wale and seated herself on a stone bench. "Why anyone should wish to walk about in this cold, drafty place, I am sure I do not know," she observed petulantly. "It is damp and dirty, and there is not even one thing of interest to keep a person from being bored to distraction. How can you expect me to sit here, frozen to the quick, and pretend to be amiable?"

Kate patted her reassuringly on the arm. "I have hopes that the wind will put some color in your cheeks, my love. Then we shall take a drive in the park; and who knows whom we shall meet?"

"Oh," Serena said, brightening suddenly. "I shall sit here until I am feeling more the thing." She gave her cousin a broad wink.

Kate quickly led Wale down onto the lower terrace. He glanced back over his shoulder toward the huddled form which was perched on the edge of the stone bench, her face stubbornly turned toward the brisk gusts which were whipping through the trees. "So Serena has fallen in love with Diremore," he observed.

Kate gasped. "Certainly not, sir! How can you suggest such a thing?"

He grinned at her. "I have known Serena since she was young enough to sit on my lap. I think I understand her moods fairly well."

Kate looked at him earnestly. "You are exceedingly fond of her, are you not?"

"I am," he agreed. "I think of her as one of my little sisters."

Kate's brow tightened and she opened her mouth to protest, but Wale had already dropped onto his knees in front of some bushes and was pushing leaves aside, peering into the damp peaty recesses beneath them. With a sigh, Kate knelt beside him and scrabbled with her fingers through the wet debris.

"This is the perfect place to find amphibians," Wale observed. "The gardeners here are not such gudgeons as to rake away all the life, as they do in so many other places. Here is a hole. It may be the home of a small toad."

Kate began to dig vigorously with her fingers.

"Here, let me do that," he urged, poking both his hands into the damp earth. "There is no need for you to muddy yourself."

Kate smiled at him. "Water and soap will put everything to rights again quickly enough."

For several minutes the two scientists dug energetically, scooping out the dirt as they worked and piling it in little mounds beside them. Leaning forward eagerly, they moved twigs aside and scraped gently to the bottom of the hole. It was empty.

They both straightened up, sighing with disappointment. For a moment they sat considering where to look next, then they moved to a fountain which was plashing happily into a lily-filled basin. Here Kate and Wale swished their hands in the water to rinse off the worst of the mire. A careful examination of the lily pads and mossy areas around the edges of the pool disclosed three small frogs, all of which were familiar to the Duke. "We have these at home," he told her. "If we could only find the frog you had in your hands last night."

"If we do not," Kate told him, "I shall search tonight when he is rambling about in the dark."

Wale nodded. "But it should be easier to find his hole now while the light is good."

Beyond the fountain, they attacked a raised bank of peonies. They had cleared another carpet of leaves and were scraping the soil back and forth with their hands when Kate laid a muddy paw on her companion's sleeve. "Shh," she warned, and pointed to a pair of bright eyes which were observing them from around the corner of a heavy stalk. Cautiously Wale reached out and closed his fingers around a tiny frog, scooping it toward himself tenderly. He plunged a begrimed hand into a pocket, drew out a small box, popped the specimen into it, then stuffed it back into his coat, leaving a trail of mud and pebbles sticking to his garments.

They straightened up and smiled at each other.

"It is not the frog we found last night," Kate pointed out.

"No," he agreed, "but it is an interesting one."

She peered into his face. It was a nice face, enhanced by a benevolent expression, and with his color heightened by the sharp breeze and his hair tumbled over his forehead, Kate found herself wondering why Serena was not enchanted with him. How her cousin could prefer the oily Diremore to this straightforward, attractive young man was more than she could fathom. She noted that he was looking back at her in the same considering way, and she was about to tell him that Serena was an extremely lovable girl, now old enough to be courted by young men who appreciated an excellent though modest maiden, when she saw something move on a tree limb that was just behind Wale's head.

"Oh!" she exclaimed; and stepping around him, she caught hold of another branch and swung herself lightly up into the tree, then dove toward a small hole in its trunk and plunged her hand in.

"Good God!" Wale exclaimed, reaching up his hands to catch her if she came careening down again.

Kate straightened up. "I have him. It's the one you wanted . . . or its twin."

"Please!" he cried again. "Hold onto something! You're going to fall!"

"Oh, no," she assured him. "I never fall. But I shall have to sit down and hand him to you. I don't want to crush him."

She held out her fist toward him. Inside it she could feel the frog thrashing wildly.

"For God's sake, Cousin!" Wale roared at her in consternation. "Hold onto that other branch! You are making an old man of me! I shall catch you if you come tumbling down, but you still may injure yourself."

"I am not going to fall!" she told him crossly. "Will you put that notion out of your head! And will you please reach your hand up here so I may put the frog into it? He is wriggling inside my fist and I am afraid he will escape or I shall squeeze him."

There was a sudden roar from the terrace. "Well, Serena!" came the Earl's booming voice. "Look who has dropped by to pay us a call!"

Kate turned to observe the newcomers, who were in plain view from her perch in the tree. Beside the Earl, the Duke of Nellingham was walking stiffly, an elegant Malaga stick in one hand, which he leaned on from time to time while he pressed his other hand against the small of his back, as though endeavoring to relieve some discomfort which lodged there. His crumbled face was more disreputable than ever in the glaring light of day, his eyes swollen with brandy and lack of sleep, and his massive array of wrinkles only partially brought under control by liberal applications of maquillage.

"Yes, yes," Nellingham mumbled, grinning in an effort at cheerfulness and thereby displaying two rows of stained and crooked teeth. He made a sweeping bow toward Kate.

"Ah, charming! Your humble servant."

With some difficulty he straightened himself out of his

66

bow, emitting a hiss as his bones and muscles settled themselves, protesting, into their proper places again.

"Your daughter," he told Deverill in a loud, ringing voice, "vies with the sun to cast radiance over this garden."

"My daughter!" the Earl exclaimed. "That is my niece, Kathryn Ashworth. My daughter is over here." And he indicated the bench where Serena's bonnet was visible to Kate through the shrubbery. Deverill turned back to scowl at Kate.

"Kathryn!" he roared. "What are you standing on? From here it looks as though you are up in that tree."

"I am, sir," she explained. "It was necessary for me to climb up here to catch a frog."

"Frog!" he exploded. "What are you saying? You have no business catching frogs—you are no longer in the schoolroom. Come down from there immediately, miss!"

"Yes, sir," she said.

"Wait, wait," he protested as she made ready to swing herself down. "You'll injure yourself. Who is that with you?" He peered through the bushes that screened Wale from his sight.

"It is his Grace of Asgar, sir."

"Well, you cannot fall on him," Deverill muttered. "Most improper. Wait there and I shall summon Timothy."

Serena had risen from her seat and walked to the balustrade where she stood watching Kate anxiously. Nellingham joined her.

"I say, Miss Ashley," he said, peering at her through his quizzing glass, "you'll find this dashed amusing, but it looks from here as though you are standing in a tree." And he laughed heartily, breaking off suddenly to fall into a deep, rattling cough. When he had cleared his lungs, he jerked an elaborate lace handkerchief from his cuff and dabbed his mouth.

"Yes, yes," he chuckled. "All these witty young ladies." And he bowed again to Serena, who was watching him with an expression of acute distaste on her face.

Wale, on the ground beneath Kate's tree, held up a hand to her. "Come down. Cousin," he urged. "I'll catch you.

67

There's no need for his lordship to fetch a footman and create a stir. Just take my hand and put your foot on my shoulder."

Kate hesitated. "If I did not have this frog in my hand, I could swing down with no difficulty whatsoever."

"It is all right," he assured her. "I'll catch you. Just step down."

"Very well," she said, "but I dislike muddying your coat."

She put her foot on his shoulder, and as she sprang down, he caught her around the waist and swung her easily to the ground.

"Here," she said, pushing her fist toward him. "Let us pop him into a box before he escapes again."

Wale rummaged in a pocket and brought out another container. As soon as they had stuffed the captive into it and closed the lid, they made their way up the steps onto the terrace. Serena and Nellingham were still standing at the balustrade.

"Honestly, Katie!" Serena exclaimed indignantly. "I shall not comment on your eccentric behavior."

The Earl and Timothy appeared through a window and came out onto the terrace toward them.

"Ah, you are down," Deverill observed. He gave Timothy a nod of dismissal. "And here is his Grace of Nellingham come to pay a call. Isn't this a pleasant surprise, Serena?"

His daughter tilted her head back to look sullenly at the ruined Duke. With a cold nod, she curtsied. He took her hand and pressed it to his lips. Immediately, however, he let it go and fell into a new fit of coughing. When he had recovered, he turned to greet Kate. She held out a muddy hand to him.

"Good God, child!" Deverill exclaimed, peering down at the hand. "You can't expect Nelly to kiss that! And look at your gown! What in God's name have you been doing? The front of your skirt is caked with mud."

Kate looked at it unhappily. "Oh, dear," she said. "It is quite ruined, I see. I was kneeling in the flower beds."

"Kneeling . . . !" He began to sputter. "Whatever . . . Good God!" He turned to Wale. "And you, sir! Have you been kneeling in the flower beds also? I shall speak frankly to you, my boy, your appearance is a disgrace!"

Wale began to laugh. "I fear you are right, sir."

Nellingham, hearing Wale laughing, joined him and for a moment they chuckled together, the old Duke interspersing his mirth with a rattling cough from time to time. The Earl watched him impatiently, then turned to his daughter.

"See here, Serena," he reminded her, "his Grace of Nellingham has come to pay . . ."

"Yes, yes, I know," Serena interrupted him crossly. "He has come to pay a call. But I am not in the mood for callers. I am wearied to death . . . I am exhausted . . . I am miserable!" And before anyone could answer her, she ran across the terrace and disappeared into the house. Kate and the three gentlemen stood staring after her in surprise.

Suddenly the Earl let out a bark of laughter. "Daresay she was funning. Naughty puss! But my niece is not exhausted and miserable, are you, Kate? You are delighted to see his Grace of Nellingham, are you not?"

"Yes, indeed, sir," Kate assured him.

He turned to Wale. "And young Wale is delighted to see you again."

"Certainly, sir," Wale agreed.

"Wale?" the old Duke exclaimed. "Would this be Randall's boy? How is your father, sonny?"

Wale made a solemn face. "Deceased, sir."

"Dead!" Nellingham cried. "I can't believe it! He and I were at Oxford together. When did it happen?"

"Seven years ago, sir."

"Seven!" Nellingham exclaimed. He scowled at him angrily. "Why was I not informed?"

For a moment Wale was caught off balance, but he quickly regained his aplomb, nodded his head solemnly, and assured the Duke that he would investigate the oversight. Nellingham stood musing unhappily.

"An accident of some kind, I collect. Your father was a young man in the prime of life."

69

Wale shook his head. "No, sir, I am sorry to say that he died of natural causes. The doctors informed us that it was port and brandy which deprived us of our gracious lord. That and a special kind of pastry which he favored."

"Good God!" Nellingham exclaimed, and began to stride up and down the terrace, restlessly swinging his stick.

"Here, here, now, old man," Deverill murmured in a soothing tone. You must not take it so much to heart."

"*Old* man!" the Duke exploded. "*Old* man, indeed!"

"Come, come, Nelly, you know that is merely an expression. I meant nothing by it."

"I should hope not! You are the same age yourself!"

"Yes, yes," Deverill agreed.

"I am in the prime of life!" Nellingham announced. "Many long happy years ahead of me. In fact, I am on the verge of matrimony." He stopped pacing and cleared his throat. "Decided to settle down and produce an heir. Looking for a pretty young girl with a docile temper and about thirty thousand pounds."

Deverill laughed. "Every unmarried man in England must be looking for such a paragon." He turned to Wale. "Isn't that so, Drew?"

"Well, sir . . ." Wale began. He glanced at Kate, his face reddening.

"I shall not settle for less," Nellingham informed them. He raised his stick and shook it at the Earl. "I have something to offer a young lady. One of the first families of the realm . . . closely connected to the throne . . ." He stopped suddenly as his gaze fell on Deverill's sundial which provided a focal point for a flower bed at one side of the terrace. He stared.

"Is that sundial accurate?"

"Yes, of course," the Earl said in confusion. "Sundials are, as a rule—allowing corrections for time of year and so forth."

"Then I can't understand why I am standing here in your garden. That sundial reads a full half hour before noon . . ." He peered at the ground around his feet. "Yes, you see? There are no shadows here. That means it is approximately noon—much too early for me to be up and about. I can't understand what's gotten into that man of mine to send me out at such an hour. Excuse me, old fellow, I must be getting back to my rooms. This will not do at all."

Before Deverill could protest, the Duke strode across the terrace toward the house. The Earl muttered in consternation and hurried after him.

Kate giggled. "Poor shatter-brained old man. I suppose everyone behaves in a befuddled manner after the age of fifty."

"Oh, no," Wale assured her. "It's just that Nellingham has lived a dreadfully profligate life. He has addled his brains. Gone through one of the largest fortunes in the country, I have been told." He clucked his tongue. "Such a difference one finds among members of a family. His heir—who is one of his cousins—is the most sober and responsible fellow alive. If he succeeds to the estate, he'll restore the family's fortunes in no time."

Kate nodded. "I am confident that Serena will never consent to bestow her hand on Nellingham."

He looked troubled. "I hope not. Serena expects a knight in shining armor to come into her life. It would be cruel to pitch her into a life with a gazetted fortune hunter like Nellingham—and a dissolute old roué in the bargain. No, no . . ." He smiled suddenly. "We must offer her a proper partner who'll give her the affection she deserves."

Kate listened to him, smiling, and she felt a little surge of excitement as she realized that he was talking about himself.

"I am confident she will soon realize her own heart and return to the man she truly loves," she assured him. She gave him a speaking look.

He nodded. "And I shall do everything in my power to bring about such a union."

He caught her hand and lifted it toward his lips; but as it neared his mouth, he paused, and observing the layers of mud which caked every part of it, he turned it from side to

71

side in an effort to find a clean spot. Finally he kissed the top of her wrist, then let it fall.

"I must take myself off and let my man do what he can for me," he said.

"Yes," she agreed, looking down at her own muddy skirt. "But I shall take Serena out to enjoy the air this afternoon. We shall make every effort to be in the park during the Promenade."

"Ah," he said, smiling, "I shall look for you there."

CHAPTER 6

After she had bathed and changed her gown, Kate was tempted to search out her aunt and engage her in a "council of war." The more she thought about the conversation she had had with Wale, the more she was convinced that she should work out a foolproof plan as fast as possible and hurry Serena into marriage with him, because there was always a chance he would lose patience with the girl if she showed herself to be too capricious.

She wondered why there had been, as yet, no sign of her sister, Lorna. Knowing Lorna as she did, she was confident that sooner or later—probably sooner—she would contrive a visit to town—"to dance and laugh and smile at them all and put their heads in a whirl"—and if Lorna arrived before the knot between Wale and Serena was tied, all would be lost. There was no doubt in Kate's mind that Lorna would attach the Duke and marry him immediately, such a delightful combination of attributes and dignities as this young man possessed.

It gave Kate a twinge to think of Wale and Lorna together; there was such a disparity in their worth. She was musing thus, scowling darkly into her dressing table mirror, when her door opened and Lady Fanny peered in.

"My dearest," she began, "is your cousin here?"

Kate shook her head. "I was about to go in search of her."

Her ladyship turned away. "Then she is still in her room, agonizing over Diremore. I must insist that she not mope herself in this manner. If she continues to weep and carry on, that swollen face of hers will reveal the truth and the entire ton will soon be laughing at us." She shuddered and turned away.

"Wait, Aunt," Kate said, hurrying after her. "We must plot together for Serena's good. I have been speaking to Wale this morning, and I am confident that he loves her— has done so since she was a child. And in her heart of hearts, I am confident that she loves him, too. This infatuation for Diremore is a passing fancy. But we must move cautiously, you and I, to be sure she realizes her true feelings. And we cannot allow Wale to become alienated before they are united forever."

Lady Fanny wrung her hands. "Oh, dear! It is so difficult! I thank heaven that I have only one daughter. I am convinced that everything will go awry and the poor dear girl will spend the rest of her life in misery."

"No!" Kate said stoutly. "She shall not! I will strain every fiber of my being to insure that such a tragedy does not come to pass."

Lady Fanny opened the door to Serena's room and the two of them peered cautiously in. Serena, crumpled in a chair by her dressing table, saw them and began to sniffle.

"No, no, no," her ladyship protested, bustling in. "We must have no more of this. You must inure yourself to suffering, my dearest. All of life is disappointment and heartbreak, you know—a vale of tears—and we must learn to bear it bravely. Besides, pining over someone else's betrothed is very bad ton."

Serena sniffled loudly. "I cannot face the world," she bubbled. "I shall lock myself up and never show my face again."

"Nonsense!" her ladyship exclaimed. "If you are not going to make an effort for yourself, you must make it for Katie. She has come to visit you, hoping for a Season of pleasure; you must not withdraw into a shell and forsake her. If you have no interest in finding a suitable husband for yourself, then you must help me find a worthy husband for her."

Serena raised her face to her cousin and gave her a wet smile. "Yes," she said, "I shall devote my life to making others happy. We must find the perfect husband for Katie. Is there anyone you prefer, love?"

"Well . . . no," Kate said. "Not at this time."

"Then we must introduce her to many more young men, Mama," Serena urged.

"I have the most delightful notion," Lady Fanny exclaimed suddenly. "We shall give a masked bal for Kate's formal presentation to Society. Everything shall be a blend of mystery and romance; then at midnight there will be an unmasking, and we shall present our lovely Kathryn to the world. I am confident that every young man in London will pay court to her, and she will need only to select the one she prefers."

"Wonderful!" Serena agreed, suddenly cheerful. "Masquerades are the most exciting things! I shall have a blue-satin domino and Katie shall have one of cherry silk."

Kate smiled. "I have never attended a masquerade."

"Then we must make it the most enchanting masquerade that has ever been given," Lady Fanny smiled. "And we shall begin to plan immediately—you two must help me— our refreshments, our decor, our guest list." She put a hand thoughtfully to her cheek. "What would you think of a Venetian theme? We can have our ballroom decorated to represent the palaces which front on the Grand Canal. I wonder if we could somehow contrive a gondolier poling his gondola about the room."

"That would be splendid!" Serena exclaimed, leaping to her feet. "How can we contrive such a thing?"

"I have no idea," her ladyship admitted. "We must think on it. In the meantime, we must set about our work. We shall go immediately to order the invitations and your dominoes. And I must select a suitable costume for myself and have Madame Antoine begin work on it." She waved her hands. "Quickly, Serena, put on your clothes. On our way to the shops we shall take a turn in the park. You may show off your new blue walking dress and Katie may wear her cherry merino."

Serena, turning toward her dressing room, caught sight of herself in her mirror and was momentarily startled by the ravages which had been wrought by her bout of self-pity. She inhaled sharply. Then her lower lip began to tremble. "If Katie wishes to wear her new dress, then I shall wear mine," she told them, "but I cannot take any pleasure in it."

At half past four, Lady Fanny's barouche drew up in front of Deverill House and the three ladies trooped down the steps and were handed into the carriage. The day had remained bright, with brilliant sunshine, but a piercing wind was now blowing, and it kept their fur collars flattened against their cheeks, and their fingers tucked safely inside their muffs. Their horses, unnerved by the gusts, danced in their traces, swinging their rumps from side to side.

No sooner had the Countess's carriage entered the park than it began to encounter friends. Diremore and Tiffany cantered past them in Diremore's curricle, Tiffany waving gaily and Diremore managing to give them a respectful bow despite the fact that he was controlling a spirited team. Serena quickly turned her swollen face away and hid it behind her muff, whispering in a stricken voice, "Good God, Katie! Did he see me?"

"No," Kate assured her. "I am confident that he did not. He is too busy managing his team."

But a moment later the Marchioness of Gyle rumbled past in her enormous landau. She nodded solemnly to them and called in a voice which could be heard all the way to Scotland. "Serena, my dear, are you unwell? You look positively hagridden."

"Beast!" Serena hissed through her clenched teeth, and kept her face turned resolutely away.

The Marchioness moved on, calling cheerful insults to

others of her acquaintance, and Sonny's wife, Letitia, immediately drew up beside Fanny. Mounted on a prancing white Arabian mare, she was clad in a dashing habit à la Hussar. Fanny wished to chat with her daughter-in-law, but the moment she was alongside them, a blast of wind rocked the carriage and the startled mare shied away. She was quickly cut off by the Duke of Nellingham, who was taking the air in his sporting curricle with his competent groom in command of the ribbons.

Nellingham bowed formally toward the Deverill carriage. "Your ladyship," he murmured, looking at Fanny curiously. "The name escapes me." He peered at the crest on the side panel, and his eyebrows rose. "Ah, Deverill's coach." He beamed at Serena. "So this is the little heiress I've heard so much about. I should consider it a great honor if you would present me one day, your ladyship."

Before Fanny could speak, he saluted them gravely and the curricle pulled away, disappearing into the crush of carriages and horsemen. For a moment the three ladies sat staring after him.

"Well!" her ladyship exclaimed. "Cork-brained old humgudgeon! He should be locked up somewhere, out of harm's way."

They were watching the Duke's retreating back when there was a new rattle of harness and another curricle drew up alongside them. Wale, adroitly managing a team of magnificent-matched grays, greeted them with a smile.

"Ah," Kate said, brightening. She put a hand on her cousin's arm and wiggled her eyebrows at her. "Here is our friend, Serena."

Her face still turned away to hide its ruined condition, Serena raised a hand in silent greeting. Wale laughed.

"Come, come, Reena," he protested, "has our friendship come to this? You used to hurl yourself into my arms, you were so glad to see me when you were a child."

"Of course she is glad to see you!" Kate exclaimed.

"Of course she is!" Fanny agreed.

Wale laughed again. "I realize that I am not such a dashing blade as some . . ."

77

"Of course you are!" Kate insisted.

"Of course you are!" Lady Fanny assured him.

Wale made no attempt to answer them, but sat laughing good-naturedly while Kate and Lady Fanny tried to think of an artful way to start a conversation between Serena and the Duke. Before they could do so, they were diverted by the Undersette carriage, which had drawn up on the other side of them.

"Frances, my dear," Lady Undersette called to her, "you must allow me the honor of presenting my nieces to you." She gestured toward a pretty blonde with pink cheeks who was sitting beside her. "This is Charlotte," she announced. "And this . . ." she indicated a little girl with curly black hair who was sitting alongside Clarissa on the facing seat, ". . . is Arabella." Both Clarissa and her little cousin were fondling a fluffy white fur muff, which the child was stroking and twisting on her lap.

"My dears!" Lady Fanny exclaimed, smiling at them. "How charming!"

At that moment the Duke of Nellingham's curricle reappeared, making its way back through the crush of carriages and riders. He bowed toward Lady Fanny. "Ah," he said. "It is Lady Deverill, is it not?" And to everyone's surprise, he removed his hat and made a sweeping bow toward them. Unfortunately he held his hat for a split second in front of his coachman's face, and during that lapse, the unfortunate driver came to grief.

Miscalculating the distance between the Undersette carriage and his own, he guided the curricle too close. His wheel hub struck against the Undersettes' with a resounding clack and jarred both vehicles so hard that the Undersette team and Nellingham's both let out whinnies of alarm and lunged against their traces.

Wale's team also lunged forward in surprise, Letitia's Arabian, with a squeal, took flight and disappeared down Rotten Row, and to everyone's amazement, Arabella's muff suddenly came to life. It sprang from her lap and flew off, sprouting legs, two wild black eyes, and a tail with hair sticking out stiffly in all directions. Landing on the front of

78

Lady Fanny's bodice, it dug in its claws. Her ladyship let out a piercing scream that was immediately echoed by horses on all sides of her, and the entire park promptly surged into violent motion. Dust whirled around their faces as a fresh gust whipped through the shrubbery, horses lunged, carriages lurched against each other.

Arabella leaped to her feet and began to jump up and down, screaming at the top of her lungs. Squealing and trumpeting, Lady Fanny swiped wildly at the kitten, trying to brush it off its perch. The cat flattened its ears and jumped again.

This time it landed on the dashboard of Wale's curricle, and as he struggled to hold his plunging team, it bounded again, landing on the bridle path directly in front of a placid chestnut hack which rose abruptly onto its hind legs. Before the horse's hooves had come down again, the kitten had shot off across a patch of open ground, under three mounted riders, then under a carriage, whose team immediately panicked and began to kick and pitch.

Arabella, sobbing hysterically, tried to scramble to the ground, but she only managed to tumble from one conveyance to the other, landing in a scrambled heap in Lady Fanny's lap.

"Good heavens!" her ladyship exclaimed. "My dearest dear!"

Kate, also watching in horror as the kitten continued its death-defying flight, leaped to her feet. She sprang up onto the side of the barouche and leaped lightly across onto the dashboard of Wale's curricle.

"Don't!" he cried, grabbing for her skirt. But she was past him and leaping lightly to the ground. "Stop!" he shouted.

Miraculously unscathed, the kitten raced along the ground, a tiny silver streak undulating through the grass. Kate rushed after it, scattering carriages and riders on every side of her until the kitten reached a tree and flew up its trunk into the safety of its upper branches. Kate caught hold of a stout cross-branch and swung herself up and out of sight inside the wind-tossed foliage. Arabella, in the Dev-

79

erill carriage, was howling shrilly. There was a steady can-
tata of shrieks emanating from the other conveyances
which surrounded them. A short distance away, Tiffany,
after glancing around to be certain she had a respectable
audience, let out a dramatic sob and fainted into the arms
of her fiancé.

"It is all right," Kate called down to Arabella. "Your
kitten is unharmed. But it is so frightened . . . Ouch!
Naughty, naughty!"

All eyes were rivited on Kate's tree. There was violent
activity in the upper branches—leaves thrashing and plain-
tive howls from the cat.

"Stop that!" Kate's voice commanded. "Now stop, I say!
You nasty little beast! Don't you dare! Ouch!" There was
silence, then another violent upheaval within the foliage,
and finally Kate exclaimed, "Ah, now I have you, demon
child! You shall not escape again."

Immediately the tips of a pair of white kid boots appeared on the lowest branch. They were followed by a
wind-whipped cloud of cherry merino skirt cascading down
over the feet as Kate seated herself. The eagerly waiting
spectators held their breath.

Kate caught hold of another branch, leaned forward, and
looked down out of the thick foliage. Wale, who had somehow divested himself of his team, was standing on the
ground below her, looking up. His face was extremely
white. But before she could tumble off her perch or disgrace herself by jumping down into his arms and granting
her well-wishers a vulgar display of limbs, a bright blue
high-perch phaeton with yellow-picked wheels pulled up toward the tree. The driver, a young man dressed in the
height of elegance, raised his whip to salute the Duke.

"Hello there, Froggy," he chirped in a high, strident
voice. "If you'll move aside, I'll rescue the lady."

Wale stepped back, and the new arrival guided his team
under Kate's branch. He raised a hand up to her in an easy
gesture; she stepped effortlessly into the vehicle, seating
herself beside him. The kitten was clinging frantically to
the front of her left shoulder.

Her escort grinned down at Wale. "Just like old times, eh Froggy? Got ahead of you here. Score one for yours truly." And he let out a sheeplike laugh.

Wale gave him a tight smile. "Chalk up one for your side, Bleater."

With a gracious bow, the young man turned his perch phaeton away from the duke and guided it back to Lady Deverill's carriage.

"Oh, my dear, my dear," Lady Fanny sobbed from under the brim of her bonnet, which had been knocked down over one eye, "I have never been so terrified!" Tears welled out of her eyes. "I thought surely I would see you crushed."

Kate, with the assistance of Timothy and her rescuer, stepped down into her aunt's barouche and put her arms around her.

"There was nothing to fear," she protested.

"One hears of such dreadful accidents . . ." Fanny put a trembling hand to her heaving bosom and sobbed helplessly for several seconds before she remembered that her niece's rescuer was still sitting in his carriage alongside her own. She dabbed her nose with a bit of lace.

"Mr. Lester," she chuffled. "So grateful to you."

He bowed. "Humble servant, your ladyship." And touching his whip to the brim of his hat, he urged his team forward and out into the stream of conveyances which had resumed their promenade.

Lady Fanny was sobbing into her handkerchief, hiccuping every two or three breaths. Kate quickly straightened her bonnet for her and reached into her reticule for her vinaigrette. As Wale strode up to the side of their barouche, his face still gray, he hissed at her, "I had not thought to see you alive again this day, Cousin." Then to Lady Fanny, he frowned and asked, "Is there anything I can do to make you more easy, ma'am?"

She shook her head.

"Is there any way we can prevent a repetition of this sort of thing?" he continued. "I fear your niece is bent on self-destruction."

81

"Oh!" her ladyship wailed. "I shall speak to her uncle. He must take a firm hand with her." And she sobbed and hiccuped so violently that Kate felt a surge of alarm.

"Serena," she said, putting out one hand to her while she encircled her aunt's shoulders with the other and hugged her reassuringly, "may I please have your vinaigrette? I fear my aunt is going to be ill."

Serena sighed. "Strange that I had never noticed before . . ."

Kate turned to her in annoyance. "Please, quickly! I need it now!"

Serena was staring into space. "Note the skill with which he handles the ribbons, Katie. He is a member of the Four Horse Club, you know."

"Serena!" she snapped. "I need your vinaigrette before my aunt has a violent attack of the vapors."

"Oh," Serena said, and dipping a hand into her reticule, quickly brought out the tiny bottle and handed it to her.

As soon as she had uncorked it and stuck the aromatic spirits under Lady Fanny's nose, Kate turned back to her cousin, who was still staring at the rapidly disappearing figure on the seat of the high-perch phaeton.

"Who is that man?" Kate asked.

Serena smiled. "It is our neighbor, Young Lester. How could I have thought that he was not worthy of my notice?"

Kate opened Lady Fanny's collar, untied her bonnet, and after pulling it off, began to fan her with it. "Sir," she called to Wale, "I must get my aunt home where we can minister to her properly or she is going to be quite ill, I fear."

Lady Fanny hiccuped behind a hand. "I am all right, my love."

But Wale, who had been watching them with concern, turned toward the coachman and gave him a command. A moment later they were in the line of carriages which was making its way out of the park. Serena craned her neck to catch a last glimpse of Young Lester's departing figure.

"Look there, Katie," she urged. "The sun is behind him. He has a halo."

"Good heavens!" Kate exclaimed indignantly. "How can I think of tulips with high-perch phaetons at a time like this?"

But as the carriage clattered over the cobbles and Lady Fanny's breathing became more regular, Kate found her thoughts returning to Young Lester. A match between him and Serena was not so desirable as an alliance with the Duke, certainly; but it was infinitely more fitting that she should lose her heart to a rich young neighbor—though not a peer—than that she should pine away in hopeless yearning for Lord Diremore.

CHAPTER 7

Lady Fanny enjoyed a restful night and by the following morning was nearly herself again. She still felt unequal to the task of discussing Kate's behavior with her husband, however, and was relieved to discover that during his peregrinations the night before he had heard the story of their adventures and was quick to give his niece a thorough scold.

"Naughty puss!" he chided. "There shall be no more such antics! Your behavior has given rise to all sorts of nonsensical rumors. Sumpton asked me if it is true that you are one of a family of contortionists who have been performing at the court of the Czar."

"Good heavens, sir!" she exclaimed. "How could such an absurdity be considered?"

"That is not the worst. My addlepated friend, Nellingham, came out of his fog long enough to inform everyone at Watier's that he had seen you fluttering about inside a tree during a visit he paid to us, and he suspects you of being a . . . a sphinx in disguise."

Serena threw up her hands. "A sphinx, indeed! How can he be such a goose? A sphinx had wings, it is true, but it had a lion's body. Certainly there is no sign of paws or a tail protruding from Katie's gown."

"I collect he referred to me as a *harpy*," Kate said,

frowning. "That was the creature which was half bird and half woman. But my uncle is too kind to use the word, considering its present connotations."

He waved a hand impatiently. "Perhaps he meant harpy, but he said *sphinx*."

"No one believed that, certainly?"

"No, no! But they are spreading the story, nonetheless. Of course, poor Nelly was hooted out of the place. Such laughter and ridicule, not even he deserved. Especially since there was a kernel of truth to his tale."

Kate hung her head.

"So you see, my dear," he continued, taking her hand and giving it a comforting pat, "you must give me your solemn word that there shall be no more flying up into the trees."

Kate nodded meekly. "I promise, sir."

Her ladyship, much comforted, led her daughter and her niece into the yellow morning room to partake of a strengthening breakfast. After they had fortified themselves and risen from the table, Lady Fanny withdrew to the library where she addressed a masquerade invitation to Young Lester, sending it off promptly to be delivered by a page. Serena, in her most becoming gown and with her hair arranged à l'Anglaise, took up a position in the blue drawing room and began to pace restlessly back and forth while she awaited Young Lester's arrival. Shortly after two o'clock the door opened and their first caller of the day arrived; but it was Wale, not Young Lester who strode into the room.

Her ladyship hurried forward to greet him, displaying such warmth and enthusiasm that Kate suspected her of not yet relinquishing all hope in that direction. As soon as he had been reassured of her complete recovery, she led him to her daughter and said in a purring voice, "Well, Serena, my dear, look who is here."

Serena greeted him listlessly. "I trust you are well, your Grace," she observed, with no sign of interest.

He bowed, then turned to bend over Kate's hand. "And here is our fair sphinx, I see, with her feet on the ground."

Both Lady Fanny and Kate opened their mouths to protest, but before they could speak, Serena, who had been deep in thought, brightened suddenly and, putting a hand on Wale's arm, said, "Drew? You know Young Lester, do you not?"

He nodded. "I know him well. We always called him 'Bleater' because of that sheepy voice of his."

Serena drew herself up haughtily. "*Sheepy,* indeed! His voice is delightful!"

Wale grinned at her. "Is it? And I'll wager you approved of the showy way he rescued Miss Ashworth yesterday in that ridiculous rig of his. Leave it to old Bleater to take the center of any scene."

Serena sniffed. "I should appreciate it very much if you would be so kind as to refrain from calling him 'Bleater' in my presence."

"Oh?" He shrugged. "Very well."

"Besides," Serena went on, "he is quite the most dignified . . . the most heroic person I know. Have you ever seen anything more . . . well . . . *heroic* than the way he languidly reached up a hand and guided Katie down?"

Lady Fanny, who was standing behind Wale, scowled at her daughter and tried to give her a speaking look. "Dear Drew appears to great advantage in his curricle," she pointed out. "I have always considered a curricle the most thrilling of all vehicles."

"No, no!" he laughed. "A curricle is quite safe. There is no one less heroic than I, I assure you."

"True," Serena agreed. "You are like Willie and Sonny—not a bit romantic. None of you can compare to Young Lester."

Lady Fanny gritted her teeth and Kate, despite her determination to support her cousin's burgeoning romance with her neighbor, was tempted to protest. But at that moment Judson announced, "Lord Elfan, your ladyship."

The Countess put out both hands and hurried toward him with an exclamation of relief. "Ah, my dear sir! How delightful to see you!"

Elfan, somewhat taken aback by the warmth of this welcome, hesitated for a moment, then strode forward to greet her, kissing her hand with fervor. "Dearest ladyship! . . . blooming again after your ordeal . . ."

He bent briefly over Kate's hand—more lingeringly over Serena's. ". . . Radiant this morning, ma'am!"

She smiled. "Tell me, Lord Elfan, are you acquainted with Young Lester?"

He hesitated. ". . . Bit . . . yes . . . rather forward chap . . . wouldn't you say?"

She drew herself up haughtily. "Not at all. His rescue of my cousin was quite the most heroic thing! Managing that team of horses in the midst of all those plunging teams . . . It brought to mind Mr. Scott's thrilling poem. 'O, young Lochinvar is come out of the west,/ Through all the wide Border his steed was the best.' "

Elfan knitted his brows. ". . . Steed, ma'am?"

"I am referring to his high-perch phaeton," she explained.

"Oh." He was thoughtful for a moment. ". . . I'm not familiar with that poem. About a high-perch phaeton, you say?"

"Certainly not!" she exclaimed in exasperation. "It is about a romantic rescue. Young Lochinvar kidnaps the woman he loves and carries her away on his steed. Can you imagine anything more thrilling?"

"Hmm," he mused. "Kidnaps . . . thrilling . . ."

Lady Fanny snorted. "I should think it the most uncomfortable thing in the world! Being snatched up when one least expects it . . . jolted and thrown about . . . most distressing!"

Serena gave her mother an indulgent smile. "Mama," she chided, "you are not the least bit romantic."

"That is correct," her ladyship agreed. "I prefer to have things arranged in the proper way." She turned to give Wale a complaisant nod.

"Well, I prefer excitement," Serena announced. "And heroic deeds."

Elfan stroked his chin thoughtfully. "Yes, yes," he

agreed. "Heroic deeds . . . devilish fine way to do things."

Kate was watching Wale, who was leaning against a mantelpiece on one side of the room, chuckling softly. It occurred to her that, rather than being too solemn and lacking humor, as Serena had once charged, his Grace was rather the opposite, finding something to amuse him in even the most serious situations. At the moment he stood grinning at her while the other young man was nodding solemnly.

"Like to establish myself as heroic sort," Elfan observed. "Perhaps . . . feign injury . . . challenge someone to a duel . . . meetings at dawn . . . that sort of thing . . ."

"No, no!" Lady Fanny exclaimed "That would be dreadful!" She turned on her daughter crossly. "Such nonsense you are putting into his head, my love! You shall tumble Lord Elfan into real harm and some innocent person may even be killed."

Serena's face paled. "I had not intended anything so extreme, sir. I had thought only of daring rescues—that sort of thing."

Lady Fanny fluttered her hands. "Let us turn our attention to happier subjects. Let us speak of the costumes we shall wear to our masquerade. I have decided to be a dryad. What character shall you assume, Lord Elfan?"

"I . . . not considered," he admitted. "If you could suggest . . ."

While Lady Fanny and Serena seated Elfan on a sofa and began to enumerate a long list of possibilities, Wale drew Kate aside.

"So Serena now has a tendre for my friend, Lester," he chuckled. "Infinitely more suitable than Diremore!"

"Well . . ." she began. "I cannot believe her heart is completely lost to him. It was a twist of fate which made him appear so grand."

Wale nodded. "Life is governed by such twists—at least, so I am told."

She was frowning. "You must not despair, sir. You are quite as heroic as Lester, I am confident."

89

He shook his head. "I am not heroic, Cousin."

"Of course you are!"

He shook his head again. "I am not. True heroism occurs only during time of war, I believe."

Kate frowned. "If Serena were to fall into a raging torrent and you threw yourself in to save her—that would be heroism, would it not?"

He smiled. "Perhaps. Where do you hope to find a raging torrent in London?"

"We must contrive a peril," she pointed out, planning rapidly. "If I were to take her riding in the park tomorrow morning and I could somehow cause her horse to bolt . . ."

"Wait," he protested, raising a hand. "That is much too dangerous."

"True," she agreed. "We must contrive a peril which appears to be dire but which is in reality quite safe—merely an illusion."

He made an impatient gesture. "That was not what I meant. I meant that it is extremely dangerous to guide the lives of others. To contrive a union between Serena and any young man is, perhaps, to plunge her into a life of eternal woe. What if, for example, she were to marry Lester, then discover that his habits or attitudes are abhorrent to her? She would be condemned to a future of quarreling and misery. And it would make you unhappy also, I am sure, to feel that you were instrumental in bringing about such a tragedy."

"But she has known you since she was a child and you have always been fond of each other," she pointed out. "How could such a match lead to quarreling and misery?"

"Oh," he said, his eyebrows rising suddenly. "You are suggesting that I make an effort to win her myself?"

She nodded.

He was frowning. "Of course," he began, "I realize that it is what my friend, Lady Deverill, wishes; and it is natural that she would prefer to have her daughter marry a man

90

whom she knows—and one she is confident will never mistreat the girl. But . . ." He turned to look at her searchingly. ". . . Is that what you wish, too, Cousin?"

"Yes, yes," she said, leaning closer to him. "If you could do it quickly . . ."

He shook his head and turned away from her. "I shall be happy to introduce Lester into this house and bring him into Serena's company as often as possible so that nature may work her wiles on them if they suit each other; but I will not exert any effort to promote a match, and I will not try to win her myself."

Kate stared unhappily down at her hands. "Very well. Then perhaps you will encourage Young Lester to call on us. Lady Fanny has sent him an invitation to the masquerade, but as yet he has not replied."

"I shall go talk to him immediately," he said, "and urge him to return with me."

An hour after leaving them, he returned without Young Lester. "He is reluctant to intrude himself," he reported. "And nothing I could say would change his mind. Says everyone will sneer at him if he 'breaches your citadel'—accuse him of expecting your gratitude, that sort of thing."

"Then we must send his lordship to call on him," Lady Fanny said; and summoning her husband from his study, she bustled him into a lavishly corded and tassled Polish coat, and sent him on his way, escorted by Wale.

A few minutes later, while Serena was pacing up and down the room, and Kate and Lady Fanny were pretending to be engrossed in their embroidery, the door opened and Judson announced, "The Marchioness of Gyle . . ." Resplendent in burnished copper velvet and plumes, the lady brushed him aside impatiently and strode into the room.

"Now, Frances, my dear," she said without allowing her ladyship time to greet her, "I have been thinking about this party of yours and it is all wrong—all wrong! Why you should be such a silly goosecap as to embroil yourself in a ramshackle enterprise like a masquerade, I am sure I do not know; but since you have done so, I consider it my duty to help you out of this pickle. To start with, the Venetian theme will not do—no, not at all."

"But I . . . " Lady Fanny began.

"Do not interrupt me! I have given it my consideration and you must do as I say. You shall change the theme from Venetian to Parisian—so simple to turn this house into Versailles. And you must let me advise you on your menu; none of those disgusting little puffed lobster things you are so fond of serving. Where is your list; let me look at it. And most urgent of all, you must move the date of the party from Wednesday to Thursday so that it will not conflict with that little musicale of Caro Lamb's. Not that anyone will go to hear that wretched cellist of hers again; but it would be dreadful if someone we especially wished to attend our masquerade—Lady Heatherington, for example— should decide that duty dictates an appearance at Caro's . . ."

"But, Augusta," Fanny protested, "we cannot change the date. The invitations have all been sent and many acceptances already received."

"That is immaterial," the Marchioness snapped, "You must do as I say, my dear. You know very well that I know much more of the world than you do."

Lady Fanny fluttered her hands. "Yes . . . well, of course, you do, Gussie. Your knowledge of the world is indisputable."

"Yes," the Marchioness agreed. "Now let me see your menu."

Lady Fanny sighed. "It is in my desk."

"Then come along," her cousin insisted, linking an arm through hers and bustling her out through the door. "I have other things to accomplish today before I dress for Lady Sefton's dinner party."

They disappeared into the hall and for a time the Marchioness's distinctive voice could be heard booming from the upper regions of the house. Finally she roared her way down the staircase again and Kate and Serena, waiting nervously inside the blue drawing room for Lady Fanny's return, were relieved to hear the front door open and her ladyship's voice piping farewell. A moment later she came back into the room and sank onto a sofa.

"Oh, dear!" she breathed. "She is gone. Such a woman— I love her dearly, of course, but her visits are always so fatiguing. She has changed every plan we have made for our masquerade."

Kate and Serena both clasped their hands anxiously. "What are we going to do?" Serena asked.

Lady Fanny smiled impishly. "I said, 'yes, yes, yes,' to everything she suggested; but I told her that everything was contingent on Deverill's permission. Thus we shall do as we please, and tell her that it was Dev's decision."

The three were chuckling happily over Lady Fanny's subterfuge when the Earl strode into the room. Fanny clasped her hands in relief. "Thank heaven you did not arrive five minutes sooner, my love," she exclaimed, "or we should all have been in the soup."

He raised his eyebrows and Fanny was obliged to explain the outcome of the Marchioness's visit.

"Certainly," he told her. "When you have made your final arrangements, tell her that I have put my foot down."

"But Papa!" Serena exclaimed. "What of Young Lester? Did you talk to him?"

"Of course!" he told them, smiling with satisfaction. "Dashed affable young fellow. Quite to my liking." He nodded vigorously. "Devilish knowledgeable, too. Said 'Yes, indeed, sir!' to almost everything I proposed."

Serena was beaming. "Did you talk about me, Papa?"

He turned to her in surprise. "Why no, puss. Shouldn't expect me to push you forward like that. For the most part we discussed the new trade agreements we've made with France, and of course, we talked about how to make a little extra on *change*."

"But you talked about our masquerade, certainly. Did he accept the invitation?"

Deverill's eyebrows rose. "Dash it all, didn't even think of it. We were going on about investments and such. You couldn't expect me to remember a mere party . . ."

He broke off as Serena's face crumpled and, pressing a hand to her mouth, she fled from the room. "What's this?" he cried. "What's this?"

Lady Fanny wagged a finger at him. "Fie on you, sir! You know how much these bals mean to young girls."

Kate hurried toward the door. "I shall go to her, ma'am."

She found Serena in her room, prostrate across her bed, sobbing bitterly. "You see, Katie?" she blubbered. "It is as I feared. Even with my new eyebrows, Young Lester has not noticed me. Your spells have been delightful and have made me feel so much more beautiful, but I am still the most mousish girl in England; and when Young Lester meets me again he will most likely bow and say 'Enchanted' or some such rot, without realizing that we are lifelong friends."

"How can that be, since you have known each other and been neighbors for so many years?" Kate protested.

"He may not have known I existed," Serena admitted with a sigh. "I came out of the schoolroom such a short time ago and have only seen him once or twice. He was at Lady Sefton's bal last year, as I remember. Although perhaps that was not he. I may have seen him at the Undersettes' musicale the night that moaning Signor Signatelli sang all those dreary songs. Or . . . no, that was Sir Percy Bucklemeer, who married the Spanish countess . . . Well, I don't remember precisely, but I collect I have met him somewhere."

Kate held a soft linen handkerchief to her cousin's eyes. "Here," she urged, "wipe away your tears. We shall find a way to attract Young Lester, although Wale says it is a mistake to interfere in other people's lives and I fear he may be right."

"Well," Serena announced, "I consider it selfish and heartless of him to criticize our actions. This is an entirely different emotion from the one I felt when I thought I was in love with Diremore, and I am sure I shall waste away and die if I do not marry Young Lester. I have made up my mind."

She blew her nose shrilly into the handkerchief. Kate began to walk up and down the room, deep in thought. "Very well," she said. "I shall be obliged to cast one of the most powerful of all spells. It will render Young Lester helpless. But it will be extremely difficult; and you must be positive before we start, that this is what you truly desire. Because if I bind him to you and you change your mind, it will be extremely wicked of you."

Serena clasped her hands with delight. "Of course I am positive!"

"Then we must begin to prepare the spell immediately, if it is to ripen in time for our masquerade."

Serena bounded off the bed and capered around the room. "Wonderful!" she exclaimed. "Wonderful! What ingredients shall we need?"

"I have most of them in my bag," Kate told her. "But we must procure a bird."

Serena paused in front of her. "A bird? What kind of bird? Stuffed? A picture?"

"No, no!" Kate explained. "It must be a real, live bird. A young, energetic one. A canary or a finch would do, if we can find a suitable subject."

Serena gave the matter her consideration. "The first place which comes to mind where one may purchase birds is Bartholomew Fair. That is where the Undersettes buy pied wagtails for their conservatory every year. They are very pretty darting among the ferns and tropical plants." Serena smiled suddenly. "Once they had a peacock which strutted back and forth and was beautiful to watch, but it screamed so dreadfully during a dinner party they held for Prinnie that they were obliged to send it to the country—at least, that is what they said, although Willie insisted that they ate it."

"A pied wagtail would do nicely," Kate said, ". . . if it is a proper pied wagtail. We must go to Bartholomew Fair and see what is available."

"Oh, no!" Serena exclaimed. "We cannot go there ourselves! It is a terrible place—most dangerous for gentle young ladies! Mama would never give her permission or take us there herself. We must send Timothy to purchase what we need."

Kate shook her head decisively. "That is impossible. I must select the bird myself. He cannot be just any kind of bird; he must have that certain extra something which indicates that he is more than just an ordinary bird—you know what I mean. I must look each prospect in the eye, and the one which cocks its head and peers back at me with more than a merely birdlike expression on its face shall be the one I choose."

"They all have a rather blank expression, don't they?" Serena suggested.

"Oh, indeed not," Kate said. "There are some which have a sort of magic in them. Like a pooka, though not in such a marked degree."

"A pooka? I thought they were only in folklore. I did not realize there really were such things."

Kate shrugged. "I do not know positively about pookas; but I know that there are individual birds and animals which have more of a certain ingredient than others, and that I must find one such bird in order to make the spell work."

"But we cannot go to Bartholomew Fair!" Serena insisted. "It is quite impossible! No member of the ton would ever be seen there at this time of year."

Kate mused for a moment. "Then we shall disguise ourselves and make our way there in secrecy. My aunt will not know of our excursion, and if anyone sees us, they won't recognize us. We shall disguise ourselves as . . . let me see . . . chimney sweeps? No, that would be too difficult, besides making it necessary to rub soot on our faces, which might damage our complexions. Perhaps we should be vendors of some sort."

"No, no," Serena said with a shudder. "The place is really much worse than you realize. It abounds with all sorts of sinister and evil persons. There are pickpockets and thieves and slavers who kidnap girls and spirit them away to use in who knows what hideous manner." She shuddered again. "I should be terrified to go there."

"Very well," Kate said, planting her hands on her hips. "I shall be obliged to go alone. I am not afraid of the lower orders. I once attended a fair in a neighboring town and found myself called upon to deal with three gypsies and an erstwhile tavern keeper. And there was a tatterdemalion with a swollen jaw and an onion sticking out of his ear who tried to charge me a shilling for tuppence worth of ribbon. But I managed very nicely, thank you."

"Oh, dear," Serena mourned, wringing her hands. "I cannot bear to think of you going there alone."

"Then come with me. It will be an adventure; and I am confident we have nothing to fear. We shall protect each other. If we encounter real perils, we can always summon aid by screaming."

Serena frowned for a moment, then her brow cleared. "Very well, we shall stand together. I shall be terrified, but I would rather march into the jaws of death than allow you to be carried off into a life of suffering without a staunch friend at your side."

Kate clasped her hand. "I knew I could rely on you. What sort of disguise do you suggest?"

Serena thought for a moment. "Let us be fish peddlers . . . 'Sweet Kate and Sweet Serena Malone.' We can walk through streets wide and narrow shouting, 'Cockles and mussels! . . .' that sort of thing."

"But we would need a wheelbarrow," Kate pointed out, "which will be difficult to obtain without arousing suspicion. And I fear that if we assume an identity which requires shouting, we would draw attention to ourselves and, perhaps, be recognized. Just think how dreadful it would be if someone were to say, 'Good God, Lester, that fishmonger is the spit and image of Deverill's daughter!' "

"Good gracious, yes! That would never do."

For several seconds the two girls mused. Finally with a sigh, Kate said, "We must enumerate the possibilities and choose among them. If we could procure trousers and ragged shirts we might disguise ourselves as tatterdemalions or pickpockets. We could also be link boys. Or, if we could somehow obtain seamen's garb, we could be sailors."

Serena frowned and shook her head. "I think we should not find it easy to pass ourselves off as sailors. They have a strange way of walking, I am told."

"You are probably right," Kate agreed. "Though I should enjoy such a masquerade. No, we must content ourselves with being women of some sort. We could wear our plainest gowns and cover them with aprons . . . and perhaps dust flour on our arms and faces. We could be piemen—or piewomen, I should say."

Serena sighed. "Yes, I fear it must be piewomen. Not very romantic figures, alas, but the costumes are within our reach." She hesitated, then added in a wistful voice, "We could not pose as cyprians, of course."

Kate clucked her tongue. "Certainly not! If we were recognized, we should be completely undone. It would be necessary for us to withdraw to the country and lead a hopeless existence forevermore."

Serena nodded. "I realized it would not be at all the thing. When shall we go to Bartholomew Fair?"

"Tomorrow," Kate said, ". . . when my aunt is busy with the decorators who are preparing the ballroom for our masquerade."

CHAPTER 8

The girls' plans for their sortie into London's netherworld
fared badly from the start. They discovered, on checking
through their wardrobes, that neither of them possessed a
simple dress of drab color which might pass as a piewoman's costume. And after removing all the trim from two
wool walking dresses and fabricating large linen aprons
from bed sheets which they purloined from a cupboard,
they looked each other over and were obliged to admit that
they had a decidedly theatrical air and resembled nothing
so much as a pair of young ladies of gentle birth who were
masquerading as members of the working class.

To make matters worse, before they could use the aprons
and dispose of them surreptitiously, the thefts of the bed
sheets were discovered by one of the maids and traced to
Serena's closet, whereupon the housekeeper confronted her
young mistress indignantly, chiding her in the same tone of
voice she had used when a three-year-old Serena had hidden a raspberry tart under a cushion on a white satin sofa
and sat on it to conceal her crime.

Serena, who had always been afraid of that redoubtable
woman, immediately began to sniffle and stumble over her
words. "Oh, Mrs. Kemp . . . I . . . we only . . . don't
you see?" And Kate felt herself obliged to step into the
breach quickly and fabricate an elaborate lie, a thing she

was always loath to do—she had long ago decided that honesty was the best policy, being the safest, in the long run.

Therefore, she told Mrs. Kemp that they were in the process of preparing a delightful surprise for Lady Fanny—something of an artistic nature to be revealed at the masquerade bal—and that bed sheets and a cup of bread flour were vital ingredients.

Mrs. Kemp munched her jaws for a moment, considering, then, with an arch smile, assured them that she would not divulge their secret. She even went so far as to promise them a cup of bread flour, which she would hide in the urn on Serena's bedside table.

Somewhat heartened by this upswing in their fortunes, the two girls began to feel more optimistic about their venture, and the next morning, after they had eaten a strengthening breakfast and while Lady Fanny was in the ballroom setting the painters to work on the masquerade decorations, they collected their aprons and little sack of flour, tied on their bonnets, and hanging their umbrellas over their arms, made their way stealthily down a back stairway and out through a service entrance.

As soon as they had closed the door, they pulled off their bonnets and pelisses and tied them into a bundle. With their umbrella tips, they pushed the bundle up onto the top of the garden wall, then over, allowing it to fall into some bushes on the other side where they hoped to retrieve it later in the day. They had just succeeded in pushing the bundle out of sight and, as it fell down inside the garden, both had said, "Ah," with satisfaction, when they turned to find themselves face to face with Timothy. He had come up behind them and was standing in the walkway with an enormous parcel on one shoulder. Before Serena could check her surprise, she gasped, "Oh!" Kate scowled at her.

"Oh, my goodness!" Serena exclaimed, letting out an artificial trill of laughter. "It is you, Timothy!"

"Yes, miss," he said, considering them solemnly for a moment. With a frown, he turned his attention to the top of the wall where their bundle had just disappeared.

"Just fancy, Katie," Serena giggled, "it is Timothy, the very person we wished to meet. Remember, I said, 'Timothy is the one who can give us directions to Bartholomew Fair'? I said that yesterday, Katie, when you were writing a letter to your sister, Lorna." She turned to Timothy with a smile. "Miss Kate is sending her sister a list of all the places which a young lady of gentle birth must avoid, and she wishes to give her instruction on where *not* to go."

Kate scowled at her. "What nonsense! We do not need to know where it is, Serena; we need only inform her that she must stay away from it." She slipped an arm rather roughly through Serena's and bustled her along the walkway toward the front of the house. As soon as she believed herself out of earshot, she hissed, "You goose! Do you think he is going to accept such a farradiddle?"

"But it occurred to me that we do not know how to find the place," Serena explained.

"We shall hire a hansom cab and order the jarvey to take us there. Now Timothy knows where we are going, and I am confident we can count on him to spoil our plans. If he does not run immediately to my uncle, I shall be very much surprised."

As they reached the end of the flagway and prepared to round the corner, the girls glanced back. Timothy was standing where they had left him, frowning, the parcel still perched on his shoulder.

"You see?" Kate scolded. "He is making up his mind what he should do. We must escape from here as fast as possible or we shall be undone. Where can we find a hansom?"

"Willie says they are invariably passing on the next street and may be obtained at the corner," Serena told her.

"Then let us put up our umbrellas and hold them very low to hide our faces. Quickly, now, if we are to make good our escape."

With their arms locked, the umbrellas nestled on the tops of their heads, and their bundle of aprons and bread flour clutched between them, they walked as fast as dignity allowed to the corner. Willie's prophecy proved correct: a hansom was making its way slowly toward them as they arrived. Although the jarvey raised his eyebrows when they informed him of their destination, he helped them into the cab, clucked to his horse, and they were on their way.

During the ride they endeavored to complete their disguise. Despite the closeness of the quarters, they managed to assemble their aprons and tie them around each other. They combed out each other's curls and pinned their hair in round, tight buns at the back of their heads. Then they decorated each other with flour, rubbing it thoroughly over their arms, patting it on their faces and in their hair. When they had finished, they sat for a moment looking at each other, then burst out laughing.

"We look like pierrots," Kate giggled, brushing some of the powder off her cousin's face. "You have only two eyes staring out of a white mask."

They were still attempting to clean each other's faces with the hems of their dresses, when the hansom stopped and the jarvey came to the door to inform them that they had arrived at the place in Smithfield where the fair was held. When he saw the change which had come over them, he gaped in amazement.

Serena paid him and the two girls made their way toward the rows of shops which had become permanent fixtures in the area. Both stared about themselves for a moment, surveying the rows of stone-and-plaster buildings with narrow flagged passageways between them. The sun was shining warmly on them, casting a golden glow over the rather prosaic facades.

"I had expected it to be more sinister, had not you?" Serena observed.

"In truth I had," Kate admitted. "Although the populace is disreputable enough."

She paused to watch a pair of ragged urchins scutter toward them, one without shoes and both so filthy that Kate was not surprised to see one of them put up a grubby hand and scratch savagely at his head. Almost immediately a slatternly woman with a tousled mop of greasy brown hair and wearing a low-cut dress which exposed a more than adequate expanse of grimy bosom, darted out of a doorway, grabbed the urchins by the arms and, banging their heads together, chattered at them about *dicked nobs* and *flash morts* and, after a glance back over her shoulder at Kate and Serena, bustled them off down a flagged walkway between two leaning buildings. The girls stepped closer together.

"That was rather sinister," Serena observed. "She was talking about us."

"Yes," Kate agreed. "We must stay out in plain sight between these rows of shops; I think we shall be safe there—if we do not suffocate from the smell before we have completed our business."

"We must dispose of our umbrellas," Serena whispered, wrapping up the strings of her reticule around her arm to shorten them. "They will surely draw attention to us, as no one else is carrying one."

Kate nodded. "We are already attracting more than enough attention in these bizarre costumes—somehow we have gone awry in our conception of piewomen. But if we quickly buy some pies to carry, that may successfully explain our being dredged in flour."

Glancing about themselves with exaggerated nonchalance, they strolled to a stall which was filled with wooden toys. While the proprietor was endeavoring to sell a dancing man to a customer, they leaned their umbrellas against the front of the building and hurried away, plunging quickly into an alleyway and joining a crowd which was moving briskly between a row of shops.

There were shops on every side of them bursting with merchandise. Some were filled with leather goods, others piled with bolts of wools; there were some candy shops and shops piled high with crockery—as well as fruit and vegetable stalls. After they had penetrated the area a short distance, they came upon a small shop which had buns and sweet rolls stacked in the rear, and little decorated cakes along the counter in the front.

"These look delicious," Serena observed, moving toward them. "Shall we buy some?"

Her cousin shook her head. "We must find pastries. If we each carry a large pie in one hand, we shall present precisely the appearance we are trying to achieve."

They pressed on and a few shops farther along the way found a house with a small booth in the front devoted entirely to pies. "Ah," Kate said with satisfaction. "I shall have two of those nice large ones, please."

The pieman surveyed them curiously, one eyebrow rising. "A shilling each, miss," he told her.

She dug into her reticule and pulled out the two shillings, accepting one of the pies for herself and passing the other to Serena. The pieman was still watching them suspiciously.

"Be ye after winnin' a wager, miss?" he asked her.

Kate considered him for a moment, and as she looked into his knowing eyes, she nodded. "Yes," she said. "How did you know we were not bakers?"

"Them purses," he said, pointing to her reticule. "Too grand by far."

"Really?" she said, peering down at hers resentfully.

"Nor a pieman's wife wouldna come to market wi' flour all about," he went on. "She'd tidy 'ersel'."

"Oh," Kate said. "Well, it is not the piemen and their wives whom we hope to deceive, fortunately. You'll not give us away, will you?"

He shook his head and made an elaborately innocent face. "Not I, miss. For a shillin' a shot I can 'old me tongue."

Serena, carrying her pie balanced precariously on one hand, had moved ahead of Kate. She waved her free hand. "Come along, Katie, and look at these linens. Such a supply! If we had only brought a footman, we could have replaced the ones we stole from Mrs. Kemp for mere pennies. And there is the drollest little wooden dog in that toy stall over there; do we know a small child who might enjoy having it?"

"Shh," Kate warned, putting a finger over her lips. "Do not speak of footmen. That pieman has already penetrated our disguises, and there is no telling who might discover us next. Let us find the bird shop and make our purchase quickly. We must escape from here before some sort of misfortune befalls us."

"Ah, there!" Serena announced, pointing across the way. "I believe there are birds for sale in that house beyond the one which has all those . . . Is it possible those are chamber pots? I had no idea one could purchase chamber pots in a shop."

The crowd had swelled, and it took some jostling to clear a path across the intervening area. Halfway there, a large woman dressed in black and with a commanding voice, caught hold of Kate's wrist and announced in wringing tones, "Ah! That looks clean. How much is that pie?"

"It is not for sale," Kate told her, trying to pull away from her grasp.

"Not for sale!" the woman exclaimed indignantly. "You are a pieman's wife, are you not?"

Kate was about to deny the charge hotly, but caught herself in time and said reluctantly, "Well . . . yes."

"Then how much?"

Kate frowned. Serena's back had already disappeared into the crowd. "Two pounds!" she announced.

"Two pounds!" The woman released her wrist and stepped back in dismay. Immediately Kate scooted away from her, darting among the passersby and coming out a moment later on the other side of the passageway.

To her amazement, she found Serena down on her knees in front of a disreputable-looking constable, weeping bitterly and pleading for mercy.

"Good God!" Kate exclaimed. "What is this all about?"

"Oh, Katie!" Serena sobbed. "He says we must have a license. He is going to take us away to prison."

"License! Whatever for?"

"Fer vendin' pies, ma'am," the constable informed her, glowering in an appropriately stern manner.

Kate's heart fluttered with alarm, but she quickly rallied her courage and returned the constable's scowl.

"Vending!" she cried. "Indeed! Who is vending, pray?

105

We have just purchased these pies and have no intention of selling them."

"But Miss said . . ." he began.

"Pooh! She thought you were the stranger who was to pay off the wager," she told him with a false peal of laughter. "Why, just a moment ago a woman made an effort to buy my pie, and I sent her away with a flea in her ear."

He looked at her dubiously for a moment. "Ask the man in the pie shop down the way," she said quickly. "He knows we are not vendors."

Still unconvinced, he nodded and moved away from them, but when Kate glanced at him a moment later, he was still watching them suspiciously. She dragged Serena to her feet.

"Here, here now, my love," she chided. "You must not give way like that. Certainly this is a strange place and we must be alert against dangers, but we must not anticipate disaster in every word that is spoken to us."

Serena, nodding, dabbed her eyes with a handkerchief, then stuffed it back into her reticule. Both girls peered around for the bird shop. Suddenly Serena exclaimed, "Katie, look at that advertisement! I cannot believe it, but it is announcing performances of a 'learned pig,' which can 'spell, read, cast accounts, tell the points of the sun's rising and setting, tell the hour to a minute by a watch, and discover the four grand divisions of the Earth. And when asked a question, he will give an immediate answer.'" She turned to her cousin thoughtfully. "What are the four grand divisions of the Earth?"

Kate shrugged. "I have no idea."

Serena clasped a hand to her cheek. "Good God! Is it possible that this pig is more intelligent than you or I?"

Kate surveyed her cousin's face with its tearstreaks and spatters of bread flour. She nodded. "Considering the way we are managing our affairs today, I believe it is quite possible."

"Then, by all means, we must pay a visit to such a marvel! He is performing at the George, and the price is only three pence. That is certainly a bargain."

106

"We don't have time to view educated pigs," Kate told her. "We must find our bird vendor and make our purchase, then escape from here before we come to grief. Every moment we remain here, our danger of discovery increases."

Serena sighed. "It is a pity. There is also a bill advertising a motion, which would be delightful to see. 'Lifelike characters, singing and dancing . . .' Does that not sound wonderful?"

"Yes, it does. What is a motion?"

"It is dolls made to move with wires. And the plays they present are exceedingly amusing. Willie viewed a motion at one of the fairs, and he said there was also a monkey which made insulting gestures when anyone mentioned Napoleon's name . . . though, when I think of it, I am not certain it was in the same performance."

"Indeed, we must view all these things one day," Kate agreed. "There is a dumb show and some rope dancers advertised over there on that other wall. I should like to see them, too, but now we must forego these pleasures, find our bird, and escape. As soon as this crowd passes us, we shall make our way across to that house, which has what we want, I am confident."

For a moment they were jostled by a crush of nondescript shoppers, who surged around them, exuding dust and the odor of rancid perspiration and garlic. Balancing their pies aloft, the two girls squeezed through, then made their way down the alleyway and discovered, to their relief, a small shop which was piled to its ceiling with cages, each occupied by a flitting, chirping bird. There were innumerable varieties—finches, canaries, warblers, and a few more resplendent birds with touches of red, blue, or green, all leaping from perch to perch, cheeping and trilling. Kate approached the vendor.

"I am looking for a small, alert bird to purchase," she explained to him.

"Aye, miss," he assured her. "I've every sort."

She leaned forward to examine a row of brown birds

who were imprisoned in yellow wicker cages. "Come, come," she called to them. "Which one of you?"

As she waited, peering from one captive to another, a brown canary with a bright yellow throat suddenly opened its beak and began to sing. The bird in the next cage quickly joined it. Singers on the opposite side of the shop also burst into song, trilling and rolling, and suddenly the shop was ablaze with music. Kate held her breath; passersby stopped to listen.

As suddenly as the performance had begun, it ended. There was a clatter of desultory chirps, then silence. Kate set her pie on top of a low stack of cages and sighed.

"Exquisite," she breathed. "It's fairy land. How wonderful to have such a shop. You are surrounded by music."

"Aye, miss," the vendor agreed, grinning at her through a ragged set of broken and blackened teeth. " 'Tis a pritty little chitterin' they makes."

Kate shook herself and glanced up the wall. "May I look at that sober little sparrow in the green wooden cage? No, no, the next. The one who is peering down at us."

As she stepped closer to examine her prospective purchase, there was a scurrying sound in a cage near her feet. "Sweetums," hissed a breathy little voice.

Kate stepped back in surprise. Clinging to the bars on the side of its cage, a little green parrotlike bird with yellow face was cocking its head on one side then the other. "Sweetums," it chattered. "Give me a kiss."

"What is that?" Kate asked the vendor. "I have never seen such a bird before."

" 'Tis a budgigaster, or some such name," the vendor explained. "Werry rare, he be. Brought from Orstralier by a lady like yersel'."

"I'm a pieman's wife," Kate corrected him.

"Yes, miss," he said.

Kate tipped her head to examine the bird curiously. "He appears to be quite tame," she observed.

He clicked his beak at her. "Sweetums," he hissed.

Kate and Serena giggled.

" 'E be a rare un," the vendor acknowledged, taking him

out of his cage and holding him up on a wand. "Torks better'n yer dooks an' earls, 'e do. Nice pet fer a gentle-born lady. Shake orf that flour 'an let 'im perch on her finger, miss."

Kate held out her hand and the bird jumped onto her index finger, then promptly scampered up her arm to her shoulder, where it snuggled against her neck and began to tug at the hair behind her ear.

"Sweetums," Kate coaxed him.

He clicked his beak at her.

"Come, come," she urged, "let me hear you talk."

But he refused to speak again, merely cocking his head on first one side then the other while he clicked and made soft squawking sounds in his throat.

"I'll take him," Kate informed the vendor. "He is the very bird I need." She coaxed him down onto her finger again and held him out to the vendor. "What is the price?"

The vendor was looking her over appraisingly. "Ten shilling," he said; then as he saw the dismay on her face, added quickly, " 'im bein' so rare an' all."

Kate thought for a moment. "Does that include the cage?"

He nodded.

"Very well," she said with a sigh.

She reached for her reticule, which had slipped out of position on her arm. For a moment she groped without success, then she peered curiously down into the folds of her skirt. To her surprise, the reticule had disappeared.

"My reticule!" she cried. "Did I put it down with my pie?"

She and Serena turned quickly to the low stack of cages, but the pie sat alone where she had set it.

"Have you lost it?" Serena asked, putting her own pie down beside the other.

"Has it been stolen, you mean?" Kate retorted. "That is more to the point. Well, my love, I shall be obliged to rely on you to pay for the bird."

But Serena was staring at her own arm, her mouth open and her face ashen. "Katie!" she gasped. "My reticule is also gone! See? The ribbons have been cut. The loop remains, where I twisted it an extra time around my arm, but the reticule has vanished."

Kate examined the strings as Serena unwound them from her arm. "It is true," she muttered. "How goosish we have been to walk so innocently through this crush without making any attempt to defend our property. We deserve to be robbed, I assure you!"

"But, how shall we be able to return home without money to pay our way?" Serena protested, her lips trembling. "We can never walk there, for it is ever so far; and I did not even notice the route we followed coming here." Her breath caught in her throat.

"Hush," Kate urged, alarmed by the wild look in her cousin's eye. "Things are not so hopeless as they seem."

"They are as bad as they can possibly be!" Serena wailed. "There is no telling what may happen to us. I have feared from the very beginning that we would be bundled into a carriage and spirited away to a lowering castle in the Pyrenees." Tears began to pour down her cheeks.

"You must not cry!" Kate told her. "Your tears are making the horridest marks on your face. They are mixing with the flour and forming rivulets of paste running down your cheeks."

Serena, in an heroic attempt to comply with her cousin's request, raised up her head and took a deep shuddering breath. Suddenly her expression brightened.

"Look!" she cried, pointing into the crowd. "There is my reticule!" And before Kate could catch hold of her to stop her, she plunged forward and disappeared into the crush of milling pedestrians.

"Wait!" Kate protested. "Serena!" But her cousin had already turned a corner and passed out of sight beyond a candy stand. "Oh, for heaven's sake!" Kate muttered, rushing after her.

Around the corner and beyond the candy shop, she found her cousin engaged in a violent altercation with a large, angry woman who smelled strongly of onions. "No, certainly you do not look like a thief!" Serena was assuring

110

her between sobs. "I see now . . . it is not a bit like my reticule."

Kate quickly slid an arm around her cousin's waist and tried to guide her away. "There, there," she said. "An unfortunate mistake."

But to her surprise the woman grabbed Serena by the elbow and pulled her back. "Try to fool me, will ya!" she shouted. "It's a trick to steal our purses. I want the watch!"

Kate pulled the other way. "How dare you, madam! Unhand her!"

The woman pulled again, jerking them both so hard that the two girls were obliged to hop around in a circle to keep their balance. "I want the watch!" the woman roared.

"Certainly!" Kate snapped. "By all means call the watch! I shall see that you are suitably punished for accosting young ladies and dragging them about by the elbow!"

A large crowd had gathered around them and it hummed with excitement at this announcement; but suddenly a silence settled over it and members of the motley throng began to step back to provide an open path for a tall elegant figure in blue superfine and white kid. Kate had never realized before what an imposing sight Wale presented when he stood at his full height and looked down his nose.

"What nonsense is this?" he asked in a voice which had a decidedly icy edge to it.

"Oh, Drew!" Serena sobbed, "Thank heaven you are here!" And she collapsed into a crumpled heap. "This woman . . . I . . . she . . ."

Kate pulled her impatiently to her feet. "It's a ridiculous misunderstanding," she told him.

"Of course," he said.

"But, sir. . . ." the woman began. She hesitated, looking from Wale to the bizarre young women. Finally she sighed. "Yes, sir," she said, and dropping him a curtsey, turned away quietly, and disappeared into the crowd. Within a few seconds, the onlookers had faded away quietly, also. Serena sniffled. Kate scowled belligerently. Suddenly Wale grinned.

"What are you?"

"We are piewomen," Kate explained. Then she sighed. "But I fear no one has been deceived by our attire."

"I'm not surprised," he said, trying not to laugh aloud.

He offered each girl an arm. "Come along and I'll take you home. Have you completed your business here?"

"No, we have not," Kate said. "We came to secretly purchase a bird, and we have been robbed of our reticules. If you have ten shillings in your pocket and will pay for the bird I selected, I shall repay you as soon as we are safely home."

"Ten shillings?" he asked in surprise. "Is that what birds cost? I'd have thought the price was more like three or four pence at the most."

"But this is an extremely rare bird," Kate explained.

"Very well," he said. "Where is it?"

"Over this way," Kate told him, breaking away and hurrying ahead to lead the way.

Serena clung tightly to his arm as he followed her cousin along a walkway, pushing through the crowd. "Well, Reenie," he said, looking down at her streaked and grimy face, "you have had an adventure. But it's a very dangerous chance you've taken coming to a place like this. I'm happy to discover that you've come to no real harm."

"I, too," she admitted, and began to weep into her sleeve.

"Don't cry," he urged her. "You'll melt yourself."

Halfway to the bird stall they encountered a tightly packed crowd which had gathered around a magician, and Wale paused to watch as the illusionist extricated a long string of sausages from a bystander's ear. While he and Serena were both engrossed, Kate came bustling back to them, shivering with indignation.

"Come along quickly," she urged. "The vendor is trying to raise the price. He claims that he has another customer and must charge me one whole pound if I wish to have the bird, but I collect he has merely decided that we are a clutch of fat pigeons which are ripe for plucking."

"And what was your reply to him, ma'am?" Wale asked,

112

turning away from the magician and guiding Serena in pursuit of her cousin.

"I said I shall snatch off both his ears, and perhaps his nose as well, if he does not behave himself."

Wale nodded approval. "That should teach him not to trifle with piemen's wives."

When they reached the stall, they found the vendor standing with both feet planted and his lower lip protruding obstinately. His eyes narrowed at the sight of his Grace, but he quickly steadied himself and scowled belligerently.

"I'll not back down, sir," he told him. "The price be one quid, an' that be final! This 'ere budgigaster be worth arry bit on it."

Wale picked up the cage calmly and held it out in front of himself at arm's length. "I doubt that it is worth even ten shillings, but I shall give you that amount at this time . . ." He laid the coins on a nearby shelf. "And if you do not consider it fair, you may come to Asgar House and discuss it with my secretary."

The vendor's face reddened. "An' ooh d'yer think yer be, sir, the Dook-er-York?"

"No," Wale said gently, "the Duke of Asgar. Please do not hesitate to visit my secretary if you feel yourself cheated."

Before the vendor could contrive a reply, Wale guided Kate and Serena out of the stall and headed them back along the passageway between the rows of shops.

"Do you think he'll come to Asgar House?" Kate asked as they hurried through the crowd.

Wale shrugged. "He may. If he does, Blythedale will know what is fair. I have no idea what a budgigaster—or whatever it is—is worth."

In a few moments they reached the street where they had entered the fair. A closed carriage was drawn up nearby, and on its seat Timothy was endeavoring to hold the restless horses in check. His face relaxed when he saw Wale coming out of the fair with the two girls in tow; but after he had stared at them goggle-eyed for a moment, the muscles around his mouth began to twitch and he turned away.

Wale bundled them and their bird cage into the carriage, took a seat beside them, and rapped on the frame for Timothy to proceed. Kate sat frowning thoughtfully to herself.

"I do not understand," she began, "why Timothy went to you instead of to my uncle, when he suspected us of putting ourselves in danger."

Wale chuckled. "He did not go to me exactly. When I arrived at Deverill House to pay an early call on Willie, and found Timothy standing on the front pavement with a parcel of bed sheets on his shoulder and a troubled expression on his face, I surmised that you were at the seat of his malaise."

Serena's face rumpled and she began to weep.

"Oh, dear," Kate said with a sigh. "What is it now, love?"

"It has all been so dreadful—so frightening!" She reached out a hand to accept Wale's handkerchief. "And I am convinced we still have a great deal of suffering ahead of us. When my father discovers what we have done, he may send Katie home to the country again. And I shall be alone . . . forever."

Wale took her hand and gave it a soothing pat. "Don't worry, Reenie. Timothy assures me that he can smuggle you into the house so that no one will know of your escapade. But . . ." He turned to each girl in turn, making a solemn face at her. "You must give me your sacred word that you will never go off on your own like this again. Smithfield has been notorious for centuries, and any number of terrible things might have happened to you. In the future if you need a bird—or a cow or elephant or whatever—contact me without delay and I shall contrive to supply one—in the deepest secrecy, of course."

Serena was watching him earnestly, nodding and sniffling.

"Do you give me your word?" he asked them.

"Yes, yes!" Serena assured him. "I promise!"

"Miss Ashworth?"

114

Kate frowned. "There are times when it is impossible to take you into our confidence. You would not understand some of our needs."

"I would try," he told her.

She shook her head.

"You must promise," he insisted, "or I'll be obliged to relate your adventures to the Earl."

Kate shrugged. "Then I must promise. And I do."

She turned to look out the window at the passing scene. He watched her solemnly. Finally he sighed.

"I wish I knew," he said, "what other schemes you have running around in your head."

CHAPTER 9

For the next few days, Kate worked diligently on the spell to ensnare Young Lester. Every morning she brewed fresh herbs and poured a small amount into Sweetums's water before she made a libation of the rest, pouring it onto the ground in the garden. All the while, she chanted softly and made gestures with her hands. Then she collected Sweetums's birdseed for the day and carefully rubbed it against Serena's cheeks and arms and across her bare shoulders while she intoned magic words.

Serena was fascinated, and although she developed a slight rash from having the rough grains passed over her skin, she bore up bravely when Kate reminded her what end they had in view.

"If you are still in love with him, that is," Kate added.

"Of course I am in love with him!" Serena exclaimed. "Do you think me an inconstant feather-brain?"

"No, no," Kate hastened to assure her. "But I thought that perhaps you might have transferred your affections back to Asgar after the way he rescued us so neatly from Bartholomew Fair. Just think how fond he must be of you to come rushing so quickly to your aid."

"And I am exceedingly fond of dear Drew," Serena assured her. "But you have observed, I am sure, that he is not the least bit romantic. On the other hand, Young Lester . . ." Her face took on a blissful expression. "He is a real man."

Kate nodded politely.

With Timothy's aid they had managed to slip into the house and repair their appearances sufficiently to return to their abigails and receive only minor scolds from those ladies. Neither the Earl nor the Countess suspected them of subterfuge. Only once had there been a minor crisis when they had been helping Lady Fanny decide whether to set extra garden tables and chairs among the banked camelias at the north end of the ballroom. Her ladyship, having had a long day of decisions and alarms, felt suddenly faint and asked Serena if she could use her vinaigrette. Having had her best little vinaigrette stolen with her reticule at Bartholomew Fair, her daughter was obliged to hand her a little blue one with gold scrollwork over its sides.

"You are using this one now, my pet?" her ladyship asked her. "Have you tired of the jewel-encrusted vinaigrette which your grandmother used for so many years?"

Serena cast a despairing look at Kate. "I had meant to tell you, Mama," she explained in stumbling accents, "but with all the planning for the masquerade, I forgot. I fear I have lost it. When Katie and I went walking yesterday, I put it in my reticule, but when I returned, it was gone. I must have knocked it out onto the path when I removed my handkerchief."

Lady Fanny, much agitated, for "it was your grandmother's favorite vinaigrette, presented to her by the Duke of Orleans after a visit to his palace," sent Timothy to search the park. He returned an hour later empty-handed and with such a glowering expression on his face, that Serena kept thanking him in an apologetic voice until Lady Fanny stared at her in surprise.

Kate quickly diverted her ladyship's attention to the decorations, and she forgot the vinaigrette as she proceeded with preparations for the bal.

To silence the Marchioness—who made daily visits to Deverill House, issuing orders and countermanding Fanny's—Fanny had compromised and adopted one of her suggestions: she was changing the locale of the bal from Venice to France and was transforming Deverill House into Versailles. At all hours of the day and night, nurserymen could be found making their way through the rear of the house carrying shrubs and trees in enormous pots as they turned the ballroom into an elaborate garden. The front staircase was to be lined with topiaries which were to give an impression of an avenue lined with trees. A gentle, winding stream filled with colorful fish was being contrived along one side of the room, little white iron tables and chairs were to be scattered about, and an actress, who was to impersonate Marie Antoinette, had been engaged to stroll near the north wall brandishing a crook and herding a small flock of sheep—which had been the most difficult of all the commodities to procure, as Lady Fanny had insisted that they be well behaved and that the merchant who provided them guarantee that they would not leave hideous droppings on the turf near the diners. The guarantee being refused, Lady Fanny subjected herself to a great deal of soul searching, but finally decided to engage the services of the sheep despite everything, and appointed one of the smallest stableboys to follow them about with a rake and a pail.

Banks of flowers were being arranged on all sides of the room, little paths constructed along the edges of the dance floor; herbaceous borders were introduced. All of London was waiting with bated breath for the glorious evening to arrive. A rumor reached Lady Fanny's ears that the Countess of Heatherington was planning to attend as Cleopatra in a costume which was said to have cost twenty thousand pounds. It was even being whispered that Prinny might lend his august presence to the festivities for a few minutes.

Kate and Serena were in a fever of anticipation. On the day before the gala event, their dominoes were delivered by Madame Antoine's messenger, Kate's a beautiful shade of cherry satin and Serena's an equally luscious sky blue. They had masks to match, which they found irresistible and wore about the house, trying to find someone who would pretend not to recognize them.

"Masks are not really becoming," Serena admitted finally, tossing hers down onto Kate's dressing table and beginning to apply some of Kate's darkening liquid to her eyelashes.

Kate was working with the little green bird, whispering to him and holding him close to her face. "Love undying," she murmured. The little bird cocked his head on one side, then leaned forward and caught her lower lip in his beak.

"Ouch!" she squeaked, hurling him away. "You little wretch!"

Serena laughed as he fluttered onto the dressing table. "Naughty boy," she chided.

Kate smiled in spite of herself. "I think he is possessed by the devil."

Serena picked him up on her finger and brushed his soft body against her cheek. "I shall miss him," she said. "Do you think there is a way we can influence Young Lester to bring him back to us—as a gift, perhaps? Can you contrive a spell of some sort?"

Kate shook her head. "If I can contrive a way to get Sweetums into Young Lester's house, I shall consider myself fortunate. Now that we have readied our spell, we must transfer it to the vict . . ." She hesitated, then finished, ". . . to the *subject.* We must somehow get Sweetums into his bedroom so that the magic will wash over him for at least eight hours."

"How are we going to do that?" Serena asked.

Kate shrugged. "I have not the faintest notion. I have racked my brains to no avail and strongly fear that we must enlist the aid of a loyal servant—in other words, Timothy."

"Never!" Serena exclaimed. "He will undoubtedly inform my mother."

"I am confident that he shall not," Kate said. "He has kept faith with us concerning Bartholomew Fair. In fact, I fear he is our only hope. We shall take a walk in the park and request my aunt to send him with us as escort. Then we shall be able to approach him with our problem."

But when the two girls appealed to Lady Fanny it appeared that their scheme was destined for failure, as her ladyship announced with an angry air of finality that under no circumstance could she spare Timothy until everything was in readiness for the masquerade. "For he is the only person who can reach the tops of the topiary trees and secure the ribbons—not to mention lifting things which would otherwise require two men."

Eventually Kate and Serena were obliged to make their way downstairs to the ballroom and stumble over bundles of sod and garden implements until they found Timothy in an alcove affixing bunches of fern to a molding. When Kate explained that she desperately needed his assistance and he had assured her that he could not leave his post until all was in readiness for the bal, she sank onto a white garden chair and frowned deeply, cudgeling her brains to come up with a solution to her problem.

After a moment she was aware that the footman was peering at her anxiously, his face rather white. "Please, miss," he urged in a straitened voice, "with your permission, I beg of you, please don't go and do anything dangerous. If you can wait until the day after tomorrow . . ."

"But I can't," she insisted. "If you cannot help me tonight, I shall be forced to throw caution to the wind and manage by myself."

"No," he protested. "Please, miss!"

"Then you must help me," she said.

"Very well. What would you have me do?"

Her mind raced quickly. "You must meet me by the garden door at midnight. And be sure to leave a window open so that we may get back inside if we should, by some mischance, be locked out. Our purpose is to free the little green bird inside Young Lester's house."

He made a gesture of protest with his hand.

"If you would rather not help me . . ." she said quickly. But he shook his head. "And one other thing," she added. "I shall need to disguise myself as a kitchen maid. Can you obtain some clothes for me?"

"I shall try, miss," he promised.

121

With a conspiratorial nod and smile, she took Serena by the hand and they made their way out of the ballroom.

"He will desert us," Serena informed her when they were once again in Kate's sitting room. "Or he will report our follies to my mother. I could tell by the expression on his face that he did not like our plan."

"But he will help us," Kate insisted. "He is a good man—and loyal."

She was standing by the window, looking out through the tangled branches that formed a barrier between the Earl's and Young Lester's house. Suddenly, as she watched, a sash on the second floor, which was visible through an opening in the leaves, was thrown open and Young Lester himself leaned out.

"Serena!" Kate gasped. "Look!"

Serena scampered to her side. "Why, it is he! It is he!" Clasping her hands in delight, she capered around the room, doing a minuet step for half the distance then a waltz for the remainder.

"Whiskey, whiskey!" Sweetums hissed from his cage, also dancing back and forth on his perch.

Kate was scowling thoughtfully. "Do you think that is his bedroom, Serena? If it is, I believe I can reach the window from that tree alongside it. I shall put Sweetums in my pocket and run along that branch . . ."

"Never!" Serena cried, halting alongside her and trying to clasp her in her arms. "You gave my father your solemn word that you would not so much as set foot in a tree!"

"I know," Kate said with a sigh, "but we are in such desperate straits. And I shall have Timothy on the ground to catch me in case anything should go wrong—which it certainly will not!"

"No, no, no!" Serena insisted. "I will not have you in a tree!"

"Then you would prefer to abandon the entire plan?"

"Yes," Serena said. "I will give up Young Lester rather than have you risk your life!"

Kate, surprised and more than a little gratified by her

cousin's display of affection, was temporarily disconcerted, but a moment later she was busily planning again.

"Very well," she said, "if you feel so strongly, I promise I shall not enter his house by tree. It should not be necessary, at any rate. I am confident that Timothy can contrive a way to get me into the house. Then we shall need someone to create a diversion of some sort to draw the household's attention away, during which time I, disguised as a kitchen maid, shall dart through the corridors to Young Lester's bedroom and release Sweetums. That should not be too difficult, now that I know the location of the room. I do not see how our plan can fail."

Serena, who could visualize any number of ways the plan might fail, frowned to herself. "How shall you explain the presence of a kitchen maid in Young Lester's bedroom, if you are discovered?"

Kate was thoughtful. "That is a problem, I see. I shall disguise myself instead as a charwoman. What could be more natural than to find a charwoman cleaning the master's room?"

"At midnight?"

"Well," Kate said crossly, "I shall have to avoid being discovered."

She was interrupted by a gentle rapping on the door, and opening it, found Timothy outside with a small parcel. He wiggled his eyebrows at her.

"Here is that package from the draper, miss—the things you asked be sent."

"Oh, yes, thank you," she said, taking the bundle and quickly closing the door.

Inside the wrapper she found a shabby but clean dress, an apron, and a mob cap. Kate quickly stuffed them into her bed between the headboard and the pillows.

"Now," she said, "it only remains to devise a disturbance which will divert Young Lester's household."

But by eleven thirty that night, they had still not managed to contrive a foolproof scheme. Early in the evening Lady Fanny had offered to escort them to the Marchioness's for a "nice little dinner party with an early return to bed." Kate had quickly conjured up a throbbing headache and Serena had wondered aloud if she were not also on the verge of suffering from a like complaint, as she had a strange tautness in both her temples. Her ladyship had then sent them both to bed with trays of tea and toast. Ordinarily she would have suspected duplicity when Brill reported to her that the two young ladies were bouncing in and out of their rooms to visit each other; but with the masquerade bal pressing in on her, Lady Fanny merely waved a hand and reminded the abigail that everyone was in a high state of fidgets over the coming activities.

At eleven forty-eight Kate stood in front of her pier glass, examining herself in the guise of a charwoman. "I think it will do, don't you, my love?" she asked Serena, who was sitting beside her, frowning anxiously at her reflection.

"No, I don't," Serena told her. "There is something wrong. I collect it is your hair."

"Of course," Kate agreed, stuffing her fashionable curls up under her cap. "How could I be such a widgeon? What other silly mistake am I making?"

"I think you are all right now," Serena said. "Although you would be more convincing if you were bent and hideous from a lifetime of suffering and overwork. Perhaps if you added a bit of soot to your face . . ."

"I shall rub some dirt on it when I get out into the garden," Kate told her.

"But, Katie," Serena mourned, "I am so frightened. We know nothing about the way real charwomen behave; and I am convinced you will make a mistake and be discovered. If you are, you will be ruined forever; what reason can we give for your lurking about Young Lester's house in the dead of night? And to be found in his bedroom would be the end of enough! Nor is there any way we can explain such odd behavior, as the truth is as bad as any lie one could manufacture, in addition to which I doubt that anyone would believe it. I am convinced that we should give up our plans and let fate take charge of my romance."

Kate shook her head. "Fate cannot be relied upon. It is

constantly pitching young girls into dreadful circumstances. Besides, I am loath to waste all the effort we have expended on this spell. We shall instead put our trust in chance and hope that it will provide some propitious twists and turns which will assist us in our endeavors."

So saying, she took Sweetums out of his cage, rolled him in a fine lace handkerchief, and stuffed him into her apron pocket.

Serena sighed. "Be careful, Katie."

"I will," Kate assured her.

She found Timothy waiting for her in the morning room. He came out of the darkness as soon as she entered, and motioned for her to follow him. Then opening the door, he escorted her out onto the terrace.

"I thank you for your assistance," she whispered to him, but he put a finger to his lips.

They moved silently across the garden to the wall which separated Young Lester's property from the Earl's. There Timothy parted some vines to reveal a small door. Pulling a key from his pocket, he inserted it in the lock and pushed the door slowly open. Kate bent her head and stepped through.

On the other side she straightened up in surprise. The Duke of Asgar was sitting on a stone bench. He unfolded his ample length and rose to greet them.

"What are you doing here?" she hissed.

He bowed formally. "Timothy was kind enough to inform me of your need," he explained, "and I am here to be of service to you."

"What on earth do you think you can do?" she snapped.

He shrugged. "What needs to be done?"

She stood thinking rapidly. "Well," she said at last, "you may be of use after all. If you wish to be helpful, you may create a disturbance on the other side of Young Lester's house to draw everyone's attention to that side. That will be of great benefit to me."

"And what will that accomplish?" he asked. "What is the object of this charade?"

Kate bit her lip. "I shall not tell you, sir. This is a most

125

secret matter, and I suspect that you are not sympathetic."

"Whiskey, whiskey," hissed a little voice in her pocket.

"What the devil!" Wale exclaimed. "Is that the green bird?"

Kate turned away from him. "If you wish to be of assistance to us, sir, you could perform a great service by repairing to the other side of the house as quickly as possible and creating a disturbance there, for if I linger about in this garden, I shall certainly be caught."

"That is true," he said. "But you must give me your word that you will not attempt to enter the house."

"How can I promise such a thing!" Kate exclaimed, stamping her foot. "I must somehow contrive to get the bird into Young Lester's bedroom. And may I ask why you are here interfering? It is the most unsettling thing to have you forever popping up where I least expect you, even when you assist me out of dreadful scrapes."

"I am here for Timothy's sake," he retorted. "Have you given a thought to what will befall him if he is discovered abetting your goosish schemes? He will certainly be turned off—if not sent to prison."

Kate was suddenly grim. "That is true. Timothy, you must return to Deverill House immediately."

Wale's stern expression melted suddenly. "No, I shall make everything right. If Timothy and I are discovered, I shall say that I am playing another prank on Lester. He will consider this escapade in keeping with what he knows of me. Besides . . ." He laughed softly. ". . . I am eager to know what his reaction will be when he finds a talking bird flying about his bedroom. I shall 'chalk one up for Old Froggy.' "

He scowled again. "But you must remain out of sight. There will be a terrible scandal if anyone discovers that you are participating in this foolishness. You would be sent home in disgrace and Lady Fanny's heart would be broken."

"Yes, you are right," Kate agreed reluctantly. "Then I shall send Timothy inside with the bird."

"So be it," Wale observed. "I shall go and create a disturbance. And the quicker the better." Turning on his heel, he disappeared through the shrubbery.

Cautiously Kate and Timothy made their way to a rear door of Lester's house. As they passed along the wall which contained the window of Young Lester's bedroom, Kate looked up at it unhappily. "I should not have been able to get inside by using a tree anyway," she told her companion. "There is nothing close enough to enable me to jump across to the window."

Timothy was silent.

They had no sooner reached the rear door of the house than they heard a strange medley of cries arising from the other side of the building. A horse whinnied somewhere and several voices were raised abusively. Inside the house Kate could hear sounds of confusion. She quickly pulled Sweetums out of her pocket. He was still tightly rolled in her handkerchief.

"Whiskey, whiskey," he scolded.

"Here," she whispered, sliding him into Timothy's coat pocket. "Be certain that he does not escape until you reach Young Lester's bedroom. Then you must release him. But only there."

Timothy had slipped a wire into a keyhole and was turning it slowly. In a moment there was a click and he gently slid the door open. But immediately he pulled it closed again as the sound of excited voices rose within.

"It's no use, miss," he whispered. "They've not been lured away."

"That incompetent Wale!" she muttered. "He is not a very accomplished conspirator. Very well, then, follow me."

She made her way hurriedly around the side of the house. Young Lester's window was dark, lying in the shadow of a great elm. Kate stood back and tried to estimate the height of the sill.

"If you could lift me onto your shoulders," she suggested. "No, perhaps that would not be high enough. A little more, perhaps. After I've gotten onto your shoulders, could you lift me the rest of the way on your hands?"

127

He stared at her. "I could, miss, but a gentle-born young lady like you would surely fall."

"Not I," she assured him. "I am as agile as a squirrel."

She glanced up at the window again. "Come, let us at least try," she urged him. "There can be no harm in that."

"But will it be any use?" he asked, looking up at the pane. "Is it open?" Then he added, "Aye, a bit. Enough, I should say. Well, if you wish to attempt it . . . I can catch you if you fall."

And so saying, he fished the bird out of his pocket and handed it back to Kate. As she received it, Sweetums wriggled inside the handkerchief.

Slipping off her shoes, Kate put one foot into the cradle Timothy made for her with his hands.

"Toss me," she urged him. He did so, and an instant later she had put her hands against the wall and vaulted up onto his shoulders. He stood motionless for a moment, startled by the ease of her success.

She reached up a hand. "It is barely out of reach," she whispered. "I shall try standing on your head."

Immediately she stepped up onto his mound of thick brown hair. Caught unaware, he staggered against the side of the house. There was a thump as he banged his face against the wall. He groaned. Kate peered down anxiously over her shoulder.

"Timothy," she hissed, "are you hurt?"

"No," he grunted. He put up his hands for her. Grasping both her ankles, he raised her slowly up.

"Excellent!" she whispered. "I can reach now. Just a moment." She pulled Sweetums out of her pocket, pushed him through the opening, and gave the handkerchief a shake. She could hear the bird flutter to the floor.

"There," she hissed in triumph. "He is inside. You may bring me down."

Timothy lowered his hands slowly. As soon as Kate's feet were securely planted on his shoulders and he had released his grasp on her ankles, she dropped lightly to the ground.

"Thank you, thank you!" she exclaimed, catching his hands and swinging him around into the moonlight. "You are the most excellent and accomplished conspirator I have ever had!"

But to her dismay, as she jerked him around into the light from a nearby window, she saw that his eyes were full of tears and there was blood running from his nose. She gasped.

"What have I done to you?" she hissed.

"Yes, what has she done to you?" echoed a voice in the shrubbery as Wale strode out of the darkness and joined them. "Good God! Has she broken your nose?"

Timothy mumbled something about being quite all right and, no, no, not in pain, sir. Wale, however, turned on Kate and wagged a finger in her face.

"Devil's daughter!" he chided. "You must forsake this life of crime once and for all."

"But I . . ." she began.

"Please, sir," Timothy warned, "someone is coming."

"Yes, we must get away from here," Wale agreed, bustling them toward the wall. A moment later he had hurried them through the gate and locked it behind them.

"Now you must go immediately up to your bed and force yourself to be honestly and deeply asleep within five minutes," he told Kate.

"But," she protested, "who is to minister to poor Timothy?"

"I shall minister to him, have no fear," he assured her. "Your assignment is to gain your bed without further incident."

She nodded and, after slipping quietly into the house through the open window, scurried upstairs, reaching her room without incident. It was not until fifteen minutes later that she was discovered by Lady Fanny in Serena's room, whispering with her about the fate of her escapade.

"What!" cried her ladyship. "Is it possible that you two are still awake and buzzing together about the masquerade bal? What am I to do with you girls? If you do not sleep, you shall be hagged and miserable the entire evening—and after all the effort I have made in your behalf. Fie on you! Into your beds immediately and to sleep! I had no idea you could be so naughty!"

CHAPTER 10

Lady Fanny's bal masque did not begin as auspiciously as she hoped—and had every reason to expect after her tireless efforts and careful planning. The first clouds arose on the horizon when Marie Antoinette arrived to take her place on the turf of the ballroom.

"Yer not tellin' me I'm to 'erd these 'ere woolies?" she cried in dismay. "I know nothin' o' sheep, I swear! That great lowerin' black 'un'll tip me a settler."

"Nonsense," Timothy assured her, endeavoring to maintain his dignity despite the large piece of sticking plaster astride his damaged nose. " 'E's gentle as a lamb." Then as the actress scowled at him indignantly, he quickly corrected himself, "as a kitten, I mean."

But Marie was determined not to be lulled into a false sense of security, and it was not until Judson himself had proven to her that the sheep were perfectly docile—by prodding the black one seven times in the side with the crook before it emitted a feeble bleat—that she tied the ribbons of her shepherdess cap resignedly under her chin and took up her post.

Thereafter, for a time, all appeared to be progressing nicely. Lady Fanny emerged from her dressing room resplendent in the Grecian draping of a dryad with a spectacular headdress of intertwined branches that had been encrusted with gems and hung with gossamer webs. She had accepted the accolades of her staff and had smiled happily to herself as she overheard the muffled exclamations of an underservant whispering to a colleague, "Coo! Ain't she beautiful! Queen Mab 'ersel'," when she began her final check of the Tuileries Gardens and discovered, to her horror, that the entire west side of the room was beginning to wilt. In great perturbation she gathered all the footmen and maids together and set them to spraying the flowers and foliage with ice water. This soon produced large puddles on the edge of the dance floor and a new brigade with buckets and mops was pressed into action.

"Everything is going wrong," she mourned as she hurried into Serena's room to ascertain the state of the young ladies' readiness. "I fear some dreadful disasters are in store for us."

"Oh, certainly not!" Kate protested. "I am confident your party will be the crush of the Season."

She turned away from the mirror where she had been adjusting her loo mask, and her eyes fell upon her aunt. With an exclamation, she threw up both hands. "Aunt Fanny!" she cried. "What a marvelous costume! You look like the faerie queen herself, and not a day over sixteen years old."

Her ladyship wriggled with pleasure. "I am sure it is not so splendid as that."

Serena exclaimed and rushed over to hold her mother's hand and turn her around. "Oh, Mama!" she mourned, "I want a costume like that. Just look at this dreadful, plain, uninteresting old domino I must wear. I do not have the courage to appear in such a dowdy old thing, I assure you."

"But, my dearest!" Kate protested, "You look lovely in your blue satin—and most mysterious with your mask and hood. You can see that everyone will guess my aunt's identity immediately."

"But she looks so wonderful! Such a headdress!"

"It is very heavy," Lady Fanny informed her. "I am obliged to hold myself perfectly erect at all times, for if I

132

turn my head the least little bit, I tilt over to one side and stumble into things. Of course, if I can maintain this posture, I shall appear wondrously queenly—which is an advantage, I admit: but I could never join in any of the dances, and I am convinced I shall be thoroughly exhausted and ready to take to my bed within the hour, as I already have a crick in my neck."

Serena sighed. "I suppose I must put my disappointment aside for Katie's sake. After all, tonight is her presentation."

"Indeed," Lady Fanny agreed. "And I shall be congratulated on being the mentor of *two* lovely young ladies—my own precious daughter and my very dearest niece—which will be the most gratifying thing!"

The three ladies twined their arms around each other and, after a moment of bliss, departed from Serena's room in high hopes. Music was already emanating from the ballroom and a bustle of excitement arose from the activity in that chamber where guests had already begun to arrive. But no sooner had they reached the head of the main staircase than Judson hurried to Lady Fanny's side, a look of suppressed anxiety on his face.

"A most dreadful development, your ladyship," he announced. "The sheep are eating the herbaceous borders, and the effect is no longer what we had desired."

"Good heavens!" the Countess exclaimed. "Get them out! They are presenting too many problems."

As Judson withdrew, Kate turned her attention to the guests who were arriving. Several gentlemen in black dominoes were clustered below in the entryway, closely followed by a magnificent Turk in elaborate golden robes and jewelled turban. Soon after they had started up the staircase, four young ladies in Russian peasant costumes entered through the front door.

The Marchioness of Gyle, always one of the early arrivals at any gala affair, swept into the house attired as a Red Indian princess. Her costumer had allowed herself free reign and had swathed her subject in rabbit pelts, which gave off a decidedly gamey aroma. A massive white eagle feather headdress streamed down the Marchioness's back, sparkling with diamonds and other precious stones which had been tucked into its recesses.

She began to tow her massive bulk up the staircase, breathing stertorously as she came. "What's this, Frances?" she trumpeted. "I was met outside by a flock of sheep running higgledy-piggledy down the street."

"At my front door?" the Countess exclaimed. "How is that possible?"

"They must have escaped from the boy," Serena giggled. "Such a pity we shan't have them grazing in our ballroom. So picturesque."

Lady Fanny was eyeing the Marchioness. "We have picturesqueness enough without them."

"Yes, I must see what you have contrived," that redoubtable lady announced. She stopped at the head of the stairs and stood for a moment, puffing and blowing.

"Then come along," Fanny urged her. "I shall show you everything. You will be delighted when you see the manner in which I have used your suggestions." And she led her cousin away to view the results of her handiwork.

A trio of huntsmen in forest green and with bows slung over their shoulders entered and began to mount the staircase followed by a drove of colored dominoes and, drawing up the rear, a Harlequin and his Columbine. Kate and Serena immediately recognized Tiffany's glossy curls bobbing over Columbine's mask. As the merrymakers passed their hostesses, Tiffany leaned toward them and whispered in a voice which could be heard throughout the room, "Any trees to climb in your French garden, Miss Ashworth?" And she let out a little trill of laughter which had a curiously metallic ring.

Serena closed her fan with a snap. "We should not be standing here, Katie. It is not necessary to play the hostess at a masquerade, and everyone is penetrating our disguise. Let us slip away into the throng and be mysterious."

"Indeed," Kate agreed. "By all means, let us be enigmas."

The two girls quickly made their way into the ballroom

134

to mingle with the crowd, which had already reached formidable proportions. Before they had taken many steps, a Hottentot in surprisingly civilized white shirt and breeches, but with a large knucklebone thrust into his hair, pinched Serena playfully on the cheek and announced, "Ugum wugum."

"Willie!" she laughed. "What an outlandish costume!"

"You know me?" he exclaimed in great disappointment.

"Of course," his sister giggled. "I hadn't the slightest doubt."

"Of all the whompers!" he mourned. "Such a dashed messy business smearing all this devilish soot on one's face!"

Kate put a hand on his sleeve. "No one else will recognize you, cousin. I had not the slightest notion who you were. It is only because Serena knows you so well that she identified you so easily."

"You think so?" he said, brightening slightly. "I shall find Wale and try my disguise on him. If he knows me, too, I shall give it all up and wash my face."

He wandered off and the girls again began to make their way through the thickening crowd. Serena pointed out a green domino who was lounging against a pillar. "I am convinced that is Young Lester," she whispered. "He appears to be under a spell. If he comes forward I shall grant him the first dance."

Kate, who was not convinced that the green domino was indeed Lester—he appeared much too bulky for that lithe young man—watched him suspiciously. "Whoever he is," she observed, "he is fascinated by you: he has looked nowhere else since he entered the room."

"Let us go talk to him," Serena suggested.

But their way was blocked by two friars who were conversing with a magnificent facsimile of Merlin the Wizard. Before they could approach the green domino, the Duke of Nellingham rolled up to them, spectacularly garbed as King Louis XIV in shimmering satin and lace. "Dearest ladies," he announced, and made an elaborate leg.

Serena, who was still watching the green domino, gave him a perfunctory nod.

"May I have the honor of escorting you to the refreshment table, Miss Serena?" he began. "You must be exhausted from all your activity. Dancing can be so fatiguing."

Before Serena could point out to him that no one had as yet done any dancing, he grasped Kate's hand and placed it on his arm. Kate quickly removed her hand and replaced it with Serena's, but her cousin slid her own hand from the Duke's arm and returned Kate's to its original position.

"Now, now," Kate chided, putting Serena's hand firmly back into place. "You must not be shy, my love. His Grace wishes to be of service to you."

"Yes, yes," he agreed, chuckling thickly. "You must not be timid, my little one."

For a moment it appeared that Serena would rebel; but Kate hurriedly slid an arm around her waist and urged, "Let his Grace take you for a turn about the room, my love. You can penetrate our guests' disguises and I shall complete our arrangements." She gave her cousin's arm a surreptitious squeeze. "I shall have everything in order by the time the first dance is made up. You know what I mean."

"Oh," Serena said, nodding, and turned her attention to the Duke.

Kate moved quickly away from them, pushing slowly through the crowd, toward the green domino. Before she could reach him, however, a black domino edged close to her and a voice which was unmistakably Elfan's hissed, "Miss Ashworth, I have heard the most distressing rumor. It is said that Miss Serena has bestowed her affections on Young Lester and means to announce her betrothal this very night."

"Indeed?" Kate exclaimed in surprise. "I have heard nothing which would encourage me to believe such a story. But it is true that my cousin admires Young Lester—in a way which everyone must admire him. Serena appreciates gallantry—a most romantic young lady."

Elfan nodded, and below his mask his mouth pulled down into a grim line. Kate moved away from him.

As yet she had not discerned Wale in the crowd. She wondered if he had decided, perhaps, not to subject himself to the crush. The room had filled rapidly and was now aroar with laughter and conversation. The Countess of Heatherington had indeed arrived in her Cleopatra costume and was the center of attention at one side of the room. Kate could hear Lady Fanny's voice squealing with delight as she enumerated aloud each of the highlights of Lady Heatherington's spectacular attire. The Marchioness, her feathers aflutter, was also trumpeting her approval.

The green domino had moved out of sight. After craning her neck until it began to feel stiff, Kate gave up her search for him and began to drift slowly from place to place, hoping to encounter him by chance. As she neared a bower on one side of the room, she noted a pair of lanky black dominoes leaning against a pillar, regarding her progress. One straightened up as she approached and she immediately realized that it was Wale. The other, who was of a slightly heavier build, was wearing on one hand a massive old-fashioned signet ring with one of the largest rubies she had ever beheld.

"Good evening, Miss Ashworth," Wale's voice welcomed her. "May I have the pleasure of presenting to you my friend Sir Malcolm Spencer-Loam? He has just returned from a sojourn in Russia and can vouch for the fact that you have not been performing there during the past few years."

Spencer-Loam bent low over Kate's hand. "Your servant, ma'am. I have heard about all the charming adventures you have been devising to entertain his Grace."

"Entertain!" Kate exclaimed.

"Yes, indeed, *entertain*," Wale assured her. "I was suffering from the most acute boredom before your arrival in town—in fact, I was ready to quit the city—but now I find myself diverted nearly every day. What manner of escapade have you planned for this evening, ma'am? If you will

137

inform me in advance, I'll be better prepared to act out my role."

Kate sniffed. "Indeed, sir, what an odious accusation!"

"No, no," he insisted, "I am anticipating our adventures with the utmost pleasure. Is Young Lester to be included? I see he has arrived in good time and is comporting himself with the utmost complacency, resigned to his fate."

"You see him?" Kate peered anxiously around the room. "Where is he?"

Wale hesitated. "I wonder if I should betray him. Perhaps by respecting his disguise I am saving him from harm."

"Please," she urged. "Which is he?"

"The mulberry domino near the pillar, there."

Wale leaned his face closer to hers. "But seriously, Cousin, if you would share your plans with me, I would feel much more comfortable."

"I have no plans, I tell you!" she retorted. "You must think me the worst sort of scheming creature alive." And turning haughtily, she marched away from him. It was only after she had passed the pillar against which the mulberry domino lounged that she realized she had also been rude to Spencer-Loam.

Before she could think of a way to rectify her faux pas, the first dance began to form. Serena and Nellingham were nowhere in sight. Kate scurried in and out of several antechambers, looking for them, but her efforts were to no avail. Finally, deciding that she must take matters into her own hands and keep Young Lester in readiness for Serena, she strode back across the floor toward him. Before she could reach him, however, a determined black domino appeared beside her, caught her by the hand and swung her into line beside him. The music started. She was barely able to catch her balance in time to take Wale's hand properly and march down the floor in a dignified manner.

"I must allow you to read my grandmother's diary sometime," he told her. "She had a most interesting and eventful Season the first year she was out, falling into one scrape after another. Do you believe such propensities are inherited?"

"But I am not prone to scrapes," she protested. "I never fall into them at home. I am the dullest girl imaginable."

To her surprise, he laughed aloud. They were immediately separated by the dance and each bounded away in a different direction. When they came back together again he was still smiling.

"I am awaiting the results of our last night's activities," he chuckled. ". . . Results in addition to Timothy's fancy-dress nose, that is."

Kate sighed. "Poor Timothy. He deserved a better fate."

"Indeed he did," Wale agreed.

Serena and Nellingham had joined the dancers at the opposite end of the line. Kate noted that Serena was hunched down inside her costume in an effort to make herself as small and inconspicuous as possible; Nellingham, on the other hand, was loudly humming a free-flowing obbligato to the music and dancing with exaggerated movements, pulling his knees up sharply in front of himself and pirouetting on his toes.

"His Grace of Nellingham is a lovely sight," Wale murmured. Kate could not suppress a giggle.

They were promenading along the far end of the room past the windows which led out into the garden, when a flicker of shimmering green suddenly darted in through an open pane. It swooped low over the dancers' heads, soared up toward the ceiling, then banked to its left and swept around the edge of the dance floor, fluttering high above the merrymakers' heads. There was a gasp of surprise throughout the room. As the green wings began to beat rhythmically, several dancers squealed and ducked.

The bird circled the room three times, then came down with a whir of wings and landed on Kate's shoulder. There was a moment of stunned silence when even the orchestra hesitated in surprise. During this pause, a raspy but remarkably stentorian little voice hissed, "Sweetums, Sweetums! Give me a kiss!"

The room was engulfed in laughter. "I say, that's re-

139

markable," came the familiar bleat of Young Lester's voice. "I found just such a little green bird flying about in my bedroom this very morning."

The musicians, suddenly recovering their aplomb, quickly struck up their music again and the dancers began to proceed with their set; but Kate pulled Wale unceremoniously out of line and pushed him over to the side of the room. "We must act at once or we shall be undone," she told him. "Please, sir, take the bird off my shoulder and hide him somewhere. Young Lester must not know he belongs to us, or he will suspect us of low cunning."

Wale reached out quickly to catch Sweetums, but with a sudden spate of angry chatter, the bird scampered up over the top of Kate's head and down onto her other shoulder. She turned around, presenting the bird again to the Duke. This time when Wale tried to grasp him, Sweetums rose straight up into the air, fluttering his wings and hanging, for a few seconds, over the top of Kate's head. As soon as Wale drew back, the bird dropped down onto her shoulder again.

"Whiskey, whiskey!" he croaked. There was a ripple of laughter from the dancers who were passing near them. Kate caught Wale's hand and drew him around a bank of flowers and out of sight.

"This is terrible," she muttered. "Where is Serena?"

"I am here," her cousin answered from close behind her. "I gave Nellingham to my dear Cousin Tiffany."

"Good," Kate said. "Now we must contrive to rid ourselves of this ridiculous bird."

But when she put her hand up to remove him, he sank his beak into her finger.

"Ouch!" she exclaimed. "Odious little beast!"

Wale leaned close to them and, in a conspiratorial tone whispered, "I have been thinking: there is no need to hide him, as there is no reason to believe that Lester will associate him with you. In fact, the bird should provide a fertile topic for conversation, which might promote a better understanding between Reenie and our neighbor."

"That is true," Kate agreed. "An excellent thought!"

She made a snatch for Sweetums and, catching him unaware, managed to grasp him around his middle. Quickly she transferred him to her cousin's shoulder; but he promptly hopped back onto her own and snuggled against her neck.

"Now, now, behave yourself," she protested, removing him and placing him again alongside Serena's ear. He immediately leaped off and resettled himself alongside Kate's neck. She turned to Wale. "Can you help me?"

He shook his head solemnly. "I know of no way to divert a man's affections from one lady to another when they are already fixed."

"Well," she grumbled, turning to Serena, "then we must change our dominoes. I collect that for some reason he prefers cherry to blue."

Both girls began to undo the fastenings at their throats. Kate was repeatedly obliged to push Sweetums away from her ear; he was fascinated by the glitter of her earring and kept nipping at it, often missing his mark and biting into her lobe, causing her to squeak and jump about and swipe repeatedly at him with one hand. Between times he tugged at strands of her hair which had pulled loose from her coiffeur. Wale, leaning against a nearby pillar, watched them, the muscles around his mouth twitching.

"Drew is laughing at us," Serena hissed.

"Disregard him," Kate told her. "If we concern ourselves with unimportant things, we shall not be able to change our clothes in time, and all our efforts of the past few days will be in vain."

"But if Young Lester is the subject of a powerful spell," Serena pointed out, "how will he contrive to escape us?"

"If only we could be sure of that," Kate murmured.

With an impatient jerk she managed to pull off her cloak and, sweeping the bird off its shimmering folds, dropped the garment to the floor. While she worked laboriously to remove her hood without completely disarraying her hair, she held Sweetums in her hand, taking care not to squeeze

141

him too hard. Immediately he began to struggle. Suddenly he broke free and shot up into the air. He circled once around their heads then landed on top of a bank of lilies.

"Oh, dear!" Serena exclaimed. She handed Kate her blue domino. "Come down, Sweetums. Here, pretty boy."

Kate hurried her cousin into the cherry domino and wrapped herself in the blue. When they had pulled on their hoods, she handed Serena her mask.

"There," she observed. "That is excellent."

"Except that your costume now drags on the floor and Serena's is up above her ankles," Wale pointed out to them.

"It is of no consequence," Kate informed him. "Where is Young Lester?"

Wale straightened himself to peer over the top of a privet hedge. "Bearing down upon us," he told her.

Kate looked anxiously up at Sweetums. "Can you fetch the bird for us, Cousin? I shall never be able to coax him down in time, and he is beyond my reach."

Wale put out his hand. Slowly he moved toward the little bird. It sat peering down at them, tilting its head on first one side then the other. Just before Wale's fingers closed around it, Sweetums fluttered away and landed on the top of a topiary tree.

"I say," Young Lester bleated, coming up behind them, "I could almost swear that is the very same bird."

"If you could help us catch it, sir," Kate suggested.

"Certainly," he said, and moved closer to the tree where Sweetums was perching. The bird rolled its eyes suspiciously and tilted its head.

Kate placed a hand firmly on the small of Serena's back and propelled her after Young Lester. "I am confident you two will contrive to capture him," Kate announced. Nodding her head, Serena trotted off in the mulberry domino's wake.

"And now that your duties have been discharged," Wale said, putting her hand on his arm and leading her toward an open window, "we shall find a quiet corner and converse uninterrupted."

To Kate's surprise she discovered that she was feeling

rather breathless and damp around her ears. She raised her fan and beat it briskly in front of her face.

"Oh, dear," she said, "it is the wrong color. I have forgotten to exchange with Serena."

"Are you unwell?" Wale asked her, bending toward her anxiously.

"This room is dreadfully airless," she admitted.

"You should remove your cowl and your mask," he told her.

"I could not!" she exclaimed. "It would end the mystery."

"But if you are going to faint . . ."

She sniffed and drew herself up to her full height. "Sir," she informed him, "I have never fainted in my life. Such missish behavior would never do for the granddaughter of . . . Well, you know all that."

Wale led her slowly through an open window onto the terrace. "Yes," he agreed, "I cannot remember hearing that Grandmother ever fainted."

Kate leaned her back against the balustrade and began to fan herself again. "My goodness," she murmured, "it is remarkably warm."

"Would you like some refreshment?" he asked her, leaning closer to peer anxiously through the slits of her mask. "Some lemonade, perhaps?"

Kate nodded. "Thank you. I should like that very much."

"Very well, I'll fetch you a glass. But, please," he urged, "promise me that you'll remain here until I return. I have something of the utmost importance to say to you."

"I promise," she assured him.

He turned away and quickly disappeared into the house. Kate began to beat her fan more vigorously in front of her face. The night was unusually oppressive for so early in the year. She felt a slight ripple of weakness and wondered if, by some wild chance, she were going to faint after all.

But as she stood fanning herself, a cool breeze rose from beyond the garden wall and wafted across her shoulders. Kate inhaled deeply and the waves of mist inside her head began to clear. Somewhere inside the house a clock struck eleven thirty. "Just half an hour more," she thought, "and I shall officially be presented to the ton."

It was a fine night with a clear sky and masses of stars thrown across the sky. From somewhere near at hand Kate could smell the clean scent of jasmine or orange blossoms or some such fragrance which Lady Fanny had imported in blooming pots for the occassion. She allowed herself to relax and bask in the pleasure of the moment—the caressing air, the music drifting in tinkling cascades from the ballroom, the sparkle of lights and laughter.

She was suddenly shaken from her reverie by the appearance of another black domino, who came darting through one of the windows farther along the terrace and made his way rapidly toward her. At the same time she heard footsteps on the other side of her. She was about to turn in that direction to see who was approaching, when the black domino hissed, "Serena, my darling!"

Kate raised a hand in protest. Immediately the green domino leaped out of the bushes on her right and clasped a burly arm around her waist, pinning one of her hands to her side. His other hand, he clapped over her mouth. Instinctively she swung her fan at his head, but to her annoyance, the string broke and it flew away from her, landing on the pavement some distance away.

Wildly she clutched at the hand which was grinding into her mouth. She had no doubt that if she could push it aside for a split second and let out one loud scream, Wale would instantly come bounding to her rescue. But the green domino's hand was fastened onto her face like a steel band, and it was pressing up under her nose in a way which partially blocked her breath. And he stank horribly of rancid sweat, unwashed garments, and fresh horse manure. For a moment Kate felt such a surge of revulsion that she was sure she was going to swoon.

A moment later she was bristling with anger. Never before had she been subjected to such treatment and never, she told herself, would she submit! If she could contrive to kick her captor in the shin, she might be able to break

144

free—or at least cause him to bellow and attract Wale's attention. She could perhaps kick backward, despite the awkward way he was holding her, and dig her heel into his shinbone.

But suddenly he tucked her under his arm and her feet flew out behind her, almost spinning her forward onto her nose. With her free hand she again clawed at the hand over her mouth—to no avail. The domino, with Elfan beside him, carried her quickly across the garden toward the back wall. She reached out her free hand and grasped wildly at passing shrubbery.

To her gratification, she managed to catch a small branch, but as she was jolted along, her hand stripped off all the leaves and then the branch slid out of her fingers. She grabbed again. This time she caught hold of a larger branch, but the green domino marched relentlessly on. Her arm was stretched out to its fullest length, and when she clung as hard as she could, the branch snapped off in her hand.

Then they were through a gate and into a waiting chaise. The green domino flopped onto the seat and unceremoniously dragged her onto his lap. Elfan jumped in beside him. The chaise lurched forward over the cobbles.

Kate began to struggle again. Quickly Elfan caught her free hand and pressed it to her lips.

"There, there, my precious," he crooned. "You shall not be harmed—only kidnapped in the most romantic and heroic manner. Young Lester could never devise such a delightful adventure, I assure you."

CHAPTER 11

"O, young Lochinvar is come out of the west," Elfan hummed.

Kate dug her fingernails into the domino's hand and clawed with all her strength. A growing panic was sweeping over her as she realized that her abductors might not discover their mistake until they were some distance from Deverill House. Then it might be impossible for her to return to the masquerade in time for the unmasking at midnight, and all the ton would learn of her misadventure— her name would be besmirched—perhaps her uncle would even pressure Elfan to marry her. Elfan, of all people! She shuddered at the thought.

Frantically she pulled at the domino's hand. If she could only move it enough to enable her to make a squeak, she might be able to alert Elfan to his mistake. Instead, the domino shifted his hand to a more secure position and covered her nose completely. She began to struggle for breath.

"There, there, my precious," Elfan murmured. "Be assured of my undying love. The first moment I set eyes on you, your glance smote me to the very core of my being."

Kate gave him a mighty kick with her heel. Her lungs were beginning to ache and there were stars flickering around her head.

"Ouch!" Elfan grunted, catching her foot. A moment later he was cradling it lovingly in his hand. "Precious little foot," he droned. "So sweet and tiny. It treads upon my heart."

A huge black cloud was settling over Kate's senses and her ears were beginning to ring violently. *I'm suffocating*, she thought—and with a surge of dismay, *I am actually going to die!*

She tried to thrash, fighting desperately for one last gasp of air; but her legs were melting and refused to move. Faintly and far away she heard a voice croak, "My God! Who is that?"

By this time there was a thunderous roaring in her ears and her lungs ached so painfully that she could think of nothing else. Then the chaise swung crazily and crashed against something, and she passed into a vast sea of blackness.

Later she thought that a hand was removed from her face, but she still could not breathe, as there was an horrendous weight crushing down on her. Finally she could hear a kind of buzzing and she felt herself gasping painfully. The domino was still cradling her in his arms, only now he smelled of fresh grass, and he was pleading with her in a voice which had changed to Wale's, "Katie! Good God! Can you hear me?"

"You should make sure she has no broken ribs before you squeeze her like that, Looby," chided a voice which Kate did not recognize. "You could puncture her lung or some such thing, and then we would really be in the suds."

"They are going to pay for this!" Wale swore. "I shall see that both of them pay—Elfan and that filthy executioner of his!"

"But Froggy, old man . . ." Elfan's voice began, whining and thin, "it was all a mistake—just a romantic little kidnapping to prove I could comport myself in an heroic way."

Wale's entire body began to tremble. "How dare you address me in that manner!" he roared. "Romantic little kidnapping, indeed! I'll see you in the dock for this, you scoundrel!"

148

"Your Grace . . ." Elfan protested.

"Here!" Wale called in a voice which set Kate's left ear to ringing again. "Timothy!"

There was a clatter of footfalls on the cobbles.

"Take charge of these men," Wale commanded him. "I'm going to use Elfan's chaise to bear Miss Ashworth back to her aunt."

"Yes, your Grace," Timothy murmured. "Get hold of that green one, Jimmy."

For a moment there was a stir of activity. Kate opened her eyes slowly. In a curl of black mist, she could see Timothy reaching out a hand to take hold of Elfan.

"Don't you dare lay your hands on me," Elfan snapped. Timothy hesitated.

"I'd accept his word," Wale muttered, ". . . . that he'll come along properly . . . if I could trust him."

"Trust me!" Elfan cried. He drew himself up. "How dare you, sir!"

Wale turned on him furiously. "How dare *you*, sir, kidnap Miss Ashworth!"

"I explained that to your Grace," Elfan whined. "I meant to kidnap Serena."

Wale snorted. "Of course that makes it right! Ruining a girl and condemning her to a life with you whether she wishes it or not—that's your idea of romance, Clangarry? You disgust me!"

"Well," Elfan began, then his voice trailed off. "I thought . . . Young Lochinvar and all that . . ."

Kate lay quietly in Wale's arms looking up at the underside of his chin, and a wonderful sense of peace and well-being washed over her. She glanced around them. In addition to Wale and Elfan, there was another black domino standing nearby with his cowl thrown back. His muscular hand was hanging down close to her face and on it was a huge ruby ring.

"She's awake, old man," Spencer-Loam said to his friend. Quickly Wale looked down at her. He drew her up close against his shoulder.

"Katie," he whispered, "are you hurt?"

"I don't think so," she replied in a voice which was barely audible.

His arm tightened around her and she felt his lips press against her hair. "I shall make Elfan pay for this night's work!"

Somewhere a clock was striking, its rhythm deep and far away. "Oh," Kate groaned, "I feel unwell. I don't think I can be presented at the unmasking tonight after all."

"Good God!" Wale exclaimed. "That's right! What time is it, Malc?"

Spencer-Loam consulted his watch. "Fifteen minutes before midnight? Can that be correct?"

Wale sighed. "Well, let's get her back to her aunt. At least someone at Deverill House can give her proper care—call a doctor, perhaps."

Spencer-Loam swung himself up onto the seat and took hold of the ribbons. With no small amount of difficulty but a great deal of skill, he managed to turn the horses in the narrow lane where the chaise had come to grief. A moment later the team was clattering over the cobbles, bouncing Elfan's carriage along in their wake. Wale's arms tightened around Kate.

"Do you have any pain, love?" he asked her.

"No," she replied, and realized, to her surprise, that she spoke the truth. Despite her rough handling, she was relatively unharmed. Someone had removed her cowl and as she lay comfortably in the Duke's arms, her cheek felt cool and refreshed against the smooth black satin which covered his shoulder. After a few seconds she realized that he was looking down at her. When she glanced up and smiled, he caught her fingers and pressed them to his lips. To her surprise a trickle of pleasure went through her.

"Here, here," Spencer-Loam protested as he glanced over his shoulder at them. "I must insist on the utmost decorum from you, Wale, until you have spoken to the young lady's father . . . or at least her uncle." He grinned down at Kate and finished, "These dukes think they can have everything their own way, Miss Ashworth, but be comfortable—I shall defend your good name against all comers—with my very life, if necessary."

"Good God, Malc!" Wale protested. "You will give Miss Ashworth a wrong picture of my intentions. Now, in order to preserve my own white plume untarnished, I must assure her that I, too, am ready to lay down my life for her good name."

Spencer-Loam was guiding his horses around a sharp corner. "How does one tarnish a white plume, I wonder," he mused aloud. Wale began to laugh and Spencer-Loam joined him. Kate, who had been about to slide one of her arms around Wale's neck, drew herself down into a little bundle against the side of the chaise.

When they reached the garden gate, they discovered to Kate's dismay and the young men's annoyance that it had been locked. They were obliged to bring the chaise around to the front of the house and enter at the main door. Wale was muttering to himself while Spencer-Loam tried to suppress his amusement. Kate found it difficult to move. She felt extremely weak from her ordeal, and as soon as she stood up, a wave of nausea swept over her. For a horrified instant, she looked down at Wale, who was waiting to help her to the ground, and thought she was going to collapse onto his shoulder or be violently sick.

"Kate?" he asked anxiously, reaching up a hand to her. "Are you all right?"

"No," she admitted. "I am not."

He reached up both hands to her and was about to lift her down, but she waved him away, stood for a moment until the earth steadied under the carriage, then taking one of his hands, stepped cautiously down onto the cobbles. To her annoyance it was immediately necessary for her to accept the assistance of Wale on one side and Spencer-Loam on the other.

"I shall manage very well," she told them as they mounted the shallow steps to the house. "Just a momentary weakness. Before we reach the door I shall be completely restored to myself and no one shall notice a thing amiss."

But at that moment the door was thrown open and, after one look at Kate, Judson stepped back in alarm, his composure quite deserting him. "Miss Kathryn!" he exclaimed in anguished tones. "Are you ill?"

Immediately he recalled himself and assumed a properly rigid posture. "Would you wish me to notify her ladyship?" he asked as the two young men half carried the girl into the vestibule.

"No, no," Kate said quickly. Her head was swimming and she felt herself to be in no condition to explain things to her aunt. But no sooner had Judson closed the door behind them than Lady Fanny's clarion tones rang from the head of the staircase.

"My dearest! Here you are! I have been searching for you everywhere. It is nearly midnight. But where is your cowl and your mask? And why are you coming in through the front door? Come up here quickly, you naughty girl."

"No," Kate protested. She stared up at the vast central staircase, which had grown enormously since her ordeal, and a tide of helplessness submerged her. "I could not," she whispered.

"Of course you can! You must!" her ladyship commanded. "Everyone is waiting for you."

"Damn it, Lady Fanny," Wale hissed. "She says she cannot!"

"Rubbish! I shall get Timothy to bring her up the stairs, if that is the problem. And Brill must tidy her locks."

"Please," Wale called to her in an echoing stage whisper. "We must make as little stir as possible here until you have heard the details of our adventures."

"Adventures?" her ladyship said, her determination faltering somewhat.

Wale, an arm around Kate's waist, helped her up the staircase. To Kate's surprise, she gained a little strength rather than lost it during her ascent. When she reached the top where her aunt was awaiting her, she saw that Serena had joined her mother. But her cousin was standing by the banister, gazing down into the vestibule with an enraptured expression on her face. Kate's heart sank. She turned to

152

look down. Sure enough, Elfan was at the bottom, gazing up at them. He had removed his hood and despite the fact that his hair was all on end, he presented an heroic picture. By mischance, a large candelabrum stood behind him, and its cluster of candles formed a glowing halo behind his head. Serena clasped her hands.

"Oh," she murmured.

Kate felt a surge of anger. "Serena!" she scolded. "Don't you dare! Do you hear me? I forbid it!"

"But look at him," her cousin breathed. "Like the painting of King Arthur with the light of virtue shining behind him—or was it Sir Galahad?"

"*Virtue!* Of all things!" Kate spat. "I tell you I forbid it!"

Wale and Lady Fanny were trying to help her into a small chamber at one side of the landing. "Forbid what, my love?" her ladyship asked, raising a hand toward Judson and signaling to him.

Kate hesitated.

"She forbids Serena to fall in love with Elfan," Wale muttered. "And I forbid it, too; dashed hare-brained scoundrel!"

"Well, certainly," Lady Fanny agreed. "I also forbid it." She turned toward an inner doorway. "Ah, Brill! Come quickly. You must tidy Miss Kathryn's hair. And her dress has need of straightening, also—these bows are twisted and the flounce is quite crushed. What on earth have you been about, Katie my dear, to get yourself in such a state?"

Brill immediately set to work straightening Kate's apparel, but Wale stepped between Lady Deverill and her niece. "I must take you aside and tell you what happened, Lady Fanny. It is impossible for Miss Ashworth to stand up in front of a room full of people tonight."

Somewhere in the distance a clock was striking midnight, its deep resonant tones ringing throughout the house. On a nearby mantel a tiny soprano set up a tinkling echo.

"But whatever will people think if she does not?" her ladyship protested.

"It is all right," Kate said slowly. To her surprise she was feeling considerably revived by her flush of indignation

153

toward Serena. "I think I can stand a few moments and smile at people. But then I shall slip away to my room and lie down for a time."

"What has happened?" Lady Fanny asked again. "Why are you so shaken, my dearest?"

Kate waved a hand unhappily. She took a step toward the ballroom. Unfortunately her legs were still rubbery and unreliable. Wale quickly gave her his arm. With a sigh, she leaned on him, and with Lady Fanny on her other side, made her way slowly into the ballroom.

She was able to comport herself with a modicum of dignity as Lady Fanny presented her to the guests, managing to smile and nod pleasantly to her acquaintances. She was even able to say, "Good evening, Lord Diremore," and "Tiffany, how pretty you look," in a cheerful voice, although her ears were ringing again and her knees were softening steadily.

Once, through the haze and murmur, she heard the Marchioness's voice declaiming, "Yes, she is a pretty child. But why is Wale standing beside her, allowing her to hang on him like that? Is it possible there is to be an engagement announcement as well as a presentation?"

"Oh, you must deny that," Kate whispered to the Duke.

"Certainly not!" he retorted. "I would never do anything so shabby."

"Such a nonsensical rumor will die down soon enough, my love," Lady Fanny told her niece. "But you are looking so pale! Are you dreadfully unwell?"

"Yes," Kate admitted as the room swam before her eyes. "If you will excuse me, Aunt, I should very much like to retire."

CHAPTER 12

Kate slept heavily until almost three o'clock the following afternoon and when she finally roused and tried to drag herself up against her pillows, she had to sink back down again to keep the room from spinning around her head. Serena darted in immediately and leaned over her.

"Are you awake, Katie? Are you going to get up? I have so much to tell you. So many dreadful things have happened this morning!"

Kate groaned. "Please bring a chair over beside my bed and talk to me. I shall lie here with my eyes closed and listen."

Serena quickly obeyed her, settling herself beside her cousin. "The most heartless thing, Katie—Spencer-Loam and Drew and my darling Elfan have been here talking to Papa, and those villains wish to have poor Carlton clapped into chains—transported even—at least Drew does. Spencer-Loam is rather more moderate in his feelings . . ."

"Wait," Kate protested. "You have lost me. Who is Carlton?"

"Lord Elfan, you silly. You are not paying attention!"

"I am trying," she told her.

"But if you could have seen Carlton in my father's study," Serena hurried on, "standing with his head and shoulders framed against the light, protesting his innocence of any intent to harm either you or me . . . And his devotion to me, Katie! It was thrilling!"

Kate sighed. "Is there going to be a dreadful scandal?"

"No, this is just the thing, you see. My father—and Drew, too—does not wish the story to leak out. Papa says it would be too dreadful to have all London gaggling over such a silly escapade. Everyone would infer that there was much left unsaid, and you or I would become an object—a laughing stock."

Kate sighed again.

"But Drew is so angry! He insists that Carlton must be punished, so he is to be sent away—to the continent—forever." Serena paused to sniff into her handkerchief. "At least for a year or two he will be banished from England—until Drew's temper cools, my father says, and until I forget him—which I shall never do! It is all so hideously unfair! What real harm has he done?"

"Serena!" Kate protested. "He nearly murdered me by accident."

"Aha!" Serena exclaimed. "You have put your finger on the essential point, my dearest—'by accident,' you said. He would never willfully harm a soul. In fact, he said to my father—in the most heart-shivering, marvelous voice—'Since I have had time to reflect, I am shocked by my own behavior. It is terrible to contemplate the harm I might have done to the lady's name if I had not been overtaken by his Grace. I deserve no mercy.' Those were his very words."

"Well . . ." Kate began.

"Don't you see, Katie, that Elfan truly loves me? He has been my most ardent suitor from the moment I came out of the schoolroom. He asked for my hand last year, you know, but Mama and Papa are so heartless and mercenary that they refused him. And for what reason?"

"Because he is destitute. At least, that is what Cousin Tiffany said."

Serena snorted. "Cousin Tiffany is such a thoroughly malicious person that she would never say a kind word about anyone if she could think of something spiteful."

156

"Very well," Kate sighed, feeling much too weary to argue. "I admit I can think of nothing to say against Lord Elfan except that he is a pauper and has a tendency to become muddled and kidnap the wrong lady. And he certainly has shown devotion to you, there is no doubt of that. I shall withdraw my charge of attempted murder since, actually, it was his ruthless green domino who came so near to finishing me, not he."

"There, you see!" Serena exclaimed, clasping her hands. "But what of Young Lester?"

"Oh," Serena said, tossing her head, "I have been very wrong about him, Katie. He is a most buffoonish person. After you disappeared, he capered off in pursuit of Sweetums and ran about the room for half an hour leaping and lunging in a thoroughly ridiculous way. He never found time to speak to me at all—which is just as well, as he has the most unpleasant voice and I should find it irritating to listen to that constant bleating." She tugged at the bedclothes. "Please, Katie, put Young Lester out of your mind and come help me convince my father that he must let me marry Lord Elfan."

"Very well," Kate said, crawling cautiously out of bed. "I shall do all I can. Allow me a little time to dress."

"I shall be back in half an hour," Serena promised.

But before the time had expired, and just as Brill was putting the last touches to Kate's hair, she rushed back into her cousin's room with tears streaming down her cheeks.

"Oh, Katie!" she wailed. "You must come to my aid immediately! My father says he positively will not give me to any fortune hunter—that is Elfan he means—he is tired of having me running about unmarried and is going to 'put an end to this nonsense once and for all,' he said. He is going to select an eligible man for me and publish the banns immediately. He says I must be a dutiful daughter and accept his decision."

Kate felt her heart sink. "Has he chosen Wale for you?"

"No, no! It is Nellingham!"

"What!" Kate cried. "Certainly he cannot be so cruel!"

"He can and he is! You and I must throw ourselves at his feet and beseech him to have mercy on me."

Kate frowned. "That would not avail; it would only disgust him. We must enlist your mother to speak in your behalf. He will listen to her."

Kate nodded to Brill, and the two girls rushed down the hall to Lady Fanny's room. But they found her ladyship in a recalcitrant mood, reclining on a chaise longue, fortifying herself with a tisane.

"I am so exhausted from our delightful masquerade," she told them. "Ah me, it was all so gratifying. The Marchioness said it was quite the most brilliant affair of the Season, with the little stream full of fish and all. I am only sorry the sheep were such a disappointment. But I am certainly not in the mood to argue with anyone, least of all Dev. I do wish you would accept his decision and let him publish the banns. It is so wearying the way you hop from one love to another, my precious. Whom does your papa wish you to marry, dear Drew? Or that elegant Young Lester?"

"No, Mama," she cried, bursting into tears afresh. "He swears he is going to marry me to Nellingham."

"Good God!" her ladyship exclaimed. "You must have misunderstood him."

"I didn't, Mama; I swear I did not!"

"Then I must go to him immediately," Fanny said, dragging herself reluctantly to her feet. "That will not do at all. Nellingham, indeed!" She marched out into the hallway with Serena and Kate pattering closely behind her.

"You must tell him flatly that I will never accept Nellingham—under any circumstances," Serena lectured her. "And you must tell him that you see no reason why we should not consider Elfan's suit—he has been so steady in his attentions and so devoted . . ."

Lady Fanny drew her daughter to a halt. "Now, just a moment! I shall not take Elfan's part in any argument of any kind. He has behaved abominably and I sincerely hope that I shall never set eyes on him again." She began again to walk briskly toward Deverill's sitting room.

At that moment Judson came up behind them and

murmured to Kate, "Excuse me, miss. His Grace of Asgar is below and requests to speak to you, if you are able to see him."

"Oh, dear," Kate murmured as her aunt and cousin disappeared through Deverill's door. "Please tell him that my aunt is not at home."

"But it was you he specifically asked for, Miss Kathryn."

Kate hesitated. "I think there is nothing I can do to help here," she said. "Very well, I shall speak to his Grace."

On her way down to the blue saloon, she could not keep her thoughts from wandering back to Serena's plight. She wondered if there were any way she could help her. She had no doubt that Lady Fanny would put an end to the Earl's plans for Nellingham, but after that, Serena's problem was still unsolved. If she had really fallen in love with Elfan after all . . . Kate wondered if his pockets were so thoroughly to let that there was no way of rescuing him. On the other hand, she had to admit that it was possible that his interest in her cousin was largely based on his infatuation with her fortune, as her aunt and uncle supposed. She was frowning and her thoughts were far removed from the drawing room when she entered it and crossed the floor toward Wale, who was leaning against the fireplace, watching her approach.

"Such chaos we have here, Cousin," she told him. "Everything is at sixes and sevens."

"That is understandable," he said in a strangely flat voice. "Are you feeling yourself again?"

"Yes, thank you," she said without looking at him. "Do you know Elfan well?"

His mouth tightened. "Unfortunately, yes. He was another of my colleagues at Oxford; and I can state unequivocably that he is the most consummate bufflehead in England—the country's finest. He has no peer."

Kate raised a hand. "Pray do not jest, sir. My cousin's entire happiness may depend on the events of the next few days, and I fear that my aunt and uncle are not so sympathetic as could be hoped."

159

"I can understand that," he said. "But surely a little time will heal all."

Kate frowned. "You mean she will shift her affection to someone else?"

He nodded. "Something like that, yes. At any rate, you must not ask me to render any kind of aid or comfort to Elfan. If you could have seen the condition you were in when Spencer-Loam and I reached you last night . . . I was convinced we would never be able to revive you." His voice changed suddenly and he turned to stare grimly out the window.

Kate, who was only listening to him with half an ear, sank onto the edge of a sofa, frowning to herself. "I think we are using the wrong tactics with Serena," she said. "The worst course is to thwart her. It will make her more and more devoted to him. Instead, we should bring them together and let him bounce about, making himself ridiculous while we introduce a truly heroic figure into her life."

Wale smiled. "Where do you expect to find such a man?"

Kate was thoughtful. "Your friend, Spencer-Loam?"

Wale shook his head. "They would not suit."

"Oh, I don't mean that they should marry. I mean that he should draw her away from Elfan and then allow her to pass on to some other man."

Wale chuckled. "It may work. You must somehow contrive to have him stand with the light behind him, forming a halo around his noble head—that sort of thing."

"Yes." Kate stood up and began to walk slowly up and down the room. "The main thing is not to let Serena know what we are about—it is for her own good, you see, but she may inadvertantly spoil everything. I have a scheme in mind which is just now taking shape. I may need your aid before nightfall."

"Very well," he said. "I shall station myself at Asgar House and await your command. Send Timothy to me with your instructions as soon as you wish me to act."

She turned away from him and walked restlessly down the room again. "But Serena may intercept our messages," she murmured. "I think we should have a code. What shall it be? There is not time for us to scramble an alphabet and copy out a facsimile for each of us to keep hidden in our escritoires. We must devise a simple but baffling method for communicating with each other—one which will defy discovery."

Wale rubbed a hand thoughtfully across his chin. "I have heard of a method in which every second word is read to reveal a message. That may serve."

"Oh, excellent!" Kate exclaimed, nodding her head with approval. "But perhaps if we read every third word, the message would be even more obscure."

"It might be," he agreed. "It shall be every third word." He reached out and caught hold of her hand. "And now I would like to speak of something else, Cousin. I would like to ask you if you have thought about yourself. What are your hopes for your future?"

Kate pulled her hand gently away from him and stepped back. "*My* future, indeed, sir! Do you imagine I could be thinking of myself at a time like this when Serena is in such need of my help? I should be the most selfish girl imaginable!"

"But Katie," he protested, "your world cannot always revolve around Serena."

At that moment the door opened and the lady herself rushed into the room. "Ah, here you are!" She grasped her cousin's hand. "Come quickly! The most dreadful thing! My mother has dissuaded my father from . . . well, you know. But now another terrible blow has fallen!" She turned to Wale. "Drew, if you could be so kind as to excuse us . . . we are in a most dreadful pickle!"

He ground his teeth for a moment—hesitated, frowning—then with a sigh, bowed stiffly. "Of course," he said. And bowing again to them both, he quickly left the room.

Serena stood wringing her hands. "Oh, Katie, we are undone! Papa has agreed to renounce Nellingham; but as a sort of penance he is removing us to the country. Elfan will be obliged to flee his creditors and I shall never see him again. He shall most certainly find a lovely French girl and put me out of his thoughts."

"That is unlikely," Kate protested. "He has been much too devoted to forget you so quickly."

"But we shall languish and die in the country! Such desolation there! No bals, no theater, no Venetian breakfasts! And knowing that I have brought ruin on my beloved . . . I shall die! I no longer wish to live."

"What's this? What's this?" Lady Fanny exclaimed, marching into the room.

"I say I shall die!"

"Nonsense!" her ladyship scolded. "You are not to resort to these foolish antics. Your tricks shall avail you naught. If you wish to gain any sort of domestic harmony in the future, you will smile prettily at your father and thank him for his kindness in offering you a short respite from the exhausting round of parties you have been enduring, and you will make every effort to convince him that you are delighted by his consideration. I assure you, it is the only way to avoid a life of suffering with Nellingham or some other cork-brain whom you hold in abhorrence."

Serena stood scowling, rubbing one thumb impatiently against the other. "Perhaps," she said slowly. "I shall, however, inform Lord Elfan of our departure and he will make every effort to await our return."

"That is impossible," Lady Fanny said, shaking her head decisively. "Your father has given orders that you are not to meet Elfan under any circumstances. I have already sent your regrets to Lady Sefton and to the Montagues for the dinner and rout party we were scheduled to attend this evening."

"But, Mama," Serena exclaimed, diving into her reticule for a handkerchief and pressing it to her eyes to stem the flood of tears which gushed forth, "we shall be gone for the rest of the Season, surely. It requires nearly a week to reach Deverill Abbey and a week to return. If we spend a week there—and my father will surely find excuses to delay our departure several times, as he always does—we shall be gone from town for a month or more. Certainly Elfan's affairs cannot wait so long."

"We are not going to Deverill Abbey," her ladyship explained. "Your father has decided to take us on a visit to his old friend, the Earl of Ryne, who, he claims, is his best friend in the entire world, although I have racked my brains and cannot, for the life of me, remember ever having heard Dev mention his name before. He says they were down at Oxford together—got into all sorts of jolly scrapes, so he could not be a bad sort, I collect. Also, I understand that he is one of the richest men in England, although he has become a sort of recluse and never comes to town. Well, we shall see. His seat is a mere day's journey from here, and most luxurious, I understand."

Serena and Kate exchanged suspicious glances.

"Why has my father chosen to take us on this particular visit, Mama?" Serena asked. "Does he have an ulterior motive?"

"No doubt he has, my dear," Lady Fanny admitted, "although I have not the least notion what it may be. But please, my angel, indulge your parents this one time. The least you can do to repay your father for a lifetime of love and generosity is to humor him for a week or so."

Serena sighed heavily. "Very well. I shall make every effort to be complaisant. But what of poor Katie? She came to town in hopes of enjoying the more sophisticated pleasures, which are not to be found in the country."

"Oh, do not be concerned," Kate said quickly. "My pleasure is in being with you. Town or country is all the same to me."

"How charming of you, dearest," Lady Fanny purred, giving her niece's chin an affectionate squeeze. "We shall all do very well during our little idyll, I am confident, and we shall be back in town before we have time to realize that we have left. Now I shall give the abigails their orders and set them to packing our trunks. I think your green sarsnet will be appropriate for dinner on the evening of our arrival, Serena. And I shall want you to have your blue sprigged muslin in case there is a charming young son to take you walking in the shrubbery . . ."

As Serena watched her mother's departing back, her mouth tightened with distaste. "There will surely be a son," she hissed at Kate. "I am positive of it—a scrawny, wizened, hideous young man with warts and bandy legs and every manner of outrageous blemish. Or perhaps a monstrous fat, greasy bore with prosing manners—or no manners at all. You may count on it, there is a son of this richest man in England, and my father has decided that I shall marry him instead of my darling Elfan."

"Perhaps not," Kate said, trying to reassure her; but her own convictions tended to march with Serena's. Deep down in the farthest recesses of her mind she was sure that the Earl of Ryne had a son who was everything a young lady could wish he were not.

"He may even be mad," she murmured, thinking aloud. "That may be the reason his father has withdrawn from Society."

Both girls stood in the center of the room, musing, their faces white and strained. It occurred to Kate that she might be leaving London, never to return—and if that were to be the case, she would never see Wale again. Of all the young men she had met since her arrival in town, Kate thought that Wale was the only one who would have been able to make Serena truly happy and prevent her affections from flitting about. In fact, he would be able to make any wife happy, of that Kate was confident.

"Somehow I must get a message to Elfan," Serena said, gnawing a thumbnail. "I must urge him to wait for my return."

"And I must send a message to Wale," Kate thought to herself. "It would be inexcusable rudeness to leave forever without even saying good-bye."

"I shall go to my room now," Serena announced, "and pour out my heart to that adorable man."

"No, no!" Kate exclaimed, putting a hand on her arm. "That you must not do! You must realize that any letter you send to him will surely be intercepted. It must be the epitome of discretion."

"Surely there is a way we can convey a message to him unapprehended," Serena said, scowling. "We shall give it into Timothy's care."

But on approaching the trusty footman, they were shocked to discover that he had been issued strict orders to refuse them any kind of succor, and he was firm in his refusal to do so.

"I'm sorry, miss," he told Serena, "but it would be disloyal to his lordship if I was to go skulking off with a secret letter for Lord Elfan."

"There is only one alternative left us," Kate told her cousin, drawing her into a quiet corner and lowering her voice. "We must ask Wale to help us. I realize that he is not sympathetic to Elfan's cause, but he is our only hope. We shall compose a simple letter and endeavor to set it out in a sort of cipher which Wale and I have devised. The rest shall be in his hands."

The two girls seated themselves at a small table. "We must be exceedingly clever and present a proper picture of ourselves to the world," Serena pointed out, "in case it should be intercepted." She put a finger to her chin. "Perhaps, 'O Romeo, Romeo! Wherefore art thou, Romeo?' That will let it be known that we are not mopish stay-at-homes who never receive invitations to the theater."

Kate shook her head. "The message would be, 'Romeo, thou.' That does not serve our purpose. We are going about it in the wrong way. We must first compose our message, then fit in logical words between."

"Yes, I see," Serena agreed. "That will be the simplest way."

But after working industriously for almost an hour, composing, adding, changing, and discarding, they had begun to despair of ever preparing a message which would convey their meaning while at the same time baffling any spies from the enemy camp, when Judson entered the room with a letter on a salver.

"This was delivered, Miss Serena," he observed stiffly, "but it is not quite understood to whom it is addressed."

Serena took the envelope from the tray and looked at it curiously. "Strange," she said, "it is addressed to The Honorable Kathryn Serena Deverill. What can it mean?"

Kate leaped to her feet. "Is it from Wale?"

165

"Perhaps," Serena said, turning it over in her hand. "It bears his seal."

Kate scampered across the room and bustled the butler out into the hall. "Thank you, Judson," she said, closing the door firmly behind him. She put out a hand to her cousin. "It is a secret message. Let me see it immediately."

But Serena had already torn off the wafer and was poring over it, a deep scowl furrowing her brow. "This is extremely odd, Katie. Listen: 'Unexpected dire emergency.' What on earth can have happened? Does he refer to his emergency or ours?"

"He means simply 'emergency,' " Kate explained. "And we must read on to ascertain the details."

"But the rest of the message is completely baffling: 'Your permission; must ask your leave to depart immediately to search for rare indigenous country frogs and to organize a rescue of *Robin's Fortune*. Most complaisantly I can not return with treasures in less than two bushel baskets. Weeks perhaps required. Contact those experts you customarily consult when in doubt. I shall soon arrive at Camelot. Wale.' "

Kate's face had flushed a bright hot pink. "Odious man! To write such a nonsensical note! It would surely have aroused suspicion had it been intercepted. Why, he has not been the least bit serious about our problems. I shall scowl in the most ferocious manner and refuse to exchange even the simplest pleasantries with him the next time we meet."

Serena was staring at her vacantly. "But what does this letter mean?"

Kate peered over her shoulder. "It says: 'Emergency. I must go immediately to the country to rescue my fortune. Return two weeks. I shall contact you when I arrive. Wale.' "

Serena put a handkerchief to her eyes and took a deep shuddering breath. "Then he is gone—and with him our last hope." She began to weep softly.

Kate sat down at the table again and stared disconsolately at the pile of papers scattered there, each with its line of carefully planned words endlessly crossed out and rewritten. "It would seem so," she admitted. "Though I am loath to surrender so ignominiously. A bit more effort, if we could plan it properly, would undoubtedly lift us over the barrier, to success."

"But what?" Serena sobbed. "What effort can we make?"

Kate turned and considered her cousin thoughtfully. "We might resort to one last bold and desperate measure— we might send Lord Elfan a letter by ordinary penny post. It might pass unobserved, you know, as no one would expect us to do anything so straightforward."

CHAPTER 13

Kate and Serena composed a discreet message to Elfan. They expected to be thwarted at every turn, but after secreting the letter in Serena's reticule, they were able to tie on their bonnets and walk out of the house unopposed, on the simple pretext of wishing to refresh themselves with a few turns around the square. In addition, since they were planning to walk back and forth in close proximity to the front door, Lady Fanny raised no objection to their taking only one of the pages for escort, and they were able to send him off to deliver the letter to the post.

After their return to the house, they were thoroughly occupied with preparations for their departure into the country, and Kate had no time to think of Elfan; but when she was ready to retire for an early night's sleep, she was surprised to discover that they had not received a reply from him.

"He has given up hope," Serena sobbed into her soaked and mangled handkerchief. "I shall never see him again. I have made up my mind, Katie, that I shall become a dedicated spinster and devote myself to making my mama happy in her old age."

"Come, come, now, you must be brave," Kate urged her. "If you keep up your spirits, all will come right in the end."

The morning of their departure dawned sunny but sharp.

169

The air, freshly washed by an early rain, was blowing in strongly from the North Sea, whipping the leaves furiously on all the trees and sending tradesmen's hats bouncing and tumbling along the gutters.

As Kate stepped out onto the front stoop with Serena and Lady Fanny, she was greeted by a clatter and bustle of activity, and she stopped to look about her in surprise. Arrayed in front of the house was a remarkable caravan.

At the foot of the steps sat the Earl's new traveling coach, decorated in the latest shade of blue with yellow-picked wheels and the Deverill arms emblazoned on the sides. Behind it stood Deverill's older traveling coach freshly refurbished and now filled with abigails, maids, and the Earl's valet. Behind that, another traveling carriage of still remoter vintage, but shining with new paint, was crammed to bursting with trunks and bandboxes.

In addition to the dozen carriage horses which strained and capered in their traces, there were a dozen others, either with riders or on leads, tossing their heads and prancing as the wind swept bits of twig and leaves against their legs. Four mounted guards in livery were stationed at the head of the train, straining to hold their horses in check. Timothy and another footman were mounted on capering hacks and armed to bring up the rear. The Earl, shouting happily to his entourage, had elected to ride and was astride his finest black hunter with a spare horse held on lead by an extra groom. With the three coachmen and their grooms up beside them, and three undergrooms mounted behind, the party was complete. On every side, horses danced restlessly, clattering their iron shoes on the cobbles, clinking their harness rings and chains, and creaking their leather as they strained against it. Over all came a hubbub of human voices.

Kate could not bring herself to descend the stairs without pausing for a moment to enjoy the scene. Serena also paused alongside her, and even Lady Fanny hesitated before she emitted a satisfied, "Well!" then floated down the front steps, her skirts swirling around her ankles, to be handed with a flourish into the lead carriage. With hot bricks at their feet and fur robes tucked comfortably around them, the three ladies settled themselves in their places and their coach door was closed. One of the guards raised his yard of tin to his lips. He released two brilliant notes, which soared over the turbulent atmosphere, there was a renewed clatter of hooves, and the caravan began to move. Carriage wheels rumbled on the cobbles, a horse nickered, the journey had begun.

Kate peered curiously out of her window. As she had expected, there were faces looking back at her from every side. A strolling couple, several nursemaids with their charges, and a cluster of housemaids and footmen who had contrived to find activities which would take them across the square were watching them with awe. All the lower windows of the houses along the street had faces peering out at them. Lady Fanny sat smiling benignly.

Deverill was in fine fettle, his handsome brow wreathed in smiles and his lips parting constantly to reveal his excellent white teeth. Kate had never seen him so buoyant. He cantered ahead of the train, greeting his friends with a wave of a hand and a radiant smile, pausing to chat from time to time before he moved on his way. At the Stanhope Gate, where two horsemen loped out of the park to converse with him, Kate heard him call cheerily, "Yes, a splendid outing in the country! Visiting my old friend Ryne. Best sort of fellow." And later, "Yes, glorious weather! No more of these stuffy bals."

The caravan made its way along the main thoroughfares of the city, continuing to draw stares from the populace. Shopkeepers stepped outside to watch them go by. Some bowed or curtsied, others merely gaped. Once, after the train had left the center of the city and was progressing through a ramshackle section of the metropolis, two wide-eyed ragamuffins appeared alongside Lady Fanny's carriage and began to argue loudly over whether or not such a display of grandeur must belong to the Prince of Wales himself; and for several minutes the two boys kept popping into view, first in one unlikely spot then another—on top of a produce wagon, hanging out of an upstairs window, on the edge of a low roof—peering into Lady Fanny's conveyance from first one angle then another in their effort to ascertain what great personage was secreted within.

It was while they were passing a disreputable line of broken-down shops that Kate caught sight of Lord Elfan. He was sitting in a battered chaise, watching them, his face white and stricken. When they pulled abreast of him, he raised a hand and Kate thought that he began to make a gesture toward them. But after a hesitation, he merely straightened one of the capes on his traveling cloak and his hand fell back to his side. Then he passed out of view as the Deverill carriages moved on their way.

They soon left the bustle of the city and found themselves on a quiet country road. Occasionally, as they passed a byre, a milkmaid or a child would rise to watch them goggle-eyed, some curtseying, others too awed to do so.

As they made their way inland, the wind subsided and the day began to grow warm. Deverill continued in high spirits, cantering his horse close to Lady Fanny's window, pointing out vistas of interest and praising the terrain. When it was time to rest the horses, the entourage drew up at a bustling inn. The Earl engaged a private parlor and ordered refreshments for his ladies. Serena, stimulated by the change of scene, began to tease her father about the journey.

"The Earl of Ryne has a son, does he not, Papa?" she quizzed him. "That is why you are taking us to visit him. Your friend has a son whom you consider a proper match for me."

Deverill pinched her cheek and laughed. "He does. And that worthy young man has the perfect lineage and situation. He is also most likely to be pleasing, as Ryne himself was a dashed handsome fellow." The Earl's thoughts carried him swiftly back to his youth at Oxford. "Good old Weasel! Such an excellent chap! I cannot imagine why he has locked himself away in the country. Should have come to town every year to be with his friends. Devilish fine dancer—the best of us all." He sighed. "Ah well, we shall soon be together again." He turned to his wife. "You'll like his house, Fan; beautiful place—much grander than Deverill Abbey."

Lady Fanny made appropriate sounds.

"But he'll not think poorly of us when he sees our train."

"Certainly not," her ladyship agreed.

Serena leaned close to her father and put a hand on his arm. "Papa," she said, tears suddenly mounting in her eyes, "you must not count on this match with Ryne's son. My heart is quite lost to another, as you know only too well."

Deverill scowled. "We shall see, we shall see."

After the horses had been refreshed, the entourage proceeded on its way, trotting briskly along the highroad, the harnesses rattling and the horses tossing their heads. But it soon became necessary to turn off onto a minor thoroughfare and the going became rougher. From that point on, as the train traveled deeper into the countryside, the conditions of the roads worsened. Lady Fanny began to feel strained. She tried to sleep, but each time she began to sink into the arms of Morpheus she was jolted awake by a sharp knock on the head as the carriage wheels dropped into potholes and surged out again.

"Delightful countryside!" the Earl kept calling to his beleaguered ladies. "And we shall spend the night in the most comfortable inn this side of London—the Great Bustard Cock."

When they reached the celebrated hostelry, however, they discovered that the town was preparing for a mill which was to take place on a down beyond its northern limits, and every available room within ten miles was filled with sporting gentlemen. Deverill's train was obliged to proceed farther. It was then discovered, to the Earl's consternation, that the next major town was beyond a river, and the week before, an unusually turbulent flood had brought trees and boulders down against the bridge, wiping it out and necessitating a detour of another three miles to a spot where the river could be safely forded.

Deverill squeezed out a jovial laugh and shook his head. "We now know why my friend has remained rusticating in the country, if a journey such as this is required each time he wishes to reach the city." Lady Fanny, Kate, and Serena all nodded agreement.

When they reached the ford, now nearly in darkness and with water surging against the rocks and rumbling in the river's bed, Deverill decided in favor of proceeding another two miles to a bridge, rather than risk the crossing. Night was full upon them by the time they entered the next outpost of civilization. There, to their relief, they found a proper inn with no less than three private parlors and ample bedrooms with roaring fires. Delicious aromas wafted from the kitchens and an efficient stable was available to care for the horses.

After enjoying a fortifying meal, the party repaired to their rooms and lost no time in falling asleep. But Kate was soon jolted upright in her bed by the sound of trumpets. On sliding quickly to the floor and hurrying to the window, she discovered that the night mail, filled with passengers, was lurching out of the inn yard while friends and neighbors shouted and waved farewell. Jovial countrymen were marching in and out of the inn doorway, laughing together and greeting each other with shouts of pleasure. While Kate watched, a curricle pulled up to the door and the occupant halooed for an ostler, who came running from the back of the inn. The front door slammed.

A bright full moon was shining over the scene. Kate soon discovered that this encouraged travel, for it was not long before a landau arrived and, with much conversation and laughter, several ladies and gentlemen disembarked and strolled inside. Kate could hear footsteps in the public rooms below, she could hear laughter and singing from the tavern room on the other side of the building. There were fresh aromas of food being cooked throughout the night. A constant hubbub and bustle rocked the house. When she checked her little clock, she discovered to her amazement that it was two o'clock in the morning, but the inn was as alive and active as if it were high noon.

She tried to go back to sleep, but managed to doze only fitfully. Twice she thought she had sunk into deep, refreshing slumber only to be brought wide awake by a sudden crash somewhere accompanied by running feet and shouts. The laughter from the tavern room never stopped. She arose in the morning feeling as though she had not slept at all. She was struggling into her traveling clothes when Serena joined her, heavy-eyed and cross.

"Such a place!" she growled. "I am exhausted! I did not sleep a wink last night with all the shouting and fighting and laughter downstairs. And worst of all, now when I close my eyes, I can no longer visualize my darling Elfan's face. I have forgotten what he looks like."

They joined Lady Fanny in her private parlor and found her also pale and weary. "It is strange," she observed, "that these laborers never appear to require rest."

Even Deverill had lost his joie de vivre. He came into the parlor walking with great difficulty and lowered himself gingerly onto a chair where he shifted his torso several times in an effort to find a reasonably comfortable position.

"Dashed unpleasant trip!" he muttered. "Why is it so much father than I remember? I used to travel to Ryne in a few short hours. Nothing to it in those days. But these roads have deteriorated badly." He tried to move his stiff legs under the table, groaning softly to himself.

"Perhaps we should go back to town," Lady Fanny suggested. "It breaks my heart to see you so stiff and uncomfortable, my love."

"Nonsense!" cried the Earl, outraged. "I'll have you know I'm as fit as can be—good for another hundred miles before I tire. Besides, we shall reach our destination before long. The innkeeper knows Ryne well. Hasn't seen him for a few years but remembers when he used to come through here on his way to Oxford; always stopped to refresh his horses. Handsomest gentleman he ever saw, that's the way he put it. 'The Earl of Ryne?' he said. 'Of course I remember him.' Those were his very words."

Lady Fanny, who could not help wondering why the innkeeper had not seen the Earl since he was at Oxford, began to brood over this ominous bit of information. She managed to keep her worries to herself, however, while his lordship was hoisted groaning onto his horse and she was helped into her carriage with Serena and Kate. But as the entourage wended its way out of the town and into a sunlit, verdant countryside, and the jolting of her carriage grew worse, her patience ebbed, and she finally voiced her concern.

"Do you suppose he could be dead? The innkeeper, it would seem, has not seen him since you last saw him yourself."

"I will not believe it," Deverill said staunchly. However, as the same thought had been preying on his mind, a heavy frown darkened his brow.

To add to their depression, the roads dwindled to mere cow paths. Once they were obliged to cross a marshy place and the baggage coach mired itself in the mud and stuck fast. Almost an hour was required to move the train ahead to a dry place, then return with the teams from both other carriages and help wrench the coach from its quagmire. Kate noted as they rehitched the teams to their proper coaches that most of the grooms were caked with mud up to their knees, and no amount of dragging their feet through the deep grass or scraping with sticks could completely remove it.

At a large white farmhouse, Deverill stopped to ask the way again. He held in his hand a letter of instructions which he had used on a trip he made to visit Ryne twenty-five years earlier.

"Is this Woodrill's Farm?" he asked a powerful middle-aged man who was plowing a lush black field.

"Aye," the man said, stopping his bullock. "T'was that. Old Woodrill's gone these nineteen year, God rest his soul, if it's him you be wantin'."

"No," Deverill explained, replacing his letter inside his coat. "It's the Earl of Ryne I'm looking for. His seat should be nearby. You must know it."

The man scratched his head for a moment then shook it. "No," he admitted, "I know of no such. But I be from Surrey, coom eighteen yearn." He pondered. "Happen it be down in the Wyne. We all stay oot o' that part."

The ladies were listening eagerly. "Ask him why he

176

avoids the place, Dev," his wife called to him. "Is anything wrong?"

Deverill lowered his voice to speak to the plowman, but a moment later he rode back to the carriage and, presenting a smiling face, assured them that there was no cause for concern. "He says it's merely that the roads are poor and there's a rather dense forest to pass through. It is too troublesome, so they stay on this side of it."

The plowman, who had not heard the Earl's words, raised his hat and called to them, "Not to worry, ma'am. Them witches an' sich sprits can-na harm ye in the daylight."

Deverill muttered under his breath while Kate sat up and exclaimed brightly, "Witches?"

"It is all nonsense," the Earl told them, forcing a laugh. "We shall hurry on now that we've found the right road. *The Wyne* is marked on this map I used when I passed this way before. I should like to reach Ryne's palace before dark. Another night on the road and I cannot be responsible for anyone's good nature."

Setting their horses off at a brisk clip, they soon reached the forest, which appeared suddenly in front of them as they emerged from a sunken road and made a sharp turn toward the west. The lane on which they were driving passed into it and vanished abruptly, as though eaten by the trees and dense underbrush. On approaching closer, however, they discovered that the road merely bent sharply and passed into a filtered shade, then out of sight again among the trees.

Once they had penetrated the woods, they found that it was not so dense and forbidding as it appeared from outside; but it was cold, only passing occasionally through clearings where sunlight drifted down in warming shafts. In these little patches there were flowers scattered on greenswards, and birds could be heard singing. As soon as they moved into the darkness again, all was silence and chill. Lady Fanny and Serena shivered under their fur robes and even Kate began to wish the journey would end.

Much of the time the lane was extremely narrow. It was necessary for the carriages to move cautiously between the trees to avoid becoming wedged. Finally the coach containing the abigails and Deverill's valet, being slightly rounder in the body than the lead carriage, made its way halfway through a pass between two enormous boles and ground suddenly to a halt. The horses lunged against the traces, but it stuck fast. When the coachman tried to back it out of its predicament, it would not move in reverse, either.

All three coachmen handed their reins to their assistants, dismounted from their stations, and clustered around their master for a conference.

"Such an absurd situation!" Lady Fanny muttered to her companions, uncorking her vinaigrette and holding its soothing vapors under her nose. "We never should have come on this ridiculous excursion without sending word ahead and ascertaining whether or not this phantom earl of Dev's is still alive. At times I wonder if he ever existed at all."

"It is terrible," Serena agreed. "We are all going to catch a putrid sore throat and die in this dreadful cold place."

"No, no," Kate protested. "You must not despair. We shall soon be out of here and comfortably settled at Ryne's palace with our faces washed and a cup of refreshing hot tea in our hands."

"Yes, my love," Lady Fanny said, patting her hand. "It is sweet of you to make an effort to cheer us, but please do not put yourself to the trouble. We wish to be gloomy."

Kate sighed and settled back against the squabs, and for almost a quarter of an hour the three ladies watched the men try every possible way to free the trapped carriage. They hitched all the teams to it and urged them forward while men on foot pushed the coach from the rear—to no avail. They rigged extra lines with ropes and all pulled together—again to no avail. His lordship, sitting disconsolately on his horse, rallied himself from time to time and tried to shout encouragement to them, but after they had puffed and strained until they were breathless, he called them off and ordered them to rest while he formulated a better plan. It was while he was scowling to himself, deep in thought, that Timothy and his lordship's head coachman

178

moved together and stood talking in lowered tones. Then the coachman approached Deverill.

"With your permission, sir," he began, "Timothy believes he can jack up the coach, with the assistance of the big new undergroom. Then he says he can put saplings under the wheels while she's up, and run her out easy as pie, being as how the trees taper in toward the top and he says he'll have another two or three inches of clearance for every couple of inches he raises her."

Deverill nodded. "Anything is worth a try. And I shall put my mind to devising an alternate plan in the event that this one does not suffice."

It took some time for Timothy and the other men to find and cut several saplings, then bind them together to form runways, and even longer to obtain lengths of wood which would serve as fulcrums and levers. But after setting everything in place, Timothy and the big new undergroom were able to exert sufficient pressure on their levers to raise the back wheels of the coach several inches. They repeated the process with the front wheels, and although there were dreadful screeches and groans from the carriage as it was prised from its prison, the saplings were eventually shoved under the wheels. As soon as the team was again hitched to its traces, the coach rolled free, its paint badly scarred but otherwise unharmed.

"Well, that is that," the Earl announced. "And we shall escape from this infernal wood as quickly as possible."

The three thoroughly chilled ladies in the lead coach were convinced that their deliverance could not come too soon and, to their relief, not ten minutes later the forest began to lighten, and the road, after making a sharp turn behind a pile of boulders, delivered them out of the woods as abruptly as it had plunged them into it.

They found themselves on the edge of a shallow valley, which stretched for about two miles in front of them, then ended on another rise which was surmounted by more trees. The entire vista was lush and green, with a few sheep grazing placidly to the south and several black cows to the

179

north. Directly in the center of the opposite rise stood the most magnificent house Kate had ever seen. It was vast—larger, she thought, than Buckingham House—and of a pale gray stone which was almost white and had a luminosity about it. Hundreds of windows graced its facade and acres of lawns stretched in front of it, while at its sides and back exquisitely landscaped clusters of shrubs and trees set it off to perfection. It sat gracefully basking in the late afternoon sunlight, a picture of opulent perfection which, Kate was sure, could be matched only rarely anywhere throughout the world.

Deverill, his horse drawn up beside Lady Fanny's carriage, sat gazing at it with satisfaction. "Ah," he said, his voice thickened with emotion, "this is England."

CHAPTER 14

From the murmur of voices behind them, Kate inferred that the servants were equally impressed by the sight which lay ahead, and after a moment of pregnant silence, Lady Fanny exclaimed with pleasure, "Well! Indeed!"

"It's beautiful, is it not?" Deverill said, turning to his wife. "Such happy holidays I spent here with Ryne! And the house has such a contented look about it at this very moment that I cannot but believe he is in residence there, living so comfortably that he found no need to bestir himself."

He raised a hand to the rest of his train, and the coachmen urged their horses forward. Kate and Serena could not resist leaning out of their respective windows to stare at the beautiful house as they approached it. "Certainly I should never care to leave such a house if it were mine," Kate told her aunt. "And with all these lush woods about, just think of the herbs and roots one could collect."

The horses, as though also inspired by the sight, quickened their pace, and within a very few minutes the train was half way across the valley, following the marks of wheels which had scratched the heavy turf.

From a nearer aspect, however, the house began to appear somewhat faded. Kate, watching its approach curiously, wondered what, precisely, made it less glowing than it had been from farther away, and as she stared at it for several seconds, she realized with a sudden pang that none of the windows was reflecting the light of the sinking sun. Neither did they appear to be broken, but they were dingy and clouded. "Of course," she told herself, "it would be an enormous task to keep so many windows washed and sparkling." Still she felt a faint twinge of disappointment that everything was not glistening and clean.

As they drew closer, further decay became apparent. The gardens had begun to deteriorate. The trees and shrubs which had appeared to cluster so solicitously around the main building were discovered to be standing some distance away and had only, through an optical illusion, presented their well-ordered picture. To the right of the lane a ruined rose garden bowed unhappily toward the ground with many bushes, mounding together to form a thicket. On the other side, the ladies looked out into what had once been a maze but was now one enormous scraggly plant.

They could see that the house, instead of being made of light gray stone which had silvered, was of white which had become stained and dirty. There was a window near the main entrance which was covered over with a cowhide, and as the first carriage clattered onto the weed-clogged cobbles of the front drive, they were confronted by every sign of sloth and decay. A cornerstone had broken off the copice and was lying where it had fallen, a clump of daisies spouting from its top; the front of the house was riddled with cracks, mottled with stains—dingy, broken, and sad.

"Good God!" Deverill exclaimed under his breath. "What tragedy has occurred here?"

He was answered by a trio of giggles from behind a nearby bush, and suddenly three small children scampered out and raced as fast as they could for the corner of the house. There were two boys and one girl, approximately six or seven years of age, all nicely dressed in ruffled muslin and nankeen. Before anyone could speak to them, they rushed out of sight, and for several minutes thereafter, Deverill's caravan sat drawn up in a line staring foolishly at the facade of the house.

182

"I sent word," the Earl said at last. "I wonder if it went astray."

But at that moment there came a sound from inside the main entrance—a pounding and thumping, and finally, with a groaning of timbers and the screech of wood against stone, a section of the front door began to inch its way open. Slowly, to the accompaniment of savage blows, a crack appeared, then little by little two footmen came into view, both kicking at the inside bottom of the door and leaning their weight against it. After a moment, the other half of the door began to receive similar treatment until the two had been forced a short distance apart and there was a three-foot opening between them.

"Well," announced a high, ringing voice, "that shall have to do. I had no idea they were both stuck fast. In the future, Bascomb, open them at least once every year."

"Yes, m'lord," a deep, resonant voice answered.

At that moment there appeared in the opening a little round man dressed in lush blue velvet. He wore knee breeches and a full-skirted coat with masses of lace foaming at his throat and wrists. His black shoes, which had three-inch heels, were garnished with huge buckles blazing with diamonds, while the top of him was covered by the most enormous wig Kate had ever seen—mounds of black ringlets and shining curls rising high above his forehead and tumbling halfway down his back. He clasped two plump hands together at the sight of them.

"Binky!" he chirped. "Ish Binky! Peerless, devil-may-care old Binky!"

And he stumbled down the few broken steps to rush at his friend, both arms outstretched. Deverill was obliged to scramble off his horse to prevent Ryne's throwing his arms around the animal's neck.

"Old man!" he exclaimed with forced heartiness and put out a hand to grasp his friend's.

But Ryne either did not see the hand or chose to ignore it. He staggered against Deverill, throwing his arms around him and pinning his guest's hands to his sides. After a moment of writhing together, Deverill was able to extricate himself and pat Ryne on the shoulder. Ryne kept laughing happily into his face and roaring, "Dash it, old man! Dash it all, Binky!"

He swung a free hand to pound his friend joyously and almost stumbled to one knee. Deverill quickly caught him and set him upright again.

"You ain't changed one bot—er, bit—er, jot!" Ryne told him. "Not a day older. Always was a trim devil!"

He punched him playfully in the stomach. "Those togs the latest kick? I'm out of it, you see. Good stuff . . ." He pulled at the bottom of his velvet coat. ". . . But old fashioned." He held out his arms to display his attire. "Look like the farce after the tragedy, what?"

"Certainly not, old man!" Deverill exclaimed, his face reddening. "Height of elegance. Always were."

"No, no," Ryne waved a hand. His face was also red, but had been so since their arrival and could now be seen to be generously blotched and covered with broken veins.

Serena leaned close to her mother. "Mama, can it be?" she whispered. "I could swear that our host is thoroughly foxed."

"Oh, dear," Lady Fanny murmured, "I hope not, indeed. This could prove to be such a trying visit."

At that moment it became apparent that the two earls, arm in arm, were making their way toward the carriage, though in a zigzagging manner. Serena quickly moved to the jump seat to allow her mother to be greeted by their host.

"So this is your lovely Frances!" Ryne roared, simpering coyly. "Good God, man! Such a beauty! And a mere child!"

Her ladyship, brightening visibly, put out her hand, allowed it to be kissed fervently, then descended to the ground with the assistance of a gentleman on either side.

"My Marguerite is a beauty, but nothing to compare with this girl. You're sure she is your wife and not your daughter?"

Lady Fanny laughed prettily. Turning away from the carriage, she picked her way over broken pavement and tufts of grass toward the front door, with her husband hobbling along stiffly on one side of her and her host on the other.

Serena sniffed. "And while she is escorted away with all possible gallantry, we are left to sit in this wretched old carriage."

"Timothy or someone will certainly rescue us in a moment," Kate assured her.

"I beg your pardon," said a soft voice outside the other window. Serena and Kate turned in surprise and found themselves looking into the face of the handsomest young man either of them had ever seen.

He bore no resemblance to Ryne, being tall and slim rather than short and fat, and his hair was a light-brown color with an abundance of gold shot through it. His complexion was clear—slightly tanned but with no signs of John Barleycorn's influence, and his eyes looked at them with a steadiness which could not but inspire confidence.

"Pray, allow me to present myself," he began. "I am your host's eldest son, David Gilbert Adolphus, Viscount Furth. May I have the honor of escorting you to the house?"

For a moment both Kate and Serena sat staring at him. Then Kate shook herself and quickly introduced her cousin.

"If you please, sir," she urged, giving Serena a surreptitious shove, "if you would be so kind as to assist my cousin first. She is quite exhausted from our journey, I fear."

He released the door, Serena stepped into the opening, and he put up one of his hands. But at that moment, a nail that had worked loose in a corner of the doorway caught the hem of Serena's skirt and the toe of her left shoe became entangled in the captured fabric. With a faint squeak of surprise, she pitched forward out of the carriage.

Furth threw up his hands to catch her. For several seconds she lay on his chest with her face close to his, her dress still caught fast. When he tried to lower her to the ground, she began to slide out of his arms. She squealed. He quickly hoisted her higher. Kate exclaimed. Furth began to laugh. Serena giggled. Then Kate was able to tug Serena's hem loose from the nail and Furth set her gently on the ground. They stood looking into each other's eyes, their hearts still pounding in unison.

They had been entangled in each other's arms long enough for Furth to notice the fine texture of Serena's exquisite white complexion, and she had discovered two tiny lines under each of his eyes which, she decided, lent a distinction and a dignity to his youthful good looks. They stood smiling at each other for such a long time that Kate began to wonder if they, too, were going to forget her and wander off toward the house together.

She was about to clear her throat or cough to remind them of her presence when a familiar voice on the other side of the carriage announced, "Well, this is a happy surprise! Are you following me about the countryside, or am I following you?"

Kate turned to find the Duke of Asgar smiling cheerily in at her through the opposite window.

"Good heavens!" she exclaimed. "What are you doing here?"

"Rescuing my fortune," he reminded her. "Did you receive my message?"

She scowled. "I did, indeed! And a more cork-brained pack of nonsense I would be hard put to find anywhere! You didn't even try to write a proper cipher."

He grinned. "I was short of time, I fear. My friend Furth sent me word that my Trelling estate was about to sink beneath the sea—along with Ryne, of course. There's a prodigious big hole in the main dike that keeps both these properties above water."

"How dreadful!" Kate exclaimed. "What are you going to do?"

"We are considering the possibilities at this time." He reached up his hands and lifted her out of the carriage. "And what brings you to Ryne?"

Kate hesitated for a moment, then took a deep breath and began, "My uncle decided that we were all in need of a nice quiet rest in the country, so he brought us to visit

186

his friend, the Earl of Ryne, who had digs with him at Oxford . . ."

Wale's eyebrows rose. "In other words, Deverill despaired of finding a proper husband for his daughter; feared losing his sanity in the process; remembered his old friend, Ryne; decided that his son would be the solution to all his problems . . ." He glanced toward the house where the two earls and Lady Fanny were mounting the shallow steps toward the front door. ". . . And is about to change his mind."

Kate frowned. "How can you know that?"

He chuckled.

At that moment Serena and Furth came around the carriage, their heads close together. At the sight of Wale, Serena threw up both hands. "Drew!" she cried. "What brings you to Ryne?" But before he could answer, she gave Furth a shy smile from under the brim of her bonnet and asked him, "Do you often journey to London, sir?"

"Never," he admitted. "I have too many duties here."

Kate looked around curiously, wondering what could require so much of the Viscount's attention when there was no evidence that any work had been expended on anything for many years. She turned to Wale with a quizzical glance, but he gazed pointedly off into space.

Picking their way carefully across the ruined drive—Serena on Furth's arm and Kate on Wale's—the four young people reached the front door. The girls were obliged to clutch their pelisses tightly around themselves to avoid damaging them on snags and rough splinters as they squeezed through the narrow opening.

"I must see to this door," Furth told them. "It has not been opened since Lord Dapplemyre's visit four years ago . . . No, it must have been more like ten years ago, as Richard and Thomas were eleven at the time, I remember." He shook his head sadly. "The years go by so quickly when there are sheep to shear and meadows to keep drained."

They had entered a cave of darkness inside the entryway. Furth guided them to their left along a hallway whose floor felt uneven underfoot and which had a distinctly

187

musty odor. In a moment they stepped out into a huge saloon which was flooded with light. It had, at one time, been a showplace, without any doubt, as even now, in its advanced state of decay it possessed the grandeur of a truly fine ruin. But, alas, its intricately carved plaster ceiling was liberally marked with brownish water stains; its parquetry floor was warped in several places; the silk panels which adorned the walls were hanging shredded and furry; and an entire cherub's head had broken off one side of the marble mantelpiece. Satin settees which were scattered about the room had fared no better than the structure itself. All were stained and torn—many had their upholstery patched with pieces of homespun—and all suffered from scarred woodwork, one sofa even listing sharply to the side as the result of a clumsily repaired leg.

"Well," Ryne sighed, drawing Lady Fanny close to an excellent fire, "here is my house, what is left of it. Do you remember this room, Binky? How beautiful it was that Christmas we entertained my Aunt Estella and those beautiful girls of hers. So much candlelight and satin dresses and music and good food—old Antoine was in the kitchen then. And my father still had his health. Do you remember the excellent way he managed things?"

"Yes, indeed," Deverill assured him. "One of the most enjoyable Christmases I have ever spent."

"The roof was still good," Ryne explained to him. "That's what makes the difference, you know. If the roof goes, the whole house begins to crumble."

"But good God, man! A roof can be repaired!"

Ryne sighed heavily. "Most difficult, most difficult. You patch a bit here and another hole crops up there. Slates blow away—they break. You order more and they never arrive—bog down somewhere between here and the quarry. Don't ask me what happens to them. And there are always other expenses that make it necessary to wait a few months before you do anything. How different life is from what we expect it to be." He sighed again.

Kate glanced at Wale and noted that he had folded his arms across his chest and was staring grimly at the devastation, while Furth, who stood close behind him, had pursed his lips and was scowling.

"Of course," Ryne continued, "there has never been any doubt in my mind as to where I should spend my money—what the really important things are . . ."

He was interrupted by a clatter of feet and to everyone's surprise, a lamb suddenly bolted into the room followed by two curly-haired boys in velvet trousers and white silk shirts. The lamb raced straight at Lady Fanny, who squeaked in alarm and jumped to one side. It then veered off toward Deverill. He, too, leaped aside in time to avoid collision, but the animal, veering for the third time, crashed into Ryne and sent him careening backward into an arm-chair, which, under the weight of his lordship and propelled by his momentum, promptly tipped over backward, dumping the unfortunate man onto his head. As the chair flipped over, two feet appeared briefly in the air, then disappeared.

Furth, muttering angrily under his breath, hastened to his father's rescue; the lamb raced on across the room and disappeared out another door with the two little boys at its heels.

Ryne sputtered indignantly. "Eustace!" he roared. "Eugene! Come back here, sirs! Both of you!" Then to Furth, as his heir assisted him to his feet and replaced the chair in an upright position, "It was Eustace and Eugene, was it not?"

"It was," Furth said darkly.

Ryne straightened his coat. "They shall answer for this. I shall see them in the library."

"Yes, sir," Furth said, and strode out the back door in search of the culprits.

Ryne shook himself and smoothed his tresses over his shoulders. "Incorrigible imps! I shall give them the scolding of their lives. But I shall not be too harsh. I cannot abide cruelty toward children."

"Your other sons?" Deverill asked him.

Ryne nodded. "Eustace and Eugene. Twins. And I hope you were aware of the fact that I recognized them and called them by name. I make a point of knowing all my children. I am not one of these men who can never remember a son's name or which daughter is older—that sort of thing."

"Well," Deverill said slowly, "I have always thought that rather important myself. How many children do you have, Weasel?"

"Twenty-three," he informed him.

There was a stunned silence.

"Three?" Deverill asked him.

"Good God, no, man! Twenty-three. Why do you think it's so hard to fix the roof?"

"But . . ." Deverill began, his mind running rapidly over his multiplication tables. "How could you have managed twenty-three children in only twenty years?"

Ryne snorted. "If you are calculating properly, you'll realize that it requires only eighteen years to produce twenty-three children. But it's longer than that since I've seen you, Binky. It's been twenty-seven years. And, besides, I have four sets of twins and one set of triplets, which made it somewhat easier—though not perceptibly."

Deverill was staring at his friend. "This is the most extraordinary thing, Weasel. Twenty-three children! And I had thought you would never marry. It never occurred to me that you would become the father of such a family. You always seemed such a light-hearted, fun-loving fellow—not the sort to saddle himself with responsibility. You have my respect."

"No, no," Ryne replied, waving his hands as though to drive away such unwarranted praise. "I deserve no credit. It's my wife who has done so splendidly. She is the one who has upheld our standards despite everything. It is my lovely Marguerite, who is the heart and the backbone and the fiber of this family."

As though in answer to her name, a little shriveled brown woman in a green brocade dress and powdered wig came mincing in through a doorway and advanced toward them.

"Ah, here she is," Ryne exclaimed with delight. "Come

190

here, my love, and allow me to present our guests to you."

The Countess, who, while across the room in the doorway presented a charming picture of opulence and grace, began to decay before their eyes as she came nearer to them, just as the house had done on their approach. Her gown, which at a distance had appeared to be rich and well fitted, proved at closer range to be rather too large and was mended in several places. Her head, as well as her body, had apparently shrunk over the years, for she was obliged to put a hand up to her wig to keep it in place when she bowed graciously to them. And Kate noted that, while the skin of her brow was remarkably placid and unlined, the flesh around her mouth was strangely wrinkled, as though she were missing a great many teeth. This surmise was soon reinforced by the Countess's tendency to raise her fan and unfurl it under her nose each time she spoke.

"What a great pleasure it is to have you visit me," she informed them in a sweet, melodious voice. "We are highly honored to know that you have made such a difficult journey in order to reach us."

"Yes, yes," Ryne agreed, beaming at them. "Dashed honored! Delighted!"

"And it's always delightful to have dearest Drew with us," her ladyship added, turning to wag her eyelashes affectionately at him. "Did you come with Lord Deverill and his entourage, my dear?"

"No, ma'am," Wale explained. "I've come to see what I can do about the Trelling dikes. I understand that they are leaking badly."

"What!" Ryne exclaimed. "Are those beastly dikes at it again? First the roof on the house, then the Number Seven Sluice Gate, and now the dikes! I'm sure I don't know where all this leaking will end!"

Furth, who had come quietly back into the room during Lady Marguerite's introduction, turned to his father and assumed an appropriately glum expression. "It will end, sir, with more than half our arable land under the sea. I've warned you of this repeatedly over the past few weeks."

"Oh," Ryne said, looking sullenly down at the buckle on

191

his left shoe, "is that what you've been talking about? You nag me about so many things that I've adopted the habit of not listening to you."

Furth sighed and turned to Wale. "Have you made up your mind yet what needs to be done?"

The Duke shook his head. "I hoped you would ride over the levees with me one more time while we discuss the problem areas."

Ryne clasped his hands together. "Excellent notion! Let's all go for a wonderful, rollicking ride. Binky, we can have the most delightful gallop along the tops of the dikes. There is always a cool refreshing breeze up there."

At the thought of placing his aching trunk again in a saddle, Deverill paled visibly. "Well, er . . . Weasel . . ." he began.

"No, no!" Ryne exclaimed, reading his friend's expression. "What am I thinking of? After your long journey, another ride would be the veriest bore."

Deverill sighed with relief and his friend turned to the young men. "But you two go have your little romp—make your survey and report all your gloomy observations; I shall listen to you—though I dare say we'll find things not so dire as you imagine and manage to muddle along somehow."

Lady Ryne fluttered her fan under her nose. "And if Lady Deverill will permit me, I shall escort her and her charming girls to their chambers. I am confident they will wish to rest and refresh themselves before dinner.

She led Lady Fanny, Serena, and Kate out into the dark hallway, then up a beautiful but sorely damaged staircase into the upper reaches of the house.

The hallway on the next floor, they discovered to their surprise, was in remarkably good repair. Its walls showed no signs of wetness and their coverings were still fresh and unfaded. Lady Fanny's room, on the south end of the house, was also in perfect condition. Somehow the family had managed to keep a small portion of the structure in a proper state, and as Lady Fanny stepped into her room she was accosted by the sight of shimmering yellow silk walls, perfect moldings, and a carved plaster ceiling. An exquisite white bed was hung with yellow brocade. She let out an exclamation of delight.

"Yes," Lady Ryne agreed, "it is pretty, is it not? My mother-in-law had it furbished up for the old king's visit, and Queen Charlotte herself slept in this bed."

Lady Fanny smiled at her, trying not to appear dubious.

"Actually they visited us three times before the King's illness became acute," Lady Ryne explained. "Came for the shooting, you know. We are said to have the finest water meadows in the entire realm."

The Countess of Deverill stepped to the window and gazed out at the view. Kate and Serena followed her.

"You cannot see them from here," Lady Ryne continued. "They are beyond the little wood which is behind the house. We were used to have such jolly picnics there—before our family grew to such proportions."

Lady Fanny turned to smile benignly at her hostess. "Will we have the pleasure of meeting all your children?" she asked her.

The Countess of Ryne shook her head sadly. "Not at this time, I fear. Six of our sons are at Oxford and three others are at Eton. One of our daughters is at school in Paris, two are at Miss Milton's Academy, one is with her god-mother—poor Lady Stillton is in wretched health this year and was so anxious to have Oriana accompany her to Bath—and my eldest daughter, Cynthia, is married to the Earl of Salk-Farlington. You may have met her in town last Season."

Lady Fanny could not remember having done so, and as she stood frowning and racking her brains, the house-keeper arrived and ushered Kate and Serena out of the room and down another hallway to their quarters. There, too, they discovered the house to be in good repair and unusually beautiful.

"Just look out this window," Serena urged her cousin, and they stood on the lush silk carpet and put their hands up to draw aside the richest of brocade draperies. Below them lay a waste of broken shrubbery, an abandoned fish pond that was half filled with dirt, and an elaborate marble statue of a naked athlete who had been pushed off his pedestal onto his face and was lying disconsolately in the grass.

When the ladies returned to the grand saloon, they found the gentlemen before them awaiting their arrival.

"Yes," Wale was explaining to Deverill, "I have the honor to call the Earl of Ryne godfather. And our families have intermarried several times. We have land which abuts."

"Good God!" Deverill exclaimed. "Are we near Asgar? I was aware that our route wound sadly about the countryside, but I had no idea we had come so far."

"No, sir," Wale assured him. "Asgar is half a day's journey from here. The property I speak of is my Trelling estate, which my grandfather acquired from Ryne as the result of a joke. It's not a large place, but an excellent one— quite profitable." He turned toward Ryne and would have spoken to him, but the Earl's attention had been attracted by the arrival of the ladies.

"Ah," the Earl crooned, striding to meet them, "visions of loveliness, I trow."

He offered Lady Fanny his arm. The ladies and gentlemen milled around each other for a moment and when they had sorted themselves out, Kate found herself on Wale's arm while Serena was appropriated by Furth. Lady Marguerite, with Deverill beside her, led the promenade in to dinner.

The dining saloon, they discovered, was in a state of quasi-ruin. Its magnificent table was unblemished and glowing softly in the light of the few guttering tallow candles which had been stuck into exquisite chandeliers. The lower halves of the walls were also still pristine, but the upper portions were yellowed with soot and the ceiling had darkened to gray with black areas near each candleholder.

Lady Ryne, in a gown of blue satin which had no visible darns though it was sadly out of style with panniers and lace cuffs, took her place at one end of the table and after her guests had been seated unfurled her ivory fan and nodded to the butler. Immediately a line of footmen in worn satin livery and moth-eaten powdered wigs entered, each bearing a platter. By the time everything had been set on the table, Kate decided that she had rarely seen such an impressive display, the board groaning with elaborate victuals, all served on magnificent plates, exquisitely arrayed and artistically garnished. When they were ready to begin eating, a footman took his place behind each chair.

Wale, on Kate's left, leaned close to her and smiled, nodding his head toward a golden salver of fowl prepared in a creamy sauce and distributed over a bed of fluffy rice. "I can recommend this dish to you, Cousin," he whispered. "Ryne's chef does it especially well."

Kate accepted a small serving and was munching happily when Ryne put a forkful to his mouth and waved impatiently to his butler.

"This is not right, Bascomb—not the way I like it. Take it away before it poisons one of us, and tell Pierre he's used too much saffron." He shuddered. "I need some wine to rid my mouth of such a foul taste. Pah!" And lifting one of his glasses to his lips, he downed its entire contents and set it out to be refilled.

The next dish Kate tried was a delicate mixture of sweetbreads and asparagus. She was chewing it contentedly, thinking to herself that she had never tasted them done so well, when Ryne burst out again, "Good God, Bascomb! Who prepared these sweetbreads, one of the grooms? Tell Pierre he cannot expect us to eat such pap! Take it away and inform him that there is nothing fit to eat on this table."

"No, don't do that, old man," Deverill urged. "I thought the sweetbreads done precisely the way I like them. In fact, they are dashed delicious!"

"You only think so because you're starved after that arduous journey of yours," his friend told him. "These removes are not fit for human consumption." He turned to his wife. "Is that not true, my love? What do we have that is fit to eat?"

Lady Ryne, behind her fan, was toying with a bit of soufflé on her plate. "This is passable, my dear," she called back to him from the other end of the room. "Lady Deverill, have you tasted the soufflé? It is not so tender as one could wish, but it is passable."

Ryne, who was quaffing a glassful of wine to clean the taste of the sweetbreads from his mouth, blotted his lips with a much-mended napkin.

"Try the soufflé, everyone," he urged. "My dearest Marguerite says it is not so disgusting as the rest of the food."

They proceeded through the dinner in this manner, the guests eating heartily and with much enjoyment while Ryne condemned the fare and slandered his cook. Course after course was sampled, denounced, and returned in disgrace to the kitchen, the Earl rinsing his mouth repeatedly, his face growing rosier and rosier as the meal wore on. Viscount Furth, who had his head close to Serena's during most of the meal, found his attention wandering frequently to his father's wine glass, and each time it was emptied, his expression grew more grim.

After they had finished their meal, the ladies repaired to the devastated saloon and the children were brought in to them. Those remaining at home, in addition to Furth, were six in number, three girls and three boys. Kate decided that they were some of the prettiest children she had ever met. There were Eustace and Eugene, who appeared to be about seven years old, and another boy named Gerald who was five. Two older girls and a little one about three years old completed the group. All were beautifully dressed in silk and velvet, their hair cut and combed in the prettiest possible manner. The littlest girl, whose name was Louisa, took an immediate liking to Serena and, clutching her firmly by the hand, led her around the room, pointing out places of interest to her—the spot where Ptolemy had fallen off his pony and hurt his elbow, the warped place in the floor where a huge basin had been set to catch water leaking in from the roof and where the children had all sailed boats until their mother obliged them to stop.

There was also the crooked leg on the settee which had

been broken when Lloyd and Percy demonstrated a trick they had perfected whereby they could stand one on the other's shoulders then put their heads together and balance Lloyd upside down; but something had gone awry and not only had the settee's leg been broken but Lloyd's also. It was healed now and he was at Oxford though he was still obliged to take some brandy from time to time to deaden the pain; and everyone hoped sincerely that his brandy imbibing was only a passing thing and that Lloyd did not take after the Governor.

Louisa's interest kept returning to the warped floor. "It is wonderful when it rains," she told Serena. "We have tubs and pots all over the room to play in."

Lady Ryne smiled at her from behind her fan. "But we hope we have stopped the leaks once and for all, my darling. The next time it rains we have every confidence that everything shall be right and tight inside our house."

"I hope not," Louisa murmured. "I like to sail boats."

CHAPTER 15

Furth and Wale rejoined the ladies before the earls had finished their port, and as they entered the room, Kate noted that the Viscount's face was strained and pale. However, his scowl melted into a smile the moment he found Serena seated with Louisa curled up on her lap.

"So, Lulu," her brother purred, "you have found a new friend, I see."

"Yes," the child said. "Her name is Serena and I wish to keep her here with us forever. Isn't she beautiful?"

"She is indeed," Furth agreed. Both he and Serena blushed violently and stared down at their feet.

Kate smiled at her cousin. She had never seen her so pretty, her cheeks now pink with pleasure and her eyes glistening with exhaustion.

"I have taught Lulu to play a little game of ducks and foxes," Furth told her. "Would you like to join us?"

Serena agreed to this and the three quickly walked away from the others, settling themselves at a table in a far corner of the room where they spent the rest of the evening falling into fits of laughter.

Kate and Wale picked their way to a little sofa and settled themselves for a tête-à-tête. The Duke shook his head sadly. "David told me the roof had been leaking, but I didn't expect to find anything like this."

Lady Ryne drew Lady Deverill down nearby in front of the fire and engaged her in conversation. "If it were only possible for us to go to town now and then," she confided, "what good friends you and I should be, I am confident. But until the children are established, there is no chance of that, I am told—and for many years after, I fear, as Ryne has sacrificed everything to give them a proper start in life. He refuses to let them go out into the world as paupers, you know—and I am sure I agree with him. They must each have the finest education and a proper portion to assure them respected roles in life. Alas, that does not leave much for us."

Kate and Wale exchanged unhappy glances.

Lady Marguerite giggled suddenly behind her fan. "You would have laughed to see Salk-Farlington's face when he first laid eyes on our grand saloon. He could not understand how a man could bring himself to assign a thirty-thousand-pound portion to each of his children while he allowed his roof to leak." She laughed merrily for a moment and waited for Lady Fanny to make a response.

"Well," Lady Deverill observed, "there are all kinds of people in the world—many who are not such affectionate fathers as Lord Ryne."

Delighted with this observation, Lady Marguerite nodded and fluttered her fan. "The only thing which grieves me is that poor darling David should have such a burden passed on to him. He is the best-hearted and most dutiful son in the world and deserves to have a few comforts, too. But it is left to him to repair the Ryne fortune after all the others have been suitably established, and he swears it will take fifty years to put everything right again—although his father insists it will not require more than thirty."

"But . . ." Lady Fanny exclaimed, her mouth hanging open, "even thirty years is a lifetime! Poor Viscount Furth will be obliged to devote his entire youth to hard work and deprivation while his brothers and sisters live in luxury. It does not seem fair."

"I know," Lady Marguerite agreed. "He will be Ryne, however, and that is a great honor in itself. And he has such a sense of duty toward his family that he does not begrudge them happiness." She fluttered her fan ecstatically. "Everything is going so splendidly for them all—that is reward in itself. My eldest daughter, Cynthia—you may have met her in town—married the Earl of Salk-Farlington, a most excellent fellow who is said to be one of the richest men in England. And my second son, Roderick, is an officer stationed in India, where, I am happy to say, he is building an excellent fortune for himself while doing his duty for his country. And his twin brother, John, shortly after he was ordained, became private secretary to the Bishop of Chesterstoke; we have every reason to believe he will rise rapidly in the church as he is quite the Bishop's favorite.

"And my twenty-one-year-old twins, who will soon be down from Oxford, although they are really too young to marry, are nevertheless both attached to young ladies of great wealth and prestige. Thomas is to marry Enid, the only child of Lord Garth. Poor Garth is completely bedridden now, alas, and Thomas will take charge of his fortune and estates for him . . ."

While she was talking, the two earls strolled into the room. Ryne went straight to his wife, lifted one of her hands to his lips and kissed it lingeringly.

"Do not neglect to tell them, my love," he urged her, "that Richard is secretly pledged to marry a niece of our good King George, himself. They shall have a hundred thousand between them and should be able to live very well on the income it will provide."

"True, true," her ladyship agreed. "And our Chloe, although she is only seventeen and still at school at Bath, has engaged the affections of Prince Franz Frederick of Schlibberhoelen-Stein. His principality is exceedingly small, but one day he will be its ruler and our very own child shall become a Grand Duchess. Only think how gratifying it will be."

"Indeed," Lady Fanny agreed, "it's all most remarkable."

Deverill, however, was standing beside his friend, frowning. "But I cannot approve of burdening your Furth with

201

all these expenses, Weasel. He, of all your heirs, should be left with some comforts and dignity."

"That is true," Lady Ryne agreed. "It is most unfortunate. But it could not be helped. You know how these children are—arriving when one least expects them."

There was a moment of silence. Before anyone could speak, a clatter of horses' hooves was heard on the stones outside.

"Can that be the boys coming down from Oxford?" Ryne asked his wife. "When does the term end?"

Lady Ryne fluttered her fan. "I am sure I do not know, my love. You must ask Mr. Price. He has all those things marked on his calendar."

Everyone listened again, but silence had settled over the gardens, and as they waited, they were rewarded only by a gust of wind which scraped some leaves against a window-pane.

"I dare say I was mistaken," Ryne began. Furth was rising to his feet.

"You were not, sir," he said. "They've arrived. I can hear Rolf's voice." He hurried toward a rear door. "I shall head them off until they have tidied themselves."

But he was too late. There was a rumble of marching boots in a hallway and Ryne's six strapping sons, on vacation from Oxford, burst into the room. For a moment Kate was overwhelmed by the sudden change in the room. Everything exploded into motion. Six enormous young men, all laughing and shouting joyously and stomping from place to place, reduced the grand saloon suddenly to a small overcrowded room. Everywhere Kate looked there were arms waving or children flying up into the air, or someone being lifted and squeezed. A dashing young giant with flickering dimples grasped Lady Ryne by the waist and raised her toward the ceiling.

"Mama!" he roared as he let her drop down into his arms and crushed her to his breast. "My dearest love!" And he squeezed her and kissed her repeatedly on the top of the head while she, forgetting her fan, pecked at his cheek with her little puckered mouth.

"Darling Thomas!" she trilled. "Darling Thomas!"

She was wrenched from his arms by another young man, no less forceful than the first, who squeezed her and mauled her and repeated his brother's vows of affection. He was rewarded with, "Ptolemy, my dearest love!" Kate watched in awe as the roaring and laughter continued, each son crushing his mother to his breast and slapping Furth and Wale on the back amid shouts and guffaws. Each tossed his little brothers and sisters into the air and solemnly shook hands with his father.

Then they were presented to the guests: Thomas, Richard, Rolf, Ptolemy, Kenneth, and George. To the amazement of all, it was discovered that these sons from Oxford had now grown to be exactly the same size during their absence from home—each six feet two inches tall and the perfect weight for a man of that height. Kate felt a bit weak as she looked from one to the other. In all her life she had never seen such a batch of dazzling handsome offspring.

"Have the girls arrived yet?" Rolf asked his mother.

"The girls?" she said in surprise. Then, turning to her husband, "Are we expecting any of the girls, my love?"

"Not to my knowledge," Ryne replied.

"But Oriana is on her way home," Rolf informed them. "Lady Stillton is much improved and Orie has decided to announce her engagement, if it is convenient for you at this time. Cynthia went to fetch her in her carriage and is coming to join the party."

"Delightful!" Lady Ryne exclaimed. "I shall be able to present them to dear Lady Deverill. Such a treat!" She frowned suddenly. "But poor Cynthia's room is in the most wretched condition! The roof has been leaking and the floor has buckled in one place and the east wall has begun to peel."

"Don't forget that piece of ceiling that came loose and fell onto the bed," five-year-old Gerald added. He giggled with delight at the memory. "We had to take the barrow full of plaster down the main staircase."

"And knocked the knob off one of the newel posts," Eustace laughed.

"Dreadful, dreadful!" Lady Ryne said quickly. "Not funny, Eustace."

"No, ma'am," he said, suddenly solemn. "Most unfortunate."

One of the young men, who Kate thought to be Richard, had planted his hands on his hips and was staring around himself, glaring at the room. "What has happened here, Mama?" he demanded. "This room is in a worse condition than ever! It is appalling!"

"Well, my dear," her ladyship explained, "with the water coming in as it does . . ."

"But didn't it help to put all these new tiles in last summer—all the effort with everyone up on the roof?"

"I am afraid not, my darling. Though we have done some patching since and hope that it will hold for a while. But Mr. Price says that the entire thing should be redone to make it right. Or at least the side which is now giving the trouble."

"Yes," Furth explained quickly. "For the problem is down near the eaves and the whole section above it must be reset."

"But that is a monstrous task!" the young man continued.

"It is," Furth agreed. "And the beams which have been soaked must be replaced, and the buckled sections of flooring replaced, and the walls replastered and painted."

"Well, it must be done immediately," the young man said. "If money is short at this time, you must use some of mine and delay payment until it is convenient."

The Earl stepped toward him quickly. "That is not advisable, Thomas," he said. "Unless you take your full portion into your marriage with Garth's daughter, you will forfeit some of the Earl's respect. He is monstrous high in the instep, is Garth, and we must never give him cause to value you less than you deserve."

Thomas shook one of his hands impatiently. "I care nothing for Lord Garth's opinion," he said.

"Nevertheless," Ryne insisted, "you must not put yourself in his debt. I shall not allow it. We shall find other means to repair the house."

Ptolemy, who was standing by the fireplace and thus near a window, called out to them suddenly, "Here is a carriage. It must be my sisters."

"Oh, dear!" Lady Ryne exclaimed, fluttering in a circle for a moment like a distracted hen, "I cannot allow Cynthia to see her poor devastated room. I shall put her in the Duke of Clarence's. It has always been her favorite . . ."

Before she could finish formulating her plans, there was a sudden exodus through a back doorway and a moment later shouts and squeals of delight were heard in a rear hallway. Shortly thereafter, the young men, escorting two beautiful young women and an exquisite young divine, trooped back into the room.

"My darlings!" Lady Ryne exclaimed, throwing one arm around each of her daughters while she stared in delighted surprise at the young cleric. "And John, my dearest! What brings you here?"

"I could not miss Orie's engagement party," he explained with a gentle smile. "The Bishop has kindly given me leave to spend a week with my family."

"It is wonderful!" Oriana agreed, treating everyone to a display of enomous sparkling blue eyes and luscious dimples. "And my darling Gyles will be here to join us before the night is out. He says he can no longer wait to make me the Marchioness of Drambeau."

To everyone's surprise, Cynthia's eyes filled with tears. "If you could only know how gratifying it is to be here with you all again," she bubbled.

Kenneth quickly caught her around the waist and danced her down the room. "No tears, no tears!" he protested. "This is a happy time. Fall in, fall in! A party, a party!"

And before Kate realized what was happening, Wale had caught her around the waist, and all of Ryne's children had grabbed hands and formed themselves into a circle, tucking their parents and guests in among them, and begun to sing and dance.

"The Earl of Ryne is very grand . . ." they sang. "The finest peer in all the land!"

Wale, Lady Fanny, and Kate quickly fell into the spirit of the occasion, bouncing around the circle with them; but Serena, overcome by shyness, had trouble making her feet work together, and George had to swing out of line several times to avoid trampling her. He was amused, however, and laughed with her as she struggled to catch the rhythm of the dance.

Everyone encountered some difficulty in bounding over the buckled sections of the floor, and after a few collisions with the furniture, those offending pieces were pushed to the side of the room; but on the whole, the dance proceeded nicely, with fair footwork, much laughter, and high spirits.

"Please sing, everyone!" Cynthia called to the rest of the throng. "I shall be a violin." And she let out a sweet, whining sound which rose and swooped stridently. Richard quickly joined in with some bass *oompahs*, and after he had managed to stifle his laughter, Ptolemy picked up a tenor line and pretended to be a horn.

"Oh, this is delightful!" Ryne exclaimed as he danced past Kate and Wale, who were going down the line arm-in-arm. "The happiest of times again. We must not allow the girls at Miss Milton's Academy to be excluded. Merman must be sent to fetch them immediately. How happy they will be to find things again as they used to be!"

Thus singing and laughing and bounding around the room, Ryne's family and his guests stirred their blood and improved their complexions until her ladyship, dropping exhausted onto a rickety sofa, asked her children if they had eaten supper. They discussed this among themselves and discovered that, although they had done so, they were hungry again. Kate, Serena, and Lady Fanny, therefore, bid them all a fond good night and dragged themselves upstairs to bed while the brothers and sisters, laughing and babbling excitedly to each other, followed their parents down the hall to the dining room.

CHAPTER 16

During the night a wind rose, rattling the windows and banging a shutter somewhere in another part of the house. Then the rain began to fall, the wind driving it hard against the face of the building. Kate roused slightly as she heard the roar and clatter outside. Her first thought was one of relief that the tempest had waited for them to arrive at Ryne before bursting upon them. Her second thought was for the roof overhead, and she drifted back to sleep trusting that, as everyone hoped, the leaks had finally been stopped.

In the morning, however, when she stepped out of her door and met Serena in the hallway, their attention was drawn to a murmur of activity which was just out of sight around a corner. As they made their way to an open doorway, they discovered, inside a front bedroom, a small army of chambermaids with mops and buckets working frantically to sop up the steady streams of water which were pouring down the walls. A girl with her skirt rolled up, her feet bare, and carrying a bucket full of water, hurried past Kate and Serena. She set it down hastily, bobbed a brusque curtsey, picked up her bucket again, and hurried down a branching hallway. Kate and Serena exchanged unhappy glances.

"Such a pity," Serena breathed.

Kate nodded her head. Together they made their way

down the main staircase and to the grand saloon. There they were greeted by fresh horrors. At least fifteen wash tubs were set around the room, each filling rapidly with water that was dripping from the ceiling. Torrents were flowing down one wall, which had already loosened and dropped a large section of plaster into a pile. Ryne and Furth stood in the center of the wreckage, their hands on their hips and their backs to the new arrivals.

"This certainly decides it, sir," Furth was saying. "No more half measures. The entire roof must be set right, and at once, or there shall be nothing left to repair."

"But you know it is impossible at this time," Ryne told him. "With all the children's portions coming due, we shall not even be able to make the repairs on the dikes which Drew says are imperative."

Furth threw up his hands in despair. "But we must repair the dikes! If we do not, there will be no income, and some of the other children will be deprived."

"No, no," his father assured him. "I have made all the arrangements with my bankers. They will provide the portions as they are needed, but expenditures here must wait."

Furth was silent for a moment, then said slowly, "Could not Oriana take only part of her portion at this time and the remainder later? With all his wealth Drambeau can certainly provide properly for a wife. Just think what we could do with ten thousand pounds. We could put everything into proper repair for a time."

"But Oriana would be deprived of some of her husband's respect if her portion were less," Ryne argued. "With thirty thousand she is in a position of strength and will feel the dignity and independence of it all her life. You would not wish to diminish your sister's sense of well-being, I am confident."

"Certainly not!" Furth agreed. "But we cannot delay repairs on the house any longer. One of the most beautiful mansions in England is being allowed to crumble around our ears, and we are sinking beneath the sea. Father, I appeal to you . . ."

"No, no!" Ryne wailed. "Do not use that word, David! I

cannot deal with you when you appeal to my sensibilities. I quite lose my head." He pressed a hand to his brow. "Just as I feared, I feel one of my headaches coming on. I must sit quietly in my office—alone. A drop of brandy will help to pass it off."

"Good God, sir!" his son exclaimed. "You're not going to start dosing yourself with brandy at this hour!"

"No," Ryne assured him, though in a wild voice. "Just a tiny sip to relax me and keep the blood flowing serenely in my veins."

And without further ado, he hurried out through a door at the other end of the room. Furth stood watching him in consternation, both hands planted on his hips. After a moment, he turned around.

He had not expected to find anyone standing behind him, and he gave a violent start as he discovered that Kate and Serena were watching him from the doorway. Immediately he frowned, and Kate knew he must be wondering how much of his conversation they had overheard. But as he looked at Serena, his face softened and he came toward her quickly, smiling with such pleasure that Kate turned away. When she looked back, Furth had taken Serena's hand in his and was raising it to his lips.

"Good morning, serene lady," he said in a warm, intimate voice. "Did you enjoy a comfortable night?"

"Oh, yes," she assured him. "I wakened as rested as though I had been at home."

Tucking her hand through his arm, Furth led her toward the dining room, and to Kate's surprise, chatting happily together, they walked off through a rear doorway leaving her alone and forgotten in the grand saloon. She was trying to decide whether to follow them and break into their tête-a-tête or to await the arrival of others, when she heard voices behind her and discovered that the Earl and Countess of Deverill were approaching from the main staircase.

"Dear, dear," Lady Fanny murmured as she stepped into the grand saloon and surveyed its tragic condition, "such a sad state of affairs. It will be like building a new house to put all this to rights."

"Most unfortunate, most unfortunate," Deverill agreed. "I don't see how Ryne could have allowed things to come to such a pass. Always thought him such a sensible fellow."

"And how he will ever find a proper wife for that charming heir of his, I am sure I cannot tell," her ladyship pursued. She nodded toward Kate. "You must not, under any circumstances, lose your heart to him, my love. He must have an heiress with an enormous fortune, but where they will find such a girl, I cannot imagine, as there is no father who would allow his daughter to burden herself with such a future as this."

"Indeed, no one of my acquaintance," Deverill agreed. "Do you perhaps know of a suitable girl with a hundred thousand pounds, Kate? He could certainly not manage to put his affairs in order with less."

Kate shook her head and Lady Fanny shook hers. "Of course I shall look about when we return to town and see if such a one can be found; but it is possible that Ryne will be obliged to content himself with a nabob's daughter for his son—or even a cit's. Pity. Such a charming boy."

Deverill and his lady shook their heads sadly together and began to pick their way across the dripping room to the door through which Serena and Furth had disappeared. Kate, following closely behind them, frowned to herself.

As they made their way down a short hallway toward the dining room, a rising hubbub met their ears, and on entering the room they discovered that it was full to overflowing with young people. In addition to the faces which they recognized from the night before, there were three new boys clustered together on one side of the table, each a carbon copy of the other. At the head of the table, Ryne was chuckling with Furth and Serena while he affectionately patted a beautiful little brunette who was standing alongside his chair, winding an arm around his neck and kissing him on top of the head.

"You silly old thing!" she was laughing. "We shall not know what to do with you if you go on in this manner."

Ryne pinched her cheek and called her an impudent

chit. Then he saw Deverill approaching and waved happily at him. "Come in, Binky! Come in!" he chirped. "My little Chloe is here. And you have not had my triplets presented to you. They arrived from Eton during the night. Malcolm, Martin, Hugh . . ."

The three young gentlemen leaped to their feet and performed ceremonious bows in the Deverills' direction. Chloe dropped a deep curtsey.

"I am so happy you are to be here for my engagement party," she told them, her voice throbbing with pleasure. "And I am eager for you to meet my fiancé, but he is sound asleep. Unfortunately he arrived only an hour ago and was obliged to travel during the worst part of the rain."

"Yes," Martin laughed. "He walked into the grand saloon just in time to watch the wall come down."

Ryne waved a hand impatiently. "So depressing, all these walls and roofs and dikes. I forbid anyone to mention them again."

With a smile of welcome, Wale rose from a place near the foot of the table and assisted Kate to a chair at his side. Serena and Furth, who were seated on the right of the Earl, had bent their heads together and were deep in conversation. Lady Fanny watched them anxiously. "Serena, my dearest," she called to her, "did you sleep well?"

Oblivious to everything but her companion, her daughter continued her tête-à-tête with the Viscount.

"My dearest!" Lady Fanny called again. "Serena, my love!"

Her daughter turned slowly to look at her. "Yes, Mama?"

"Did you sleep well?"

"Oh, yes," she assured her, then added with a warm smile toward Furth, "the most comfortable rest I have ever had in my life."

Instead of being comforted by this announcement, her ladyship's concern appeared to grow. Her frown deepened. She seated herself at the table and accepted a cup of steaming coffee which was delivered to her by Chloe, but her brow was deeply furrowed and after a moment she turned to Kate, who had taken a seat beside her.

"My love," she whispered, "I am appointing you Serena's protector. You must guard her night and day and insure that no matter what happens, she does not lose her heart to this charming but hopelessly impoverished young man."

Since the entire purpose of Deverill's trip had been to make a match between these two, Kate felt that her aunt's request was somewhat unreasonable. But Lady Fanny was so obviously unhappy—her brow, which was usually smooth and complaisant, now furrowed with anxiety, and her cheeks pale—that Kate, with a heavy sigh, agreed to do what she could.

Before they had time for more conversation, the Countess of Ryne entered the room, giggling happily and fluttering her fan in front of her mouth. She was immediately attacked from all sides by her energetic and affectionate children. Several of the boys picked her up and swung her around; Chloe hugged her and kissed her cheek until she squealed with laughter and begged for mercy.

She was wearing a yellow silk gown and had replaced her large powdered wig with a smaller one in natural brown which had a flat top and clusters of curls over each ear, giving her the appearance of having recently been dropped on her head.

The Earl of Ryne was tasting a dish of buttered eggs and frowning angrily over it. "These eggs are not fit to eat," he muttered. "Don't touch them, Binky. I'll have them sent back to the kitchen and something palatable brought out for you."

"Good God, sir!" Richard roared at him. "These eggs are adequate." He turned to Deverill. "You must excuse him, sir. Since the old chef died, my father has not found any food in this house fit to eat." He turned back to Ryne. "But this is the best they can do in the kitchen, sir. And I assure you, it is not wholly unpalatable. You should taste

212

the wretched stuff we are obliged to endure at Oxford." He shuddered.

Deverill quickly served himself some eggs before the platter could be removed by a hovering footman. When he sank his fork into them, he discovered that they were exceptionally tasty.

"Dash it, Weasel!" he exclaimed. "These eggs are delicious!"

"Are they?" Ryne said. He sighed. "But not so delicious as old Antoine's buttered eggs. You remember what marvelous food he sent out of the kitchen—everything perfect—enough to make you eat until you burst, even when you sat down without an appetite. Ah, Binky, you can remember the way things were at this house—the guests we had in such numbers, the parties, the food, and everything in the first style of elegance and freshness. The flowers had so much more perfume—the garden was filled with their scent; of course, there were more of them then. What grand times you had here, did you not?"

"I did," Deverill assured him. "And a grand time I am having now. I can't tell you how fine it is to meet your lovely lady and all these handsome children."

To everyone's embarrassment, a large shining tear formed in the corner of Ryne's left eye. Chloe quickly twined an arm around her father's neck. "There, now, Papa," she scolded. "You know you would not change one of us for all the tight roofs in England."

"Indeed not!" he assured her and tried to laugh goodnaturedly. But it was necessary for him to force his joviality, and the sound of it not only had a false ring but a watery echo.

The rain was continuing in torrents outside, throwing streams against the leaded windows at one end of the room.

"If only this storm would end," Furth muttered, "before we are completely washed away."

"But it is not a bad kind of storm," Ryne pointed out, suddenly determined to be cheerful. "It is just the sort of storm we like to have—enough to soak the ground prop-

213

erly without causing floods." He turned to his wife. "Is this not the most desirable kind of storm, my love?"

"Indeed," she agreed. "A charming rain. And I hope it will pass away in time to allow us our daily walk in the shrubbery."

Kate, who was not so confident as her hosts that the rain would be so obliging, glanced at the windows from time to time throughout the remainder of the meal. There was no sign of the storm's abating.

As soon as they had completed their breakfast, Ryne took his friend, Binky, to look at the library, which was still "snug and dry." Furth went off with Wale and several of his brothers to survey the damage to the rooms over the grand saloon, and Lady Ryne led her guests to a small sitting room on the south side of the house which was in excellent condition. A fire was burning brightly in the grate.

"This is my own little room," she told them. "None of my children is ever allowed to come here—not even the eldest, as the younger would then wish to enter and there would soon be wear and tear enough to destroy its delightful character." She turned to beam at Kate and Serena. "Of course, you are both welcome, my dears."

The two girls thanked her prettily, then withdrew to a corner where they could talk together while the two countesses sat close to the fire and strove in vain to find mutual acquaintances about whom they could gossip.

"Katie," Serena whispered, her face suddenly flushing with pleasure at the thoughts which were rushing into her head, "is *he* not the most sensitive, the best, the handsomest, kindest, and most generous young man you have ever met?"

"Yes," Kate agreed, thinking that perhaps Wale might be an exception, "but if you are speaking of Furth, I am much impressed by his good qualities and am appalled by the suffering to which his father condemns him."

"And to be so forgiving and so loving and generous to his brothers and sisters . . . so dutiful . . . so self-sacrificing . . ."

214

Kate nodded her head unhappily. "He will live in poverty and deprivation all his life."

Serena's face, which had grown pale, crumpled, and she began to weep softly. "I cannot bear to think of him in such straits. That such virtue should be punished rather than rewarded . . ."

While Serena was pressing a handkerchief to her streaming eyes, Kate leaned a face anxiously closer to hers. "Serena," she whispered, "you are not going to give your heart to this young man, are you? As admirable as he is, you must not, even for a moment, be tempted to place yourself in a position where you shall be obliged to share this wretched life with him. Just look at the poor Countess, if you wish to see what your future would be."

Her cousin kept her eyes downcast. "But it would not be imperative that I have twenty-three children, would it?"

"Certainly not! However, the damage has already been done to the Ryne fortune. And it is obvious that Furth shares his father's sense of responsibility toward the other children. You heard the Countess say that he has calculated it will require fifty years to put things to rights. By that time you will be sixty-nine years old, and all your youth wasted in misery. Not to mention the fact that there will be no portions for your own children, however many you decide to have."

Serena mopped her eyes. "I have no choice. I love him."

"But you loved Asgar and Diremore and Young Lester and Elfan; and each of those fancies passed quickly away."

Serena raised her head and looked steadily into her cousin's eyes. "I did not truly love them, Katie. Now I understand what my feelings were—mere whims. But I am truly in love with Viscount Furth."

Kate peered at her cousin, giving her a thorough scrutiny. And there could be no denying that Serena's expression had changed. Instead of the mulish look around the mouth that had sprung into being each time one of her lovers had been criticized, she now wore such an air of helplessness and abject misery that Kate was tempted to believe she had sunk to the depths of finer feelings and that her love was true and profound.

She turned to stare grimly into the fire. "What are we going to do?" she murmured unhappily. "Your mother and father will never countenance a marriage between you and Furth—before breakfast I overheard them talking of his plight. I am sure your case is hopeless."

"Then I shall wait until I am of age and can marry against their will."

"But then you will be harming the man you love," Kate pointed out. "Furth's only hope of salvation is to marry an heiress with an enormous fortune—and I am confident there are many young ladies who would fall in love with such an excellent young man and help mend his affairs—an heiress whose parents would welcome a viscount as a son-in-law. You cannot destroy his chances merely for love."

"But love is the most important thing in the world," Serena reminded her.

Kate shuddered. "Just see what it has done to his parents."

Serena made no attempt to reply, merely weeping softly into her handkerchief.

"Please stop," Kate whispered. "Your mother will hear you and ask us all manner of awkward questions. And when the rain ends you will wish to be with Furth. You must not show him a swollen red face which resembles an owl's."

Her cousin was immediately silent. She sighed heavily.

"Do not despair," Kate urged her. "Who knows what may occur to change everyone's lives?"

Serena bent her head close to her cousin's. "Please, Katie," she whispered, "please help me. I shall be the most miserable girl in all of England if I cannot have him. I shall never agree to marry another man—as long as I live. Can you not think of a plan which will solve all these problems?"

Kate fluttered her hands. "Solve all these problems? Serena, do you have any idea what you ask of me?"

"Yes, I know it is a great deal," she admitted, "but is

216

there not a spell you might cast which will bring sudden wealth to my darling David?"

"I have never heard of such a spell," Kate told her.

"Perhaps your mother has used one," Serena went on, reluctant to give up such an easy solution. "Can you remember ever hearing her speak of such a one?"

Kate shook her head. "I am sure she never has. We have never required a spell like that, as we have always had more money than we needed."

"Perhaps, then, your father could loan Furth some money," Serena suggested.

"Well . . ." Kate said slowly, "perhaps. I shall write him a letter and inquire."

At this point their conversation was interrupted by the Countess of Ryne, who called to them and pointed out that the rain had stopped.

"You will be able to go outside and walk in the shrubbery," she told them, rising from her sofa and coming forward. "I always enjoyed strolling in the shrubbery when I was your age and first came to Ryne. The maze was quite remarkable in those days; but, alas, after old Grendel died, there was no one who could keep it properly clipped. I wonder if it could be put to rights while you are here. Such delightful hours his lordship and I spent chasing each other about inside it. I shall discuss it with him and see what can be done."

"You must put on sturdy boots if you are to take a stroll in the garden," Lady Fanny urged.

"You must," Lady Marguerite agreed. "Although there is no danger of wetting their feet, as the walks are thoroughly gravelled. That is one thing for which we have never wanted at Ryne—gravel. It is rather a case of scraping it out of the beds than adding it to the walks, as was the case at my home."

Serena gave her a wan smile and rose to her feet. Before either of the countesses could observe her cousin's red swollen eyes, Kate also rose, tucked her arm through Serena's, and led her out of the room. They walked in silence for a moment, down a short hallway, then into the grand saloon

217

where they made their way carefully between the scattered tubs which were setting up a merry symphony of ringing plops as the water from the ceiling dropped into them.

"We must formulate a plan," Kate murmured, "to make it possible for you to walk with David. Perhaps if we could engage the cooperation of all these young men, they can each take a turn with you strolling through the house or the garden, and when you pass out of sight—behind some shrubbery or such—they can hand you on to Furth. That would serve to allay my aunt's and uncle's alarm for a time, and would give you and Furth an opportunity to know each other better."

Serena sighed. "If you are expecting me to transfer my affections again, my love, it is no use. And this time, I fear, subterfuge will not serve. You must cast a spell which will cause everything to fall happily into place."

CHAPTER 17

The two girls had reached the staircase and were picking their way carefully up its buckled risers when Serena stopped suddenly, clasped her hands together, and turned to her cousin.

"Katie!" she exclaimed. "How can I have been such a widgeon? The solution is obvious. You must put a spell on Drew and make him exert himself in my love's behalf. Cousin Tiffany has told me many times that he is so rich and powerful that there is nothing he cannot do if he puts his mind to it. And he is exceedingly fond of my dearest David. I am confident Furth's happiness is of the utmost concern to Wale." She let out a trill of merry laughter. "Here I have been suffering so dreadfully, lashing my poor brain to concoct a remedy, and a simple spell is all that is required."

"Oh, dear me," Kate began, "I don't know . . ."

Serena instantly burst into tears. "Please, Katie! If you ever cherished any warm feelings for me—if you ever loved me, even a little—take pity on me now and cast a spell. You have it within your power to make me the happiest of women or the most miserable creature in the entire world. Surely you cannot condemn me to a life of emptiness and sorrow."

"But what if I cast a spell and it fails?"

Serena grasped her hand and, crushing it painfully, sniffled, "It must not fail! I shall never ask for anything else as long as I live, if only I can have this wonderful young man for my husband."

"Very well, I shall try," Kate told her, pulling her hand away and giving it a vigorous shake to relieve her throbbing fingers. "I shall consult my book and decide on a proper incantation. But you must be patient. It will require two or three days to bring something about."

Serena wiped her nose and leaned her face close to her cousin's. "What are you going to do?" she whispered.

"I don't know," Kate said. "Let us take our walk in the shrubbery and formulate a plan."

While she was in her room pulling on some boots, she put her mind to work on the problem. It was possible, she realized, that Wale would help Serena and Furth, even if he were not under a spell—if he thought they were truly in love—and if he considered Serena worthy of the young man and not just a silly goose who was constantly landing herself in fixes. Or, perhaps, like Deverill and Lady Fanny, he would consider Furth unworthy of Serena because of the disparity in their fortunes. She realized that it would be necessary for her to have a chat with him and find out what his feelings were.

She peered at herself in the dressing table mirror, adjusting the tie of her bonnet and frowning thoughtfully. To her surprise, she found herself wondering if Wale would approve of the way the bonnet framed her face.

At that moment the door opened and Lady Fanny, Lady Ryne, and Serena bustled in. Deverill's two ladies were attired in warm pelisses while Lady Marguerite was wrapped in a velvet cloak with sable trim, which was tucked tightly up under her chin.

"Ah," Lady Fanny observed to Kate, "I see you are ready for our delightful walk in the shrubbery."

"Such a lovely time we shall have," Lady Marguerite told them as she led them downstairs and out through a side door. "We shall play a little game. We shall separate at the entrance to the shrubbery and her ladyship and I shall walk through the yews while you girls trip around through the rhododendrons. Then when we meet on the terrace we shall pretend to be surprised by the sight of each other. We used to do this with the children when they were small. Such good laughs we always had!"

Chuckling happily to herself, she led Lady Fanny down a path to their left while the two girls dutifully turned to the right and proceeded along a path which was strewn with broken branches and stones.

"Have you started the spell, Katie?" Serena asked her.

"Yes, yes, do not worry," she said. "I am working on something at this very moment."

"How soon will Drew begin to help David?"

Kate rubbed her chin thoughtfully with her gloved fingers. "I wonder if I could instead cast a spell which would cause the roof to mend itself."

"Oh," Serena sighed, "if only you could!"

Kate shook her head. "I am not sure such a miracle could even be effected by my mother, let alone a novice like myself. Although my mother has said many times that nothing is impossible—but I have often thought that many things are."

Serena wagged a finger at her. "You do not have enough confidence in yourself, my love."

"That is true," Kate admitted. "It is what my mother has said to me over and over: 'You could do so much more, if you only had confidence in yourself, Kathryn.' "

With some difficulty they picked their way along a debris-strewn walk, stepping over clumps of grass, sticks, and medium-sized stones. On one side of them was a rampant forest of conifers which had grown into an impenetrable mass. At several points they passed little lanes which branched off the main walk and entered the tangle to be swallowed immediately by the lush growth. On the other side of them was a more open aspect, allowing them a view of water and distant hills beyond a moldering pile of broken shoots and twigs. There was an occasional shimmer of color nearby where a hardy flower endeavored to push a blossom up into the sunshine.

As they inched around the sagging limbs of a large wet juniper, taking special care not to sprinkle water onto their clothing from its soaked branches, they discovered Wale and Furth approaching them on a side path. The young men were striding briskly, frowning together and shaking their heads, but as soon as they caught sight of the two young ladies, their dour expressions vanished and they both smiled brightly.

Furth caught Serena's hand, gave it a squeeze, then carried it to his lips where he bestowed a lingering kiss on her upturned fingers. Wale tucked Kate's hand through his arm and guided her away from the other two, who quickly selected another path and disappeared behind a leafy bower.

"Poor David," Wale said softly. "I fear he's Serena's latest victim. He is convinced that he has found the love of his life but must lose her because of the ramshackle state of his fortune. Such a sad tangle his father has made of things—and from the best motives. which makes it difficult to condemn him, or to reason with him, alas." He shook his head unhappily. "But Serena and David would not be a good match, I fear. David is the most loyal and constant person on earth and Serena the most fickle."

"No, no," Kate protested. "Her interest is firmly fixed this time. In the past she was the victim of fleeting infatuations with persons whom she did not even know. But now she is truly in love and I am confident that she will remain devoted to him forever."

Wale stopped and looked down at her for a moment, one eyebrow at half cock. "Perhaps," he said slowly, "if she had children to keep her mind occupied . . ." He grinned suddenly. "Twenty-three or twenty-four should be sufficient."

Kate shuddered. They walked on in silence for a moment, then she asked him, "But Ryne's financial pickle affects you also, does it not? I overheard him telling Furth that he would be unable to help with the repairs on the dikes."

Wale nodded. "It will come out right in the end, however. I'll mend them all myself and somehow contrive to

222

convince him that he has borne his share. I have always managed to work him around."

Suddenly he stopped and stared thoughtfully off into space. "If Serena were betrothed and no longer your concern . . ." he began.

Kate, pausing beside him, looked up at his face. It was a truly handsome face, she thought, with the wind blowing color into his cheeks and whipping his hair into charming clumps of tumbled locks around his ears and forehead. And he had a nice square jaw which gave him a look of trustworthiness. As she was thinking about the way his eyes sparkled when he laughed, he looked down at her so abruptly that she did not have time to rearrange her own face. When he saw her expression, his changed instantly. "Katie!" he said in a thickened voice, and pulled her into his arms.

She immediately found herself bent rather uncomfortably to one side and her neck twisted in an odd way; and with his lips crushing hers, she felt herself suffering to a rather marked degree. But she thought to herself happily, "Ah, this is what it is like to be truly in love."

"Oh!" exclaimed Serena's voice.

Kate tried to jump away, but Wale held her tightly, cradling her face against the front of his shirt.

"Don't stand there gaping," he scolded. "Leave us and spend your time arranging your own affairs."

"But my father is approaching," Serena warned him " . . . with David's father. They must not discover that David and I are determined to have each other—at least not yet—until we have had time for more discussion and decided on certain steps to solve our problems."

With a sigh, Wale allowed Kate to slip out of his arms, but he kept a tight hold on her hand, and when she tried to flee down a side path, he quickly pulled her back to his side. She saw that Furth was standing beside her cousin and had his arm around her shoulder.

"Dearest Drew," Serena said hurriedly in a hushed voice, "can we rely on your help in our hour of need?"

"Yes," he said slowly. "What would you have me do?"

"Help us plead our case with my father."

He frowned. "What could I say to him at this time?"

"Please!" she urged him. "There is so little time!" And before he could answer, she and Furth ducked around some brambles and disappeared again into the shrubbery. The earls of Deverill and Ryne immediately came into view, rounding the corner of a nearby path. They were chuckling happily together. Ryne raised a hand when he saw Kate and Wale.

"Ah," he cried, his voice bubbling with pleasure, "here you are! Come along with us to join the others on the terrace. What a happy state we are in today . . . nearly everyone at home. Only Daphnis and Roderick are away." He frowned suddenly. "Such a pity! We shall feel the pain of their absence."

"You have, however, twenty-one reasons for rejoicing," Wale pointed out, smiling.

"To be sure," his godfather agreed. "Twenty-seven, to be exact, with my dear wife, my dear guests, and yourself."

"No reason to lament, sir."

Ryne sighed heavily. "But I wish to have the others here also. Imagine what a day of rejoicing that would be."

Everyone nodded, trying to envision such a carnival. Ryne stepped closer to Wale and linked an arm through his, drawing him away from Kate.

"Let us speak of dikes, my boy. We must have a little chat, you and I, without David's interference."

Wale glanced back at Kate briefly, then allowed himself to be led away. She kept her face averted from Deverill, hoping that he had not noticed how flushed and hot her cheeks were; but he was staring off into space, frowning to himself, and without looking at her, took her hand and slipped it through his arm. Slowly he guided her along the path, behind the two men.

"I must talk to you, niece," he said in a low urgent voice. "Since our arrival I have become concerned—there have been certain exchanges between Serena and young Furth. I fear a budding friendship there, which I cannot like. He is a fine young man and under other circumstances would be a perfect match for her; but one need only look about this house to realize that an alliance between our two families is quite impossible."

Kate felt a ripple of anger. "It is unfortunate, sir," she said, maintaining with difficulty an even tone of voice, "that such should be the case, as the entire purpose of our journey was to form this alliance."

Deverill sighed. "Unfortunate, indeed. In fact, quite tragic. It is remarkable that Ryne and his wife bear up under the strain of their circumstances; and that they actually appear to be happy is a miracle. But Serena could never endure such hardships. She does not have the granite constitution which is required. Warped floors . . . crumbling plaster . . . lambs gamboling through the grand saloon! Such a family! Charming, but so ramshackle. In such surroundings, Serena would be driven into a decline, I am certain. And as a proper parent I cannot allow my daughter to condemn herself to such a fate. Besides, we know how easily her affections can be shifted from one young man to another."

Kate sighed, realizing that what her uncle said was true. Unhappily she looked up at him. He put out a hand and squeezed her chin affectionately.

"Your aunt has told me what a clever puss you are. You must weave one of your cunning schemes for us. Please, my dear, save Serena from losing her heart to this charming young man. We shall rely on you."

"But, sir," she protested, "all my schemes so far have failed. You must not depend on me."

"That is immaterial," his lordship told her, smiling and sweeping away all doubts with a wave of a hand. "Your next plan shall succeed. And if it does not, I shall assert my parental authority—I shall order Serena not to fall in love with Furth." A sudden thought struck him. "Good God, do you realize that even Elfan's affairs are not in such a hopeless tangle as Furth's? But I shall not allow her to marry Elfan either. She shall fall in love with Asgar. He is the best of the lot—rich, good-natured, of a pleasing appear-

225

ance, and he is a duke. Yes, it must be Asgar. Tell her I have decided it shall be he."

They were approaching a thickly wooded shrubbery, and could hear a babble of many voices beyond it. Suddenly there was a chorus of squeals and delighted laughter. "What is that?" Deverill asked uneasily. He turned to look around anxiously. "And where is Serena?"

"I collect we shall find her part of this merry throng," Kate suggested, leading him around a clump of bushes. "Ah, yes, there she is, being kissed by Lady Marguerite. I wonder what has happened."

Kate and Deverill stood on the edge of a weed-choked terrace which bore every evidence of having been, at one time, an exceptionally beautiful expanse of brick and statuary, with a spectacular view of rolling green meadowlands, a distant river, and beyond that the ramparts of blue and purple hills. All of Ryne's family appeared to be gathered on this terrace, and in the foreground Lady Ryne was embracing Serena while Furth stood on one side, smiling happily and accepting congratulations from his brothers. Lady Fanny was on the other side, wringing her hands in despair. The moment she caught sight of Deverill and Kate she hurried over to them, her eyes filling with tears.

"Oh, my dearest!" she exclaimed in agonized tones, "thank God you are here!"

"What, what?" the Earl demanded.

Before her ladyship could answer him, Cynthia came dancing across the terrace, holding out both her hands to Deverill. "Oh, sir!" she exclaimed. "This is the happiest of all days! My brother and dearest Serena will announce their engagement when Oriana announces hers. How wonderful to know that your family is to be joined with ours. My father's most heartfelt wish come true."

Lady Ryne came tripping toward them, fluttering her fan in front of her mouth. "Oh, Lord Bertram! . . . May I call you Binky? . . . This is such a delight! Your darling Serena shall be just the daughter I have always wanted!"

Deverill, bristling, dropped Kate's hand and moved away from her.

"Yes, yes!" Cynthia laughed. "Poor Mama has only eight daughters and is in desperate need of another. In fact, with my husband now added to her number of sons, we girls are so sadly outnumbered that we must find wives for each of our brothers with all possible haste—even the eight year olds—if we are ever to even out our numbers."

"Just think what a distinction it will be for me," Lady Ryne agreed. "I know of no other lady who has forty-six children."

Kate, feeling suddenly faint, put out a hand to steady herself, and to her relief discovered that Wale had come up beside her. He caught her hand and tucked it into his arm.

"Ah, there you are, my love!" Lady Ryne called to her husband, who had arrived with Wale. "Come hear the good news! Our darling Furth and your friend's lovely child have plighted their troth. Are we not the happiest parents in the world to acquire a new daughter in such a delightful way?"

Ryne roared with pleasure. "Binky! Best old friend! It has come to pass just as we wished it. Remember the way we promised them to each other long before they were born? And when I tried to protest and said we should wait and let them choose for themselves, you said nonsense, we should *will* it to be. Good God, man! You have had your way! And I could not be more pleased!"

"But wait!" Deverill protested in a wild voice. "I have not yet given my permission . . ."

Ryne laughed. "You gave it twenty-five years ago!"

"No, no!" Deverill persisted in a voice which was rising wildly. "This is a misunderstanding. Serena is pledged to another man."

His daughter rushed forward and grasped him by the hand. "Papa!" she cried. "Was this not the purpose of our visit—that I should meet and love your dear friend's son? Was this not why we suffered such a long and excruciating journey? You told me how much I would find to appreciate and admire in this heir of his lordship's; and it is true! I do!"

227

Deverill's face was reddening. "You misunderstood me, puss. We came merely to visit."

"But you hoped for an alliance, Papa, you must admit that. And it has come to pass."

"Good God, Serena!" he roared. "You have not even known Furth for twenty-four hours!"

"You see, Binky!" Ryne laughed. "It is a match made in heaven. Such jolly happy times we shall all have together."

Deverill turned on him angrily. "How can we have jolly happy times when the boy does not even have a solid roof to put over his bride's head? You have ruined him with your folly, Weasel! I will not allow my daughter to condemn herself to fifty years of poverty and suffering for the sake of any man, no matter how worthy. That is my final word!"

The Earl of Ryne's family, which now stood around them in silent ranks, all turned anxious faces toward Furth, whose complexion had grown ashen. He bowed stiffly.

"If you refuse, sir," he said in a trembling voice, "then I must withdraw my suit."

"No!" Serena cried, putting a hand to her throat. "I shall not allow it! You cannot be so heartless, father. I love him, and love overcomes all obstacles."

"Yes, yes," Ryne urged. "Do not be such a faintheart, David. Pursue your case."

Deverill drew himself up to his full height. "It is useless, sir. I have promised her to another man." Then as a thought struck him, he turned to Wale, who was holding Kate's hand in his, squeezing it absentmindedly from time to time. "I have promised her to Asgar," he announced. "It is an affair of long standing and . . ."

Serena put out her chin at him. "Never! I will never marry him! I love Viscount Furth."

"You will marry Asgar and that is final!" her father shouted, jutting out his chin in exactly the same way.

"Just a moment, sir," Wale intervened, raising a hand. "If you will forgive my disputing you in such a public manner, but there has never been a serious attachment between Serena and me, except the kind of affection one would expect between a brother and sister. Now that it is obvious she has given her heart to my friend Viscount Furth, I add my sincere wishes for their happiness. I also would like to announce at this time—though I deplore the public way in which it must be done—that it is Miss Ashworth I intend to marry. I had planned to speak to you this very day and ask your permission to approach her."

Deverill was shaking with anger. "What! You have pretended to pay your attentions to my daughter and all the while you were courting my niece! You are a cad, sir!"

"No, no, Binky!" Ryne protested. "That is not what he said. You are doing it too brown! My little Duke of Asgar is a most straightforward boy. He would never deceive anyone. Indeed, why should he?"

"He has deceived my daughter!" Deverill roared.

"No, he has not, Papa," Serena protested, and burst into tears. Immediately Lulu, who was standing some distance away, also burst into tears and, rushing across the terrace, kicked Deverill savagely in the shin. The crowd, which had been heretofore listening in shocked silence, came to life and a hubbub arose. Some voices chided Lulu for her conduct, others urged her on. In the midst of the confusion, Lulu heard Serena emit a fresh sob, and she attacked anew, kicking repeatedly at Deverill's legs until he was obliged to jump back and forth from one foot to the other, to keep out of reach of her sharp little toes.

"No, no, Lulu!" Ryne scolded. "Naughty girl!"

Cynthia came forward quickly and, scooping the child up in her arms, carried her away.

"See here, now, Binky," Ryne continued, "how unhappy you are making everyone! You must relent. We cannot allow these children to suffer. Poor Serena is crying so bitterly—and I have never seen David so white and stricken. You must give your permission for this match."

Deverill turned on him in a fury. "Don't burden me with your absurd problems! Such a ramshackle, irresponsible gudgeon I have never met in my life! How could you be such a cork-brained noddy as to have twenty-three children? I ask you, how could you do such a thing?"

A babble of protests rose around them from the other members of the family. Ryne frowned thoughtfully and rubbed his chin.

"I really don't know, old man. At first we were so delighted with them. Then they just seemed to keep coming along. And after the first eleven, we thought there would be no more. You can imagine our amazement when the triplets arrived . . ."

"And all this devastation!" Deverill roared, waving a hand at the ruined garden. "It is disgusting! There is no other word for it—disgusting!"

"Now, see here," Ryne chided, his face reddening. "You're being a bit harsh, Binky."

Deverill closed his eyes and shouted with all his might, "Stop calling me *Binky*! I cannot abide that abominable name!"

The hubbub rose around them again. Serena began to sob. On the other side of the crowd, Lulu let out a screech. The two countesses, in the midst of the turmoil, stood weeping and arguing together, wringing their hands and wagging their fingers at each other. Ryne, his face growing steadily redder, began to scold Deverill.

Kate, much shaken by all that had transpired, stood clinging to Wale, wondering when, if ever, they would be able to escape from the scene of such misery. But after a moment she felt him tremble and glancing up at his face in surprise, she realized that he was trying to keep from laughing.

"Do you think it is funny?" she whispered.

He grinned at her. "Do you think it is not?"

At that moment Deverill caught sight of Wale's face. He shook with fury. "How dare you, sir!" he roared. "How dare you laugh at me! Get out of my sight and never, as long as I live, let me set eyes on you again!"

"Now see here, Binky!" Ryne began. "I mean, *Bertram*. You have no right to order people about. This is my house. If I wish them gone, I shall order them myself. And I shall not order little Drew away; he is a delightful boy—I have always been extremely fond of him."

"He is a sly, deceitful, cunning rogue!" Deverill shouted.

"No, no, I protest," Ryne insisted. "And I must take exception to your highhanded manner, Bi . . . uh, Bertram. You are not so mighty as you appear to believe yourself. My loyalty must be to my godson—to little Drew. Besides, you must bear in mind that you are only an earl and he is a duke."

Deverill's face was so red that Kate felt alarmed for his blood vessels. Wale was also staring at him apprehensively.

"I shall take myself off, sir," he told Ryne. "We shall contrive to meet later."

"Very well," his godfather agreed. "It may be for the best."

Wale let Kate's hand fall away from his arm and strode quickly across the terrace. The others watched him, stepping aside to make way for his passage; but so distraught were all the participants in the drama that no one spoke to him. He quickly found a path, marched around a clump of bushes, and disappeared from view.

When he had gone, the entire audience turned to look at Deverill, awaiting his next move. He stood for a moment, furiously munching his jaws. Then his eyes fell on Kate.

"You!" he cried. "You have been at the core of this intrigue! I have nurtured a viper in my breast."

Serena let out a wail of anguish. Kate stood staring at him, her heart pounding in her throat. For a moment she hesitated—thinking of myriad replies she might make; but realizing that no balm on earth could soothe the raging Earl, she turned quickly away from him and ran off into the broken garden, bounding over rocks and scattered branches toward the shelter of the house.

CHAPTER 18

If Kate or Serena or any of Ryne's family expected Deverill to relent, they were disappointed. In a very short time he marched to the house and commanded his servants to prepare for the journey back to London. In vain did his old friend coax and cajole.

Serena, dissolved in tears and on the verge of hysterics, assured her father that she would never marry anyone but Furth—not even if she lived to be one hundred years old! "I shall wait until I am of age," she announced. "Then we shall be reunited."

Deverill ignored her threats as well as her pleas, merely informing her abigail that his daughter was to be ready to depart within the hour. Then, with Lady Fanny fluttering at his heels, he marched into Kate's room and informed her that he was sending her home forthwith. "I have treated you as a daughter," he told the white-faced girl. "I have loved you and trusted you, and all the while you have been plotting against me. I shall never forgive you."

At this point Lady Fanny was driven to protest. "It is not true, Dev! Katie would never deceive us!" But he remained adamant, and when, a short time afterward, the carriages drew up in front of the house, it was discovered that the Deverill servants had somehow been stuffed into the baggage coach, and their carriage had been loaded with

Kate's possessions and prepared to transport her home to her family. She was handed in by the Earl and sent off down the drive in disgrace. Ryne, who tried to see her off with proper dignity, was brushed aside by Deverill.

"I must say, old man," Ryne whined at his friend, "I have never seen you in such a snit. Dashed uncivil of you, if you want my opinion."

"Well, I don't want it," his guest snapped.

As the carriage rumbled over the grassy stones, Kate leaned out the window and tried to wave to Serena, who was down on her knees, pleading with her father. Lady Fanny, in disgust, had given up trying to reason with her husband. Putting a hand under her daughter's elbow, she pulled her to her feet and urged her into their coach. Kate could hear agonized wails rising from the unhappy girl. With a heavy sigh, she pulled her head back inside the carriage, settled herself among the cushions, and closed her eyes.

It was afternoon the following day that a battered chaise clattered into a grove of ancient oaks, and its three occupants scrambled out onto the mossy earth to stretch their limbs. The driver, a rough young ostler who had been hired at an inn, went quickly to the horse's head while Serena and her abigail shaded their eyes with their hands and peered around curiously.

"Well, indeed!" Serena said at last. "This is beyond anything! We have been driving in circles for nearly an hour, and these country gudgeons keep sending us back to the same empty grove where there is not a sign of Katie's home anywhere. I collect they are making sport of us and don't intend to divulge her whereabouts; though why they should wish to keep it a mystery is more than I can fathom."

At that moment Serena became aware of an unusual odor which was beginning to permeate the air. Her nose quivered.

"What is that?" she asked, and was immediately obliged to dig a handkerchief from her reticule and put it over her nose. There was a rustle of movement in the boughs over their heads.

"Oh, Mama!" came the sound of a small male voice raised in strident protest. "Are you brewing again! It's only been three days since you brewed the last time, and you know I can't stand the smell of it! Such a terrible stink! It makes me cough 'til I'm fit to choke." And to illustrate this remark, a series of light, breathy squeaks were emitted.

"Now, now, Teddy," replied a rich, purring voice, "you know it is necessary for mother to prepare this healing potion for poor old Mrs. Wynn. She won't survive another night if that fever of hers is not put to rout."

"But I'm going to cough the entire time, until you're finished."

"Then take a little walk, my dear. I'll give you a penny to go up the crag and fetch me some mugwort. There's a nice patch near old Darley's Dreath."

"I'll get some for you," the child said, letting out a trill of laughter. "And will the brewing be finished by teatime?"

"It is nearly finished now," she said.

"Good!" he said. And to Serena's amazement, there was a rustle of leaves, and a handsome little boy of not more than seven or eight years dropped suddenly out of the sky and landed not ten feet away from her.

Her first thought was that he was one of Ryne's children, somehow miraculously transported to this other place, for he was expensively dressed in a mulberry velvet suit and fine white silk shirt, and his hair was well cut and combed around his face. But she saw at once that his features bore little resemblance to Ryne's. In fact, he looked like Kate, with tumbled black hair and large dark eyes. They bulged at the sight of her.

"Spies!" he shrieked. "Spies!" And before Serena could speak or make a move to detain him, he darted across to the nearest tree trunk and bolted up into the shelter of some thickly clustered leaves.

"Wait!" Serena shouted; but it was too late.

She leaned back her head and looked up into the foliage. To her surprise she discovered that she was under a small platform. And farther along, another such platform could be seen, shrouded in leaves, and to one side, another.

"Katie?" she called in a quavering voice.

Immediately there was a creaking sound above her, and a pair of dainty black shoes appeared on a branch. They picked their way along a heavy limb, then partway down a thick, slanting trunk until Aunt Sophia suddenly came into view and stopped to look down at her.

"Yes?" she said in a faintly hostile voice. "Katie who?"

"Please, ma'am," Serena said, struggling to gather her wits, "I am trying to find my cousin, Kathryn Ashworth."

"Ah," Sophia said, "then you are Serena; and you hired a chaise at the inn last night and ran away as soon as your family settled down to sleep."

"Why, yes," she admitted. "How did you know?"

"Because it was the sensible thing to do, and the only way to solve your problems. I said to Katie last night, 'My dear, the only solution to Serena's problem is for her to run away and come here for help.'"

"Yes," the girl agreed. "I was in the most desperate straits, but I said to myself, 'What would Katie do if she were in such a pickle?'" She took a deep breath. "'She would run away,' I said; so I did." She peered anxiously up into the foliage. "Is she here?"

"Of course." Sophia came down a steeper section of trunk and reached a hand toward her niece. "Here, my dear; give me your hand."

Serena drew back, her face flushing with alarm. "Oh," she protested, "you cannot expect me to climb up into that tree!"

"Of course I do!" the woman said. "How can you expect us to help you if you won't come up and sit down comfortably? You must take off your bonnet and enjoy a nice cup of tea while we formulate a plan."

"But I can't climb trees. I'll fall out."

"Nonsense! I'll see that you come to no harm. Give me your hand."

"Please," Serena begged. "Let Katie come down to talk to me. I'll find an inn nearby where I can stay . . ."

"There are no inns nearby. The closest is more than ten miles away."

There was a scrambling sound in the foliage above them, and Kate came running down the sloping trunk. "Serena!" she cried. Throwing her arms around her cousin, she waltzed her in a little circle, squeaking happily.

"Oh, my dearest!" Serena exclaimed, giving way to a rush of tears, "you have no idea the agonies I've suffered since my father sent you away so heartlessly!"

"You must bring her up into the house," Sophia told her daughter. "Pay no heed to her protests." And without further ado, she walked back up the oak trunk and disappeared among the branches.

"Yes, my love," Kate told her cousin, "you must not be alarmed. It is perfectly safe. I have lived here all my life."

"In a tree!" Serena exclaimed.

"In several trees," Kate explained. "You will see what a comfortable place it is—nothing frightening about it in any way."

"But," Serena protested, "it is terrifying just to think of going up into a tree."

"No, no," Kate assured her. "Pretend that it's merely an inch off the ground instead of fifteen feet, and you'll see how safe it is. And to make it even easier, I'll have the steps put down—you won't be obliged to run up the trunk."

She turned to call up into the foliage, "Ryder, please put the steps down." There was a creaking protest of wood against wood, and a three-foot-wide staircase tilted down out of the nearest tree. Kate put an arm around her cousin's waist and shoved.

For a moment Serena was immovable, digging her heels into the ground; but within a short time Kate managed to push her forward a few steps.

"Oh, all right," Serena said suddenly. "I shall at least look." But halfway up the staircase, she panicked again and cried, "No, no! I cannot!"

Kate, pushing with all her might, forced her up a few more steps until they reached the narrow landing at the top. There Serena grabbed hold of a sturdy upright branch and clutched it desperately to her bosom. Cautiously she turned to survey the area around her.

"My goodness!" she exclaimed, staring. She was facing a large fanciful house which rested on a base of foaming leaves. At first glance it appeared to be made of yellow stone, but when she leaned closer to a nearby wall and peered at it intently, she saw that the masonry was painted onto the wood in a remarkably realistic fashion. The entire structure made her think of a picture in a book of fairy tales. There were turrets and tiny sloping roofs of what appeared to be slate, but were probably, she thought, trompe l'oeil wood. The windows were all prettily mullioned with tiny panes and uneven leading. One distant tower looked so graceful and enticing that she half expected Rapunzel to put her head out of an embrasure and let down her long golden hair.

"It is remarkable," she murmured. "How many rooms does it contain?"

"Only twenty-seven," Kate told her, "and most of them small—not more than sixteen or seventeen feet across."

Serena was silent for a moment, then she observed, "It is really quite extensive, Katie. Why does it not cast an enormous shadow on the ground?"

"Because it is built in pieces and scattered through the forest," Kate explained, "with little walkways running from one room to another. In that way, the sunlight can penetrate between them, and the forest life is barely disturbed. Such a delightful place it is, my dearest! Come inside and see for yourself. After you have spent some time in it, you will not be happy anywhere else."

She tried to pull Serena toward a dainty paneled doorway which stood a few feet away from them, but her cousin clung tenaciously to the branch. "No, no, Katie! Now that I have seen it, I shall go down again."

"But you must at least look into the little white drawing room," Kate insisted. "There is a comfortable sofa there, where you may rest." And she pulled fiercely on her cousin's arm while Serena pulled as fiercely in the opposite direction. Eventually Kate began to move her inch by inch until, with a lunge, Serena released the branch and shot across the intervening space to grab hold of the doorjamb and cling there as tenaciously as before.

She found herself peering into a small octagonal drawing room which had white-paneled walls and a low-domed ceiling made of bamboo strips set in an intricate pattern. A pretty little yellow satin sofa was placed against one wall. After regarding it suspiciously for several seconds, Serena suddenly took heart, released her hold on the doorjamb, and walked over to seat herself uneasily on its front edge while she grasped the back with whitened fingers.

"Well," she said, relaxing slightly, "it's not so bad . . ." But at that moment there was a rustling sound and a draft of chilling air swept through the open windows, raising the trim on Serena's pelisse, licking icily around her ears, and stirring the room—tilting it two inches to the left, then allowing it to settle back into place. She let out a shriek and with one huge bound, leaped back across the room to the doorjamb, falling upon it and again clutching it with all her strength.

Kate laughed merrily. "My dearest goose! That's only the wind. It blows through this valley every day from noon until sunset." She held up both arms and turned in a circle, inhaling voluptuously. "I love the wind! In fact, the lack of air was the thing that troubled me most when I stayed at your house in London—it was so silent and motionless, like a mausoleum—or the dreadful, wet old castle we have on Krenull Isle." She inhaled again. "Take a breath. Can you feel the difference? So much cool fresh air. There's a feeling of life about this house. So exhilarating!"

But Serena was still clutching the door frame, her face pressed against it and her teeth beginning to chatter. At that moment a door opened on the opposite side of the room and an exquisite girl struck a pose against the billowing cluster of foliage beyond her. She was wearing a light-yellow dress, which contrasted nicely with the green of the leaves, and she paused long enough to allow Serena to appreciate the perfection of her form and the sheen of sunlight on her golden hair before she put up a hand in a graceful gesture to push a curl away from her cheek and draw attention to the limpid beauty of her eyes. Then she smiled, displaying pearly white teeth and two enchanting dimples.

"Is it possible?" she murmured in a carefully tempered voice. "Can this be my cousin, Serena?"

"Why, yes," Serena said, momentarily forgetting her fear. "And are you my cousin, Lorna?"

"I am," she said, coming toward her and extending an alabaster hand. "How delightful to have you here. You and I shall be the greatest friends, I am confident. Won't you come inside and sit down?" She turned crossly to her sister. "Why did you not invite her in, Katie? She cannot be comfortable standing on the sill, clutching the doorjamb in that peculiar way. Besides, Ryder has announced that it is going to rain."

"I am to blame for standing out here," Serena explained. "I am holding on, because I do not like the way the house sways."

"Oh, I see," Lorna said, arranging herself on the sofa. "As you wish." She frowned. "I should have worn a different frock. This yellow on yellow is not effective."

Another draft of wind rose, sweeping through the tree house, soughing gently and setting everything in motion. Serena, with a whimper, clung to the door frame, her face growing as white as the drawing room walls. Unaware of her distress, Lorna went on.

"When I visit you in London, you must introduce me to all the most important marriageable men. How many dukes do you know?"

With some difficulty Serena controlled herself sufficiently to answer through rigid teeth, "Old Nellingham, of course—although—I don't know him really well, and hope I never shall. And of course, dear Drew."

"Drew?" Lorna said, perking up.

Kate gave Serena a signal to be silent, but she continued,

240

"The Duke of Asgar. He has been a dear friend for many years. Those are the only two dukes with whom I have more than a bowing acquaintance."

Lorna put a finger pensively to her lips. "Ah, yes, the Duke of Asgar. His lands surround my father's little forest here, you know. We have suffered every sort of inconvenience from that arrogant and overbearing family."

"True," Kate agreed, with a quick wag of her eyebrows toward Serena. "And the present duke is rude, overbearing, opinionated . . ."

"Why, Katie!" her cousin exclaimed. "How can you say such a thing after all his kindness to us? He is one of the dearest, most charming, generous . . ."

"Indeed?" Lorna said. "Is that possible?" She was looking down at the front of her gown. "But I must change my frock; if anyone were to arrive unexpectedly and see me wearing this one—well, it would not be at all the thing." She rose quickly and disappeared through the opposite doorway.

Serena frowned. "She is thinking of the last duke when she speaks of overbearing rudeness and the like."

"Yes," Kate agreed. Standing stiffly against the far wall, she knitted her brows and rubbed an index finger back and forth across the tip of her chin. The sun had disappeared and as a fresh gust of wind rocked the room, it brought a smell of rain. "I am going to speak to my mother," she said suddenly, and without further ado, walked out the door.

"Katie!" Serena protested in bewilderment. The breeze, now damp and threatening, was rising sharply, and it swept through the branches, tilting the drawing room roughly to one side. "Katie! Lorna! Aunt Sophia!"

At that moment they heard the muffled thud of hoofbeats on the mossy turf.

"Help!" Serena howled. "Is that you, Papa? Drew? Help me!"

The hoofbeats thumped to a halt beneath them. "Serena?" came the sound of Viscount Furth's voice. "Is that you?"

"Oh, David!" she wailed. "Help me!"

"Where are you?"

"I am up here in this tree—hopelessly trapped and about to fall out."

"How did you get up there?"

"I came up the staircase."

There was a moment of silence, then his voice came again. "There is no staircase anywhere in sight. Wait a moment while I tie my horse to this bush."

For several minutes there was the sound of hoofs shifting restlessly on the ground while Serena clung miserably to her perch. Then Furth scrambled up the trunk. As soon as he reached the landing, he stood up and looked around in surprise.

"What in heaven's name is this?" he exclaimed.

"It's Katie's home," Serena told him sulkily, "and it pitches and tosses in the most alarming way. I am confident it is going to come tumbling down any minute, taking us with it."

"Indeed, it will not!" Kate assured them. "I keep telling her that it is perfectly safe."

Furth stamped a foot on the platform. "Feels sound enough." He peered into the white drawing room. "Amazing!"

He looked across the room to the little yellow sofa. "Wouldn't you be more comfortable, my love, if you were to sit down and take off your bonnet?"

She shook her head. "I cannot let go of this jamb. The instant I do, I feel as though I am plunging into space."

Kate opened her mouth to protest, but before she could do so, the door on the other side of the drawing room opened and Kate's mother appeared with a handsome middle-aged man who was wearing a suit of forest green and a Robin Hood hat cocked rakishly over one eye.

"Ah, here you are, I see," Sophia said to her guests. "I wish to present you to your uncle, Monseigneur Harley, who will speak to you."

The gentleman cleared his throat. "Yes," he said. "As your uncle, I feel there are a few things I should say to you—remind you, for example, that when we are young we

242

have a tendency to be attracted to things that have surface beauty—pretty rocks and marbles—gems set in gold—that sort of thing."

Furth and Serena exchanged bewildered glances, then nodded solemnly.

"But when we are mature," Harley went on, "we become aware of a more profound reality—of the true worth that we often find in vessels which do not necessarily have such a glittery surface, but have a deeper beauty." He looked Furth in the eye. "Do you understand what I'm saying, my boy?"

"Why, yes, sir," Furth assured him. "And I agree with you wholeheartedly."

Harley sighed with relief. "Excellent. Then you have my permission to marry Katie. You'll never be sorry for your choice."

Kate looked up in surprise. "But, Papa!" she exclaimed. "This is not Asgar."

"It's not?" he said. "Who is it?"

"It's Viscount Furth."

"Oh," he said. He stepped across the room and shook him vigorously by the hand. "Then you have my permission to marry Lorna."

Kate waved a hand in protest. "No, no! He doesn't want to marry Lorna, either."

Harley frowned. "Who, then?"

"Serena."

"Serena? I don't even know anyone named Serena."

"Your niece," Sophia explained. "The one clinging to the jamb. Fanny's daughter."

"Oh," Harley said, brightening. "Fanny's daughter, eh? How is your mother, my dear?"

"Very well, sir," Serena said.

Harley seated himself comfortably on the sofa. "Well, well, well," he mused. "So Fanny's little daughter is about to be married."

"That's the problem, sir," Furth explained, "the Earl and Countess of Deverill are not pleased with the match. Asgar

243

is with them at this very moment, trying to reason with them—at least, he went after them yesterday with that purpose in mind."

Serena, from her post, called across the room, "I have very little confidence in their seeing reason, Aunt Sophia. The only thing which could possibly solve this dreadful dilemma is for you to cast a powerful spell and make everything end happily. Would you do that for us, please? I should be grateful to the end of my days."

Harley raised a hand in protest. "No, no, my dear. We must give ourselves time to work out this problem and only resort to your aunt's spells when all else has failed."

"But it would be so easy just to conjure up eternal bliss," Serena pointed out. "It would save us hours of pleading and reasoning."

"So it would seem," Sophia agreed. "But think of what it would be like when the magic wears off. Your parents would be angry and prejudiced again, just as they are now."

"Must the spell wear off? I've heard of enchantments which lasted for thousands of years."

Sophia smiled. "In fairy tales, not in real life. In reality everything is transitory—spells, living things—even rocks are worn away and take other forms."

"Yes," Harley agreed. "I would forego your aunt's spells, if possible. They have a strange way of bouncing back at people." He turned to his wife. "Do you remember the time you made the *magic dancing substance*, my dear, and smeared it on young Walmore's feet? It took us hours to get him unstuck from the floor."

Sophia gave him a wry smile. "I suggest that you refrain from denigrating my skills, husband, or I'll transform you into a frog."

Kate giggled. "Then Wale would put you in his collection, Papa."

Everyone laughed but Serena, who was watching her aunt wide-eyed, her face slightly pale. "Can you really do that, Aunt Sophia?"

244

The woman shook her head gently. "Unfortunately no, or I'd have done it many times."

Furth had turned his head to listen. From some distance away came the sound of hoofbeats and, beneath them, Furth's horse whinnied. "Someone is coming," he said.

"Is it my father?" Serena asked in a strangled voice.

Kate peered down through the foliage. "It's Wale."

"Thank God!" Furth exclaimed. "I trust he's the bearer of good tidings." And he scampered down the trunk. A few minutes later he reappeared with Wale at his back. The Duke paused on the landing to look around appreciatively.

"Marvelous!" he exclaimed. "So this is what you did when my father forbade you to live *on Asgar soil.* It is not only adequate, it is grand!" He smiled at his host. "Are you my Uncle Harley, sir?"

Kate quickly presented her parents to the Duke.

"Please, Drew," Serena interrupted, "tell us what happened when you spoke to my father. Did you convince him that he should allow me to marry David?"

"Well," Wale said with a sigh, "I hope I did. He was not receptive to my arguments, as you may have guessed. In fact, he refused to speak to me for several hours—threw a boot at me when I pressed him to listen. But eventually Lady Fanny insisted that he at least hear me out."

Serena smiled. "And you were able to convince him that true love would overcome all obstacles."

"No, but I assured him that you would be safe and comfortable with David because I had made up my mind to present Trelling to him, as a wedding gift."

"Good God!" Furth exclaimed. "You can't do that, Drew! It's much too generous! I cannot accept it."

Wale raised a hand to silence him. "Of course you can. If you do not, Deverill will refuse you permission to marry his daughter. Besides, I have never felt comfortable holding that property, considering the murky tactics my grandfather used to secure it from your father. Trelling has belonged to the Viscounts Furth since time immemorial, and you shall have it back, as is proper, and take your bride to

Trelling Manor, as your ancestors have done for genera-
tions. Then Kate will be free to direct her attention to other
activities than matchmaking." He turned to Serena. "You'll
like the house, Reenie. It's a pretty place—and has a nice,
tight roof."

Serena threw her arms around Wale's neck. "Oh, Drew!
Dearest Drew! If I were not in love with David, I should
fall in love with you instantly!" And she bestowed an ardent kiss upon his brow. He laughed.

Kate was frowning to herself. "But what will happen to
Ryne Palace if David doesn't marry someone with an enormous dowry? Won't it be ruined beyond all hope?"

"Out of Serena's thirty thousand pounds," Wale explained, "David can use ten thousand to repair the roof
properly and put the house back in reasonable order. The
other twenty thousand can be invested and will bring in a
fair income; and the profits from Trelling will support a
young family comfortably and keep all the dikes mended.
I'll be surprised if David isn't able to bale Ryne out of the
bankers' clutches long before the thirty years are up."

Serena threw her arms around Wale's neck again and
squeezed. "Help!" he cried, laughing.

Before Serena could draw away from him, there was a
rustling sound on the walkway beyond the drawing room,
and Lorna reappeared framed by a halo of oak leaves. She
was golden, wearing a white frock, which set off her curls to
perfection, and at the sight of Wale, she arranged her
mouth carefully to reveal a tiny glimmer of peerless teeth.

"Good God!" he exclaimed. "Lorna Ashworth! What are
you doing here?"

She dimpled at him provocatively. "I live here, sir." And
she dropped a playful curtsey, tilting her head charmingly
to one side.

"Of course," he said, chuckling. "I should have realized;
you're Kate's sister. But I can hardly believe it."

Lorna tilted her head the other way. "We have the same
name, sir."

"True. But two girls could not be more different."

Kate, her eyes round and dark, managed to say in a small, damp voice, "You know Lorna, sir?"

"Indeed I do! I've known her for years. Used to find her at my Aunt Lavinia's house from time to time when I visited there." He glanced at Harley. "Aunt Lavie's house is just beyond this wood, I believe."

Harley nodded.

Wale shook his head ruefully. "We always fought like cats and dogs, Lorna and I." Catching one of her hands, he raised it absent-mindedly to his lips. "I always considered you the most hen-witted peagoose of my entire acquaintance. Do you remember the time you got so angry that you stamped on my foot merely because I said you were no more use than a butterfly and were never going to be good for anything but sitting on a flower sipping honey?"

Lorna, who was maintaining her charm with some difficulty, smiled at him stiffly. "Yes, you were an odious boy. But now we are older and I have made up my mind not to quarrel with you anymore."

"Excellent," the Duke said. "You and I must sit down together sometime and have a nice friendly chat—brother to sister. You can tell me all about your new gowns and jewels, and the latest young men who've fallen madly in love with you."

"But we shall speak of weightier things than frocks and admirers," she corrected him. "In fact . . ." With a superhuman effort she managed to smile at him playfully. ". . . I have heard such charming things about you, I may even be induced to forgive the past and consider your suit."

"Impossible," he told her, giving her hand a comforting pat. "I have come here today to obtain your father's permission to address your sister."

Lorna's eyes widened with surprise. "Kate?"

"The very same."

"But why do you wish to marry Kate?"

He smiled. "The usual reason."

"You're not in love with her!"

"I am, indeed! So much so that I could never consider any other wife."

"Well, well," Harley said, picking up Kate's hand and squeezing it affectionately, "what do you say, Katie? Do you accept your cousin's offer?"

Kate, slightly breathless with surprise, looked from her father to Wale, then toward her sister and back again to the Duke. Suddenly she smiled. "I do," she said.

"Excellent, excellent!" Harley said as Wale lifted Kate's hand to his lips. "I could not be more pleased."

"But, wait!" Lorna protested, scowling at Wale. "If you are going to marry Kate, what duke is left for me?"

Wale and Kate exchanged solemn glances. "The only other unmarried duke I can bring to mind at the moment," Wale told her, "is Nellingham. But he will not do at all."

"Nellingham?" Lorna said. "That's a very pleasant-sounding name."

"Good heavens!" Kate exclaimed. "You can't marry Nellingham! Don't even think of such a thing!"

"Yes," Lorna said, "I might consider Nellingham." She turned to Serena. "How soon can you contrive to invite me to London, Cousin, in order to put me in his way?"

There was a sudden spattering sound outside in the trees. "Oh, dear!" Serena exclaimed. "It's beginning to rain. What shall I do? One of my arms is outside, and it's already damp and cold. It'll be soaked through in no time."

"You must let go of the jamb and come inside," Kate told her.

"No, I will not! I must stand here and catch a virulent fever—there is no other choice."

"That's ridiculous!" Kate protested. She turned to her mother. "What shall we do?"

"I'll take her to Asgar," Wale said. He patted Serena on the dry arm. "My mother will be delighted to have you pay her a visit, Reenie, and you can sit on the ground there, if you have a mind to."

While Harley nodded and tugged on a bell pull, Wale turned to Furth. "Of course, you'll be our guest, too, David. And if you'll join us, Katie, I can make you known to my mother. I've told her about you and she's most eager to meet you. You can also keep Serena company and give her moral support when her parents arrive."

Harley was making gestures to someone on the ground. He walked over to Serena. "Come along, my dear," he said, prying her loose from the door frame. "The ostler has brought your chaise, and young Furth will drive you to Asgar." With an arm around her waist, he managed to bustle her down the trunk to the ground. Furth dropped lightly out of the tree and climbed into the chaise while Wale disappeared through the foliage and returned a moment later mounted on his horse. Kate stood looking down at them from her place on a broad limb.

"Are you going to join us, love?" Wale asked her, peering up into the rain, which was now driving hard into his face.

"Yes," she said. "It has occurred to me that we should have a consultation, the four of us, and formulate a plan to prevent Lorna's marrying Nellingham. I am convinced that it would be a dreadful match."

"Come ride in the chaise with us," Serena called to her. "You'll be soaked to the skin if you stand out in this rain."

"It doesn't matter," Kate said, waving away the offer. "I wish to speak with Wale." She turned to him. "If you'll ride under this limb, Cousin, I'll jump on behind you."

He quickly maneuvered his horse under the tree and she stepped lightly down onto its rump, then while it danced under her feet, settled herself behind the Duke and slid her arms around his waist.

"What is your opinion of making a match between Lorna and Elfan?" she asked him. "He is young and pleasant enough—and personable; and Lorna has an ample portion to repair his fortune. They should be much more comfortable together than Lorna and Nellingham."

"I think she would scorn a mere earl," he told her after a moment's consideration.

"Then we must contrive a way to insure that she accepts him gratefully—as an alternative to another dreadful fate."

Wale chuckled. His powerful hunter was cantering away

from the treehouse, along a branching path which led them toward the edge of the forest. As the rain came driving down, pasting his hair over his ears and running off the ends of Kate's streaming locks, he glanced back over his shoulder at her.

"Are you going to take cold, my love?"

"Certainly not!" she assured him. "The rain never bothers me."

"Good," he said. "Then we shall make a dash across the fields."

But before he could dig his heels into his horse's flanks, she cried, "Wait!"

"What is it?" he asked, reining the restless hunter in a circle.

"Please," she said. "I must get down. There is the most remarkable toad over there." And she pointed to a mossy hummock between the spreading roots of a nearby tree.

Wale laughed. "Let him go on his way. I have no interest in toads today." And he dug his heels into his horse.

As the hunter lunged forward, Kate slid off its rump and ran toward the tree. "I must catch him, nevertheless," she called back to him. "I have never seen one quite like it before."

In consternation, Wale wheeled his horse and, cantering back past her, scooped her up onto the saddle in front of him and locked his arms around her.

"Good God!" he protested. "You must curb this tendency to do the first thing that pops into your head! This horse could have kicked you badly when you slid off like that."

"But we must catch that toad! He's an especially beautiful one."

"You are much more beautiful than any toad," he assured her, pressing his lips against her shining skin, "and infinitely more intriguing."

Kate giggled. Wale tightened his arms around her and pressed his lips against hers. The horse sprang forward suddenly, and as it lengthened its stride, bounding over the lush wet countryside, the two lovers shared a deep, delicious kiss. Then Kate, enveloped in a warm tingling glow, curled herself inside Wale's arms and murmured, "What was I saying?"

"I don't remember," he admitted.

"Let me see," she said, trying with difficulty to recapture a businesslike tone. "It was about my sister. I am aware that you're reluctant to do anything which will benefit Lord Elfan; but since you have decided that you do not wish to marry Lorna, I am no longer cross with her, and I have my heart set on happy endings all around."

"Very well," he murmured, his lips pressed close against her ear. "I find that I can forgive him."

"Good. Then if you will invite him to visit you at Asgar, Serena and I will insure that he and Lorna fall in love with each other. We shall contrive a truly splendid scheme. . ."

251

THE PASSING BELLS

by

PHILLIP ROCK

A story you'll wish would go on forever.

Here is the vivid story of the Grevilles, a titled British family, and their servants—men and women who knew their place, upstairs and down, until England went to war and the whole fabric of British society began to unravel and change.

"Well-written, exciting. Echoes of Hemingway, Graves and *Upstairs, Downstairs*."—*Library Journal*

"Every twenty-five years or so, we are blessed with a war novel, outstanding in that it depicts not only the history of a time but also its soul."—*West Coast Review of Books.*

"Vivid and enthralling."—*The Philadelphia Inquirer*

A Dell Book $2.75 (16837-6)

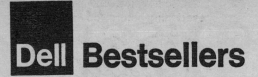
Dell Bestsellers

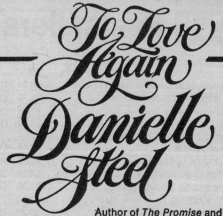